There is a mys_____ _____ _____ _____
London's most select gentlemen may
join. And once members, they may
never leave it . . . alive.

Anna Rosewood is determined to discover the truth about the death of her twin brother. Following a single clue—the symbol of a black rose crossed with a sword—she dons a mask, infiltrates a secret gathering that only a disreputable woman would attend, and encounters a dashing stranger . . .

Were it not for a promise to a dying comrade, Roman Devereaux would never have met this enchanting doxy who seems quite naïve for her profession. But he is shocked to later discover that the lady is, in fact, the fiancée of his cousin—and that she and Roman both seek information about the sinister Black Rose Society. But working together could prove disastrous, for there is no resisting the passionate fire that sears them—or the forbidden desire that could only lead to scandal . . . or far, far worse.

By Debra Mullins

SCANDAL OF THE BLACK ROSE
JUST ONE TOUCH
THREE NIGHTS . . .
A NECESSARY BRIDE
A NECESSARY HUSBAND
THE LAWMAN'S SURRENDER
DONOVAN'S BED

*If You've Enjoyed This Book,
Be Sure to Read These Other*
AVON ROMANTIC TREASURES

THE LORD NEXT DOOR *by Gayle Callen*
A MATTER OF TEMPTATION *by Lorraine Heath*
TAMING THE BARBARIAN *by Lois Greiman*
THIS RAKE OF MINE *by Elizabeth Boyle*
AN UNLIKELY GOVERNESS *by Karen Ranney*

Coming Soon

PORTRAIT OF A LOVER *by Julianne MacLean*

Debra Mullins

Scandal of the Black Rose

An Avon Romantic Treasure

AVON BOOKS
An Imprint of HarperCollinsPublishers

This is a work of fiction. Names, characters, places, and incidents are products of the author's imagination or are used fictitiously and are not to be construed as real. Any resemblance to actual events, locales, organizations, or persons, living or dead, is entirely coincidental.

AVON BOOKS
An Imprint of HarperCollins*Publishers*
10 East 53rd Street
New York, New York 10022-5299

Copyright © 2006 by Debra Mullins Manning
ISBN-13: 978-0-06-079923-6
ISBN-10: 0-06-079923-4
www.avonromance.com

First Avon Books paperback printing: February 2006

Avon Trademark Reg. U.S. Pat. Off. and in Other Countries, Marca Registrada, Hecho en U.S.A.
HarperCollins® is a registered trademark of HarperCollins Publishers Inc.

Printed in the U.S.A.

10 9 8 7 6 5 4 3 2 1

For Jay

Prologue

Sunlight shone in multicolored hues through the stained-glass windows of the church. The glow warmed the golden brown wood of the pews lining either side of the aisle before her, and dust motes danced like faeries in the sweep of light. From the front pew, her mother smiled at her, and standing before the altar, Lord Haverford awaited with the vicar.

"You look lovely," her cousin Melanie whispered, brushing a hand over her arm.

Anna frowned at Melanie, who was dressed elegantly in pink with roses in her hair. "What are you doing here?"

Melanie giggled. "I'm your bridesmaid, silly."

"Bridesmaid . . . ?" Anna glanced down. She

1

was clad in a lovely white-and-silver dress and held a posy of orchids and roses in her hands. "I'm getting married?"

"Of course you are. You've always known that."

Anna glanced at Lord Haverford again. Yes, she had always known she would marry this man, ever since childhood. But so soon? Wasn't she supposed to be doing something—?

"Come, Anna." Her father, Admiral Quentin Rosewood, appeared beside her, clad in his naval uniform. He offered an arm. "Time to do your duty."

"Yes." Her frown clearing, she slowly lifted her hand and placed it on his arm. "My duty."

He patted her hand. "You were always a good daughter."

They started down the aisle.

Anna looked straight ahead at her groom, at the vicar, at—

"Papa?" She stopped walking. "Papa, where is Anthony?"

"Come, Anna." He tugged her along.

She dug in her heels. "Papa, Anthony was to be Lord Haverford's groomsman."

"Anna, *come*. You have a duty."

"But where is Anthony? I can't get married without my brother here!" She pulled her hand away, frantically scanning the pews.

Melanie stepped in front of her, blocking her view. "Anna, do what your father tells you."

"No, not without Anthony." Growing more and

more panicked, Anna spun around, ignoring Melanie. "Anthony! Anthony!"

Her mother grabbed her arm. "Stop that, Anna! You're causing a scene."

Anna shook off her mother and turned again, coming face-to-face with her father. He gripped her upper arms, his eyes fierce. "You must not do anything to jeopardize your future! Your betrothed is waiting."

Anna looked at her fiancé, who had not moved from his place before the altar. "Lord Haverford, where is my brother?"

Lord Haverford just pulled out his pocket watch, glanced at the time, and shook his head sadly.

"Anthony!" Anna jerked away from her father, pushed past Melanie, raced down the aisle toward the doors of the church. "Anthony, where are you?"

Then he was there, standing beside the last pew. He wore his favorite coat, filthy and bloody and torn. His eyes were dark and mournful as he reached out and took her hand. "Anna, don't let it lie."

"Anthony, what happened?"

He faded, growing translucent. "Don't let it lie," he said again. Then he was gone, leaving her with nothing but the smear of his blood on her hand.

"*Anthony!*" Her scream echoed throughout the church. It grew louder and louder . . .

And woke her.

Anna sat straight up in bed, her heart pounding, her breathing little more than desperate gasps for air. Tears slipped down her cheeks, her throat tight with more to come. She buried her face in her trembling hands, rubbing her palms against her skin as if to erase the horrible dream from her memory. But she knew it would change nothing.

Anthony was dead.

With a soft sob, she wrapped her arms around her knees and rocked back and forth in a motion that should have brought comfort. But nothing could comfort her—not with her brother dead this past year. Murdered, they said, by footpads.

She didn't believe it. There was more to the story than a simple robbery. Anthony had been her twin, and more than once she had known when things were not right with him. And she had always been correct. Always.

She knew in her bones that he had not been killed by brigands. But he *had* been murdered, and she was determined to discover by whom.

With a last, hiccuping sniff, she lifted her head and focused on steadying her breathing. As her racing heart slowed, she slowly unfurled her body, stretching out her legs and running her hands through her sleep-tangled hair. When her limbs stopped shaking, she pushed aside the covers and slipped from the bed.

The letter was right where she had left it, secure between the pages of her journal. She unfolded the page, spreading a hand across the crumpled paper to flatten it against the surface of her writing desk.

There were no words, just the drawing of a sword and black rose crossed within a circle.

This was the key. She sat down, staring at the picture. The symbol had something to do with Anthony's death, she was certain of it. She had found it in a pack of letters given to her after Anthony's funeral. The letters had been written by her to her brother, bittersweet written memories that she had not the strength to look at until now, over a year after his death. The note with the mysterious symbol had been wedged between two of the envelopes.

Had he known she would search for the truth? Her parents had thought her still mad with grief and pushed aside her suspicions with a well-meaning caress of condescension. They loved her, but they had never understood her connection with Anthony. They couldn't. Only her twin had comprehended the bond, for he had shared it, too.

And now she was alone.

The pain of his loss seized her about the throat. She squeezed her eyes shut, but a lone tear escaped and splashed her hand. She tossed the drawing on the desk and stood, glancing out the window at a sky rosy with imminent sunrise. Her vision blurred, but she blinked away the moisture, sucking in a fortifying breath and straightening her spine.

"Don't worry, Anthony. I won't let it lie."

Chapter 1

❦

She had never felt so naked in her life.

Glancing furtively at the masked revelers who swarmed Vauxhall Gardens, Anna gave a discreet tug at the scandalously low-cut bodice of her favorite green evening dress. She had never worn the garment without the lace fichu, but these circumstances called for boldness.

I'm doing this for Anthony. The litany repeated in her head, playing harmony to her rising panic, as she trailed along behind the party ahead of her.

The evening had begun innocuously enough. She and her parents had accompanied some friends of her father's to the masquerade at Vauxhall Gardens. Everyone from the royal family to the poorest commoner wore a mask, adding an air of scandal to the otherwise mundane amusements.

7

The entire park was lit with Chinese lanterns, the sounds of gaiety and music filling the air. She had been content to go along and simply observe the laughter, secure in the company of her family.

And then she had seen the ring.

Her gaze drifted to it again on the hand of one of the gentlemen she followed. A black rose crossed with a sword. It was this symbol that had given her the courage to slip away from the security of her party and follow these raucous youths down darkened paths to their lanternlit private dining area.

Coarse laughter drifted back to her from the group of Cyprians who had caught the eyes of the rakish gentlemen she pursued. It had been an easy thing to attach herself to the crowd and pretend she was just another doxy. The masks they all wore would protect her identity. And if they unmasked at midnight, she would make certain to be gone before then.

"Come in, ladies," the young man in the lead invited, with a sweep of his arm. His ring glittered in the dim light.

Sucking in a deep breath, Anna fell in line behind the gaudily dressed prostitutes. She tried not to goggle at the shocking décolletage of one woman's gown, the bodice so low that her ample breasts looked to be in danger of popping out of her bodice. Another of the disreputable females had clearly dampened her skirts, outlining her limbs in a most shocking manner. All of them wore flamboyant masks, their faces enhanced by heavily applied powder and brightly rouged lips and cheeks.

Next to the colorful lot of ladybirds, her unpainted lips and simple mask struck her as somewhat conspicuous. Part of her wanted to run away, back to the safety of well-lit paths and her father's old friends. But she couldn't leave. Not when she was so close to discovering the meaning of the symbol.

Their host blocked the door with his arm when she would have entered the dining area. "What have we here?" His mouth curved in a predatory smile. Behind his mask, his eyes glittered as he swept his greedy gaze over her body. "Aren't you a tasty-looking sweetmeat?"

His audacity struck her mute. Then he traced his fingers down her bare arm. She flinched away, her gaze falling on his ring with a cold kind of terror.

His smile became a scowl. "What's the matter, sweetheart? I'm not good enough for you?"

"Leave her be." A scantily clad doxy with brassy blond curls pushed to the front of the line. She leaned against the host and rubbed her barely clad breasts against his arm. "Can't ye see she's a new girl? I've got what a man like you wants." She held his gaze boldly, a knowing smile on her ruby red lips.

Slowly the masked man grinned, then traced a finger down the bare slope of her breast. "That you do, my beauty." He cast Anna a dismissive glance. "Go in, then."

Heart pounding with fear, she hurried into the lion's den.

Roman Devereaux lounged against one of the ornate Greek columns that framed the private dining area, pondering the madness that had possessed him to accompany his young friend to Vauxhall. In truth, he knew what had driven him to bypass Stumpleton's card party in favor of attending this foolish bacchanal. He'd been concerned that Peter had fallen in with too fast a crowd.

He needn't have worried about the lad. The rowdy cubs that Peter called friends gathered around the table with the giggling doxies, pouring wine and offering culinary delicacies to the females. Peter joined in the merriment, popping a bit of sliced fruit into the open mouth of a fetching little strumpet. The wench smacked her rosy lips, then whispered something in the boy's ear that made him blush to his widow's peak.

It seemed the only thing fast about this crowd was the speed with which Peter might be relieved of his trousers.

One of the women approached, eyeing Roman's tall form like a cat sizing up a bowl of rich cream. "Would you care for sommat to eat, my handsome friend?"

"Not at the moment."

"Are you certain?" The painted blonde stroked

teasing fingers down his arm. "I'll be happy to get you *anything* you like."

"Perhaps later." He held the tart's gaze until she accepted his rejection. With a pout, she turned on her heel, sauntering back to the group around the table.

Peter hurried over to him. "Rome, come eat with us."

"I'm not hungry."

"Oh, don't be such an old stick." Peter glanced back at the dark-haired doxy, who licked her lips in blatant invitation. "There's plenty to go around."

Rome merely shook his head. There was no mistaking the brightness in the boy's eyes; lust would have its way with youth, and common sense drifted away like smoke on the breeze. At thirty-three, he felt ancient by comparison. "Have a care for your purse, Peter. Leave some of your inheritance for your children."

"I will." The young man flashed him a grin and darted back to the table and the delights of the wench who awaited him.

"And I gave up a night at the card tables for this," Roman muttered. He could have been swapping battle stories with his old comrades in arms over a hand of faro, a glass of whiskey at his elbow, but instead he was spending his evening playing nursemaid to a twenty-two-year-old youth and his wild friends.

A promise was a promise, after all.

He just hadn't known when his good friend Richard lay dying on the battlefield that the promise he made to watch out for Richard's younger brother, Peter, would include chaperoning the lad to various orgies and drinking parties.

Peter had seemed so excited about his new-found friends, a group of fencers who challenged each other to mock duels. The fascination with swords had raised Rome's concerns. These days there were so many foolish pursuits that could land a reckless young man in trouble. He owed it to Richard to make sure Peter had not gotten involved in something dangerous.

This evening he had been prepared to extricate Peter from the clutches of this set, if necessary. Instead, the deadly organization he had imagined appeared to be little more than a collection of wild bloods out to impress each other with showy exhibitions of swordsmanship, nothing more. His only concern was that the strumpet currently sitting in his young friend's lap did not include picking pockets among her talents.

Another half hour just to be certain there was truly nothing to be concerned about, and he would take his leave and claim his chair at Stumpleton's.

A movement caught his eye, and he looked away from the revelry to the young woman standing just to the side of the crowd at the table. At first glance, she appeared to be part of the merriment, but as he watched her he realized that wasn't the case. Every few moments she took another step away from the table, edging toward the door.

What was she up to?

Rome straightened. She was a fetching thing, not hard-eyed and painted like the other bawds. Her dress looked to be of a decent-quality satin, though its plunging bodice revealed a delicious amount of swelling breasts. He forced his gaze upward to note that her honey brown hair curled in fashionable disarray around a fine-boned face that looked elegant even with the simple satin mask covering half of it. Only her mouth fit her surroundings, lush and sensual and begging for a man's kiss.

He'd never seen a prostitute who looked so much like a debutante. Curious, he made his way across the room.

She saw him coming. For an instant, her eyes widened, then she glanced away and took another step toward the door.

He blocked her escape.

When she realized that he stood in her path, she took in his large form with a quick glance, then pursed her lips. He could nearly see her working out the options in her head.

"You might as well say good evening," he murmured. "I'm not going to move."

Surprise flashed across her face. In the flickering light, he could see that she was not beautiful.

Sensual, yes. Striking. Erotic, even. Alluring. It was all he could do not to bend down and taste those soft-looking lips.

"I do wish you would," she whispered.

Lust jolted the breath from his lungs, and he nearly hauled her into his arms before he realized she couldn't possibly have read his mind.

"I wish you would move," she reiterated, her soft voice nearly inaudible beneath the riot of merriment around them. "I think perhaps I've made a mistake."

"Have you?" He peered at her, noting her nervous glances at the rest of the party, the way she startled every time someone roared with laughter. "This is your first time, isn't it?"

She jerked her gaze to his, her brown eyes wide with panic. "How did you know?"

"I can tell." He reached out and took her hand, suddenly glad he had come. Her fingers fluttered in his for a moment, then quieted. "You seem rather shy for a woman in your line of work."

"Oh . . . well . . . I . . ." She stuttered to a halt, a becoming blush darkening her cheeks.

"It's all right. I find it charming." He tucked her hand into the crook of his arm, and she stepped closer, as he'd hoped she would. "My name is Rome."

"I'm A . . . Rose." She licked her lips, distracting him. "My name is Rose."

"Rose." He tested the name on his lips the way he'd taste a fine wine. "Beautiful."

"Thank you." She smiled up at him. "You're very kind."

"And you're very lovely." Expertly he turned and steered her away from the crowd at the table. The swish of her satin gown drew his attention to the body beneath the material. The swell of a hip, the bend of a knee. A quick flash of ankle. The gentle curve of her collarbone.

She was soft and sweet and lush, a siren that stirred his appetite. How long had it been since he'd had a lusty wench beneath him? Weeks perhaps. Much had happened since he'd resigned his commission and come home to England, and he hadn't wanted the complication of a permanent attachment. Or a temporary one, for that matter.

Her perfume drifted to him, the innocence of attar of roses. His body responded, communicating its wishes in no uncertain terms. Suddenly attachments didn't seem so complicated anymore. Peter was safe enough. The so-called swordsmen appeared to be little more than rambunctious university students. Why shouldn't he indulge?

He led her to an alcove in the Grecian-style temple that that served as the club's dining room, out of sight of the revelers but not lost in the darkened paths of Vauxhall. The intimate niche held a large planter. Columns, plants, and statuary completely concealed them from the others. He ducked inside and pulled her against him. She gave a squeak of surprise and flattened her hands against his chest as if to brace herself.

He laughed, tracing a hand down her spine. "There now, sweet Rose. Relax against me. Let me enjoy the feel of you in my arms."

"Heavens," she whispered.

"You really are an innocent," he mused. "Are you certain you intend to pursue this line of work?"

"I have no choice."

"Ah, like that, is it?" He stroked her back, her bottom. "I, too, had no choice but to form a career, though mine was in the military."

"There's a bit of difference between the two."

He chuckled. "There is indeed."

She shifted against him, clearly uncomfortable with their proximity. "Sir—"

"Rome," he corrected, resting a hand at the small of her back. "Sweetheart, if you intend to be successful in your new trade, you need to learn to enjoy a man's embrace."

Her dark eyes looked fathomless through the holes in the mask. "As I said, this is my first time."

"There's nothing to fear." He traced the shell of her ear, then wrapped one soft curl around his finger. "I won't hurt you. It was quite intelligent of you to tell me this is your first foray into the trade. Have you ever been with a man before?"

"Have I . . . no! No, of course not."

He brushed his lips against her temple. Attar of roses flooded his senses, and he nuzzled her hair, unable to resist her. "You are in possession of a precious gift, sweet Rose."

A breathy gasp escaped her as he traced butterfly kisses down her cheek. "I understand that such things have value to men."

"They do indeed." He nipped her chin, felt her quiver in response. "Every man wants to be the first." Unable to hold back any longer, he pressed his mouth to hers.

Dear God, she tasted sweet. Her soft lips trembled beneath his, and he moved in to take full advantage, enjoying the innocence of her kiss even as it excited him. Her fingers clamped on his arms, then slowly eased their grip. Soon she was making mewling noises, kissing him back.

"Dear God." Barely able to control his lust, he seized her hips and pulled her lower body tight against him. "You had best name your price, sweetness, for you have a buyer for your wares."

She jerked stiff as a poker. "What did you say?"

"And enough of this foolishness."

He reached for her mask, but she stayed his hand. "We can discuss terms, sir, but my anonymity is one that cannot be negotiated."

He hesitated, then nodded. "I am disappointed, of course, but I must have you, Rose. Whatever your price, I will pay it."

"I must think." She pushed against his chest until he allowed a couple of inches between them.

"If you can. My reason has deserted me." He took her hand and tangled his fingers with hers. "I will make it good for you, my dear. I swear I will. You might not get so generous an offer from someone else."

Anna stared up into the stranger's eyes. They looked to be green behind the black velvet mask, and at the moment they glittered like emeralds.

"Rose," he coaxed, his voice low and soothing. He swept his thumb along the inside of her wrist, then brought her palm to his lips. His gentle kiss made her knees buckle, and she struggled for reason.

Heavens, but what had ever given her the wild notion to pass herself off as a demirep? She could have followed the group of young bucks and claimed to be lost while still maintaining her identity as a gently bred lady. Instead, she had mingled with the crowd and allowed them all to think her a harlot.

But the madness that had grabbed hold of her when she had seen that ring had ended up leading her down the right path. She had learned from the evening's conversation that the crossed rose and sword was the symbol of the Black Rose Society, a club of swordsmen who dueled one another for sport. Her masquerade had proven a worthy sacrifice to discover the truth.

She just hadn't expected anyone to take her up on her implied profession.

"Have you forgotten me?" He tugged her against him again, and she could feel the hardness of him pressing against the juncture of her thighs. She had never felt such a thing before, but she'd had a brother and knew what it meant. Heat flooded her system, making her skin tingle and her breath catch.

Think, Anna! How could she get what she needed and still escape unscathed? "I do not know what to say," she murmured, her mind scrambling for a solution.

"Say yes." He nuzzled her temple with his lips. "I'm not young and foolish like the rest of these lads. If you came here to find a man for your bed, you've got one."

Aha. She pulled back enough to look in his eyes. "But I came here in search of a certain kind of man. How do I know you are the one I want?"

"Take my word on it."

She managed a flirtatious laugh. "I have specific tastes, sir. I like a dangerous man, one who can protect a woman." She leaned in, toyed with the lapel of his coat. "I overheard this evening that this is a society of swordsmen."

"I've a sword for you, my sweet." He pressed his hardness more firmly against her. She struggled to back away, but this time he wouldn't let her. "No," he murmured near her ear. "Stay. I like the feel of you against me."

"That's not at all the kind of sword I meant,"

she choked out. "I understood this to be a dueling club. Do you duel?"

He grinned. "Yes, I have fought a duel or two in my time."

Her heart pounding, she asked, "Have you ever killed anyone?"

A burst of surprised laughter escaped his lips. "Bloodthirsty wench! Yes, I've killed men. Is that what it takes to excite you?"

Dear God. He admitted it! "Recently?" she whispered.

"If I tell you I have not killed a man since last year, will that weaken my chances of getting you in my bed?"

Last year? Had he been the one who'd dealt Anthony his death blow? "Who was the last man you killed?"

"I usually don't know their names." He frowned down at her. "Why all the questions?"

"I'm curious. As you said, swordplay excites me."

His expression cleared. "I am an accomplished swordsman, my dear, probably more so than the young pups at yonder table." He took her hand and nipped the palm, edging her more firmly against his erection. Ripples of pleasure coursed through her at the double assault.

This was wrong, so wrong. This man might know something about her brother's death. Might even be the cause of it!

But he touched her, and rational thought flew from her mind. Was this not proof of his wickedness? Could she really be so attracted to a man who might be connected to her brother's death?

"What are you doing to me?" she whispered, her voice breaking. He rubbed against her like a cat, and her eyes drifted closed on a wave of pleasure. "We can't . . . you can't . . ." She struggled to remember her purpose, to ignore the burning in her blood.

"Oh?" Amusement softened the growl of desire in his voice. "I assure you we can." He cupped the back of her head and drew her closer for another hungry kiss. Her insides melted, then her stomach seemed to flip over as he urged her lips apart with his tongue.

His experience devastated her. Good Lord, to be taken by a man like this . . . The thought alone made her burn in parts she had never considered.

He rocked his hips against hers, setting a rhythm that her body seemed to recognize. His mouth seduced her, his hands stroking over her body with the knowledge of a man of experience. No boy was this, stealing kisses in the garden. This man had every intention of calling her bluff and making her body his.

And she wanted him to, with a passion that shook her to the core. Right or wrong, she wanted what he could teach her.

"You won't tell me your price," he murmured.

"Perhaps you need to see what I can give you. That I am worthy of the valuable treasure you possess."

Before she could gather her scattered wits, he'd swept her off her feet and set her down on a stone planter nearby. The edge was narrow, and she started to topple backwards into the shrubbery. He stopped her by bracing his arm behind her.

She remained carefully balanced between the narrow strip of stone and his warm, hard arm, completely at the mercy of his whim. He loomed above her, blocking the light from the lanterns, a tall, broad-shouldered man with thick dark hair and sharp features that managed to be attractive even as they were not handsome. His simple black mask only added to the allure of danger.

"Easy, sweetness." His voice soothed her in the darkness, the calm timbre of it playing against her nerves like silk against skin. His fingers brushed her ankle, glided along her calf.

"What are you doing?" Scandalized, she wanted to lean forward and push away his hand—that clever, tantalizing hand that made her feel things no respectable lady should feel. But her balance was precarious; she depended completely on him to hold her steady.

"I'm showing you how it can be between us. I am a generous lover, Rose." He caressed the inside of her thigh, then tenderly squeezed it.

Sensations rippled along her nerve endings,

and her eyes slid closed at the intensity. She didn't doubt his words, not for an instant.

"Trust me." He trailed his fingers up, up, up until he was *there*, slipping past all barriers to press his palm against her mound.

She gave a startled whimper.

"Easy. It's all right. I won't take what's not freely given." He rubbed his hand in a circle against her most intimate place, sending heat bursting through her. "But I want to show you what can be, if you let it."

"Dear heavens," she breathed, barely able to inhale properly.

"I can make you feel so good, sweet Rose." He stroked her sensitive flesh with his fingers, so lightly it didn't alarm her, but with such skill that she could barely remember her name when he touched her. "Just let me. Let me make you feel good." He slid a finger partway inside her and at the same time found a spot with his thumb that made her see stars.

"Oh my." She arched her back and would have fallen off the planter except for his arm around her. All the while his fingers never stopped, his thumb stroking that one place that drove her wild.

"That's it. Yes, you like that, don't you?" His voice encouraged her to give herself over, to enjoy the sensations bursting between her thighs. It was wrong, so wrong. She shouldn't be doing this.

But it was so delicious. So irresistible.

"That's it, my sweet. Let me make you feel good," he crooned.

Time lost all meaning. Her entire world became his hand between her legs, his fingers bringing forth amazing sensations that dazzled her. Her body became a creature she didn't recognize, reacting to his touch and seeming to know how to respond when her mind had no idea.

Her thighs fell open wider, and she pressed herself against his hand, desperate for something elusive that only he could give her. It was there, just beyond her reach. She would catch a glimpse, then it was gone. Then it was there again, offered to her, and taken away.

The burst came out of nowhere. One moment she was swept along by arousal, and the next, pleasure shot through her, bowing her back and dragging a keening cry from her lips. All the while she heard his voice encouraging her, complimenting her. His fingers slowed and finally stopped, leaving her shuddering in his arms.

He pulled her upright and pressed her face into his chest, wrapping his arms around her. "Dear God. Sweet Rose."

Anna. Her name was Anna. She nearly said it, then remembered there were reasons why she couldn't.

She wanted to hear her name on his lips—her real name. But Anna Rosewood would never be caught here in a man's arms. No, only Rose was so bold. Rose, who would cease to exist after this night . . .

"Now you see," he murmured, pressing a kiss to her forehead. "We are good together."

She didn't answer, merely concentrated on calming her breathing. Her body hummed with some new energy, and she was surprised her heart didn't jump right out of her chest. He continued to hold her against him, stroking her hair.

She squeezed her eyes tightly shut as reality slowly came back into focus. Good Lord, what had she done?

He was hard as a rock and dying to be inside her.

The slender woman in his arms still trembled from the force of her climax, her face buried in his chest. He patted her back, waiting for her to collect herself. He *would* have her, this delicate female who so excited his senses. No matter what her price, he would be the first man to make love to her. And perhaps their relationship would not end there.

He could put her up in a modest house, provide fine clothes and a carriage. He would visit her at his leisure, bury himself in that sweet young body whenever the whim took him, and no one else would have her.

She would be his . . . completely.

She tried to pull away. Confused, he tightened

his grip and frowned down into her face. Her mask had shifted a bit, revealing an elegant cheekbone. "Where are you going? That was just the aperitif, my dear."

"No." She pushed at his chest.

"No?" Flabbergasted, he let her go. "After that, you refuse me?"

She stumbled back a step and grabbed the edge of the planter to steady herself, raising one trembling hand to straighten her mask. "I told you before, I think I made a mistake."

"You're simply overset. It's to be expected. But if you are to make a success of this business, my girl, you can't turn away eager patrons like myself."

She gave a little shrug and glanced away. "Apparently I am doomed to failure as a courtesan."

"Not from what I saw." He stepped closer and took her free hand, then pressed it against his erection. She gave a startled gasp, her eyes wide with surprise. Her fingers fluttered helplessly beneath his ruthless grip. "I want you, Rose. You've gotten me so aroused that I can think of nothing but having you."

"I don't even know you."

"This . . ." He moved her hand over his hardness, shuddering at the pleasure of it. "This is all we need to know about each other. Name your price, Rose, and I promise I will initiate you into your new occupation with gentleness and pleasure."

She stared up into his face, her eyes flickering

with a combination of longing, curiosity, and something else. Something that held her back. Then she jerked her hand from his grasp. "Please don't."

"Blast it, woman!" He ripped the mask from his face and threw it aside. "Don't you realize how dangerous it is to lead a man on like that, then cut the strings? Not all men are gentlemen."

"Are you?" she threw back.

He stiffened. "I am."

"I've changed my mind about my profession," she said.

"Have you?" He came closer. "I can tell you are gently bred, Rose. The circumstances must have been dire to force you to this turn."

"They were," she agreed quietly.

"Then can you afford to change your mind so easily?" He tilted her chin up so she faced him squarely. "Am I really so horrible?"

Her soft brown gaze swept over his face. "No," she whispered.

"Then come home with me." He stroked the backs of his fingers down her pale throat. "Let me be the man who teaches you about loving."

She gave a quick, sharp laugh. "We're not talking about love."

"Perhaps." He fingered the chain of the cameo locket around her throat. "But we could bring each other much pleasure."

A crash erupted from the main dining room.

Rose jerked away from him, the chain of her necklace snapping with the movement. "What was that?"

"I don't know." Her broken locket dangling from his fingers, Rome edged over to the shrubbery and peered past the leaves to see into the main dining area.

A man had interrupted the party. He wore a black domino and mask that in no way hid the contemptuous sneer he turned on the young people. The sword in his hand gleamed in the flickering light, and a platter of sweetmeats lay in shambles at his feet.

"This," the stranger said scathingly, "is a disgrace." A swipe of his sword sent more plates flying from the table to smash against the stone floor.

Cries of alarm rose from female throats. "Be gone," the newcomer ordered, and the doxies turned without hesitation and fled into the night. The protests of the males fell away as the swordsman turned his hard gaze back to them. "Are you, all of you, mad?"

"Are you?" one of the youths demanded.

The stranger simply held up a hand to reveal a ring. A small ruby glittered from the middle of the crossed sword and rose pattern that Rome had seen others at the party wear. The petulant murmurs ceased at once, and a hush fell over the group.

"I am your judgment, boy," the swordsman said

to the one who had spoken. "I bring punishment to those who would put our order in danger."

The young man who had spoken dropped his gaze to the ground.

"What is it?" Rose whispered, creeping up beside him. Her small hand curled around his arm as she struggled to see through the shrubbery.

"Be very quiet," Rome murmured. His instincts urged him to disarm the swordsman, but his intellect prevailed. He was unarmed. Observation was needed at the moment.

But should this fellow use his sword on anything but china, he would act. He would protect Peter. And Rose.

"Are you mad," the swordsman hissed, "to meet together like this? So many of you in one place?" He swept all the youths with an angry glare.

"We didn't think," Peter spoke up. "It seemed harmless at the time . . ."

"It is not harmless. Only the fact that you chose a masked event has saved your miserable lives."

"That's not fair!" someone exclaimed.

"You know the rules." The interloper stabbed a piece of pear with his sword and held it aloft. "You do not meet until you are told." With a flick of his wrist, he sent the pear slice winging into the darkness. "Now go, all of you. Should you entertain such foolishness again, it will be one of you I skewer."

"But—" one red-haired lad protested.

The black-clad man pointed his sword at the speaker, advancing on him with alarming speed until the tip just touched his throat. "I am in charge here."

"Yes, sir." The youth swallowed nervously.

"Unless," the stranger hissed, "you mean to challenge me for my position."

Silence reigned.

"Is that it?" the swordsman prodded. "You mean to challenge me for my position in the Triad?"

The young man's eyes widened, and he carefully shook his head.

"No? I thought not." He withdrew the sword and turned on his heel, stalking toward the table. "Be gone, all of you. Unless you want to taste my blade in combat."

The young men scrambled to obey, tripping over the broken china and bumping into each other. They fled into the night, scattering in different directions. The swordsman stayed behind, his head cocked as if listening. After a moment, he prowled around the dining area, glancing behind columns and statuary. His gaze came to rest on the alcove where Rome watched.

Rome didn't move. The fellow might suspect that someone else lingered nearby, or perhaps he was just extremely cautious. Either way, they didn't dare risk discovery. He doubted a grown man like himself would be permitted to run off as the others had.

And he dared not think about what might happen to Rose.

Rome kept his breathing shallow and all but silent, standing as still as he could. After a long moment, the swordsman seemed to make some sort of decision. He turned on his heel and stalked from the dining area.

"Heavens," Rose breathed.

"Quite." Rome kept his eyes on the entryway in case the swordsman returned. "You did very well."

"I was too petrified to move." She stepped away from him, one hand over her heart.

"I believe he's gone." Rome turned back toward her. "Are you all right?"

"Fine." She gave him a sweet smile. "Just frightened."

"We'd best leave at once." He tried to take her hand, but she pulled it out of reach. "Come on, now. This is no time for games."

"I'm not playing any game. I told you, I changed my mind."

He gave a growl of frustration. "We need to leave this place, sweet Rose. Then we can continue our conversation."

"The conversation is finished. I have refused your offer, Rome. Now please have the good grace to accept my decision."

"Damn it." Any insistence now would make him seem a churl.

"I'm sorry." Her smile revealed her genuine regret. "You've been kinder than I had reason to expect."

"I'm not kind," he grumbled. "I'm a gentleman. There's a difference."

She laughed, raising a hand to her throat. "In any case, you have treated me quite well for a woman of my ... er ... vocation. Now if we ... good heavens!"

"What?"

She grabbed at her bare neck, then spun in a circle, staring at the ground. "My locket is gone!"

"I have it. The chain is broken." He held it up, admiring the unique cameo for an instant. Then she snatched it from his hand.

"Thank you. This locket means the world to me." She closed her fingers tightly around it.

Silence fell between them, an awkwardness he did not usually feel around women. "Are you certain you won't change your mind?" he asked finally.

She shook her head no. "I do apologize. I'm not a ... well, I'm not the type of woman to give a man false hope. I think it's best if we simply part company and forget this night ever happened."

"Can you forget?" He took a step closer to her, holding her gaze.

Her expression softened. "I have to."

"But—"

"I must go." She darted around him before he could move.

"Rose, wait!" He sprang after her as she

slipped out of the alcove and hurried for the entryway to the dining area. "You shouldn't go about alone."

She paused for a moment in the doorway. "I dare not go about with you either."

"Blast it, Rose. I said I wouldn't force you."

She gave a little laugh. "It's not you I worry about."

"This isn't over, Rose." He took a step toward her, barely able to contain himself from grabbing her like a madman. "I will find you, and we will finish what we've started."

Her lips curved in a sad smile. "Good night, Rome." Turning from him, she vanished into the darkened paths of Vauxhall.

Chapter 2

❧⁂❧

Anna awoke the next morning not knowing where she was. For one sleepy moment she thought of Anthony and reached for him with her heart. But there was nothing there.

Then memory flooded back, and her eyes popped open. Over a year ago, death had snapped the bond with her twin like a twig beneath a booted foot. Yet every morning she woke and expected to find him nearby, as he had always been, even before their birth. And every morning the bitter disappointment of her aloneness nearly choked her.

She raised her hand to her neck, but the locket that always comforted her was not there. Then she remembered. It lay across the room on the bureau, sparkling in the morning sunlight. She recalled

Rome's hand at her neck as the chain gave way . . .

Rome. Good heavens.

Anna fell back against the pillows, mortified, as memories of the previous night washed over her.

What had possessed her to allow a total stranger such liberties with her person? She laid a hand over her eyes, shocked at her own actions. She had followed that group of gentlemen to discover more about Anthony's death, not to be mauled.

A twinge of guilt pricked her. All right, perhaps mauled was not the word. Molested? No, not quite right either.

Caressed?

A ripple of excitement shivered through her at the recollection of the astonishing sensations she had experienced. Not just caressed. Seduced. Thoroughly, indubitably seduced by a gentleman who knew exactly what he was about.

And despite the chagrin that arrived with the sunrise, a sense of giddy glee made her want to hold her secret close and giggle like a schoolgirl. Finally, she understood, a little bit, what all the fuss was about.

Wanton! She rolled over in bed, cheeks burning, and tried to push the shameful . . . shocking . . . delicious memories from her mind. She had no business reliving last night's erotic adventures. She was an engaged woman—well, almost. She had no right to fantasize about a man who was not her future husband.

Instead, she should be concentrating on her brother.

The thought of Anthony sobered her as nothing else could. He must be her priority, scandalous escapades aside.

She swept back the covers and rose from bed to cross the room to the bureau. Picking up the broken locket, she flipped open the catch. Inside were two miniatures, one of her and one of Anthony.

The artist had captured her brother perfectly, from the devil-may-care grin to the sparkle of mischief in his brown eyes. His nearly black hair curled over his forehead like that of a little boy; he'd neglected to cut it, as usual. She smiled sadly, remembering how she'd badgered him about it. Then again, he'd only kept it unruly to annoy Papa.

The miniature of her was an older one, done when she was barely six. They'd both had their portraits painted that year, but Anthony had presented her with a more recent one of himself for her sixteenth birthday.

He'd always known exactly what she needed, always known the right thing to say. They were twins, completely in tune with one another's thoughts and feelings. She wondered what he would have said about her actions last night.

As the first tear slid down her cheek, a soft knock came at the door. "Anna, dear? Are you awake?"

"Yes, Mama." Sniffling, she glanced around for

something with which to wipe her eyes as her mother opened the door.

Seeing her daughter's tears, Henrietta Rosewood's face creased in sympathy, and she produced a fine lace handkerchief. "There now, darling."

Anna took the handkerchief with her free hand and dabbed at the moisture around her eyes. "Thank you," she whispered.

Her mother's gaze fell on the locket in her hand, and she gave a sigh. Taking the necklace, she glanced briefly at Anthony's miniature, her own expression softening to one of longing. Then she shut the locket with a snap. She frowned as she noticed the broken clasp. "Anna, what has happened to your locket?"

"It broke last night."

"I thought you said you had not encountered any brigands when you got lost last night?" Concern sharpened her tone as she led her daughter to the chair at the vanity table and sat her in it. "You told me that when you got separated from our party at Vauxhall that no one had accosted you."

"That's true."

"Anna." Henrietta folded her arms and gave her daughter a stern look that had served her well being married to a naval officer these many years. "Were you assaulted or not? How did your locket get broken? Heaven knows you haven't taken it off in years."

"I wasn't assaulted, Mama. My locket broke

when someone bumped into me." Seduction didn't count as assault, did it?

"Hmph." For a moment, it seemed as if her mother didn't believe her. Then she sighed, and Anna knew the danger had passed. Her mother placed the locket on the vanity table. "Well, we shall have to get it repaired then. I know how you treasure it."

"Thank you, Mama."

"I shall see to it. In the meanwhile, you will stay at home today. We are going to Lord Haverford's for dinner tonight, and I want you to look your best."

Guilt surged anew at the mention of the man she had been promised to—but not officially betrothed to—since birth. "Yes, Mama."

"Wear the yellow silk. It suits you."

Anna made another sound of assent as her mother prattled on about how she should wear her hair and what jewelry would best complement the ensemble. Having heard the lecture many times, she didn't attend quite as well as she should have.

"—and since we will be dining *en famille* with Lord Haverford this evening, I do not have to tell you to be your most charming, darling. You must make a good impression on his family. Your very future hangs in the balance."

"What? The earl's family is attending the dinner?"

"Yes." Henrietta wandered over to the wardrobe

and threw it open, regarding the dresses within. "His aunt and cousins will be joining us."

"Goodness." Her stomach fluttered as if butterflies had been let loose in it, and she pressed her palm to her belly.

Her mother caught sight of the motion and frowned. "You're not ill, are you, Anna? You wouldn't want his lordship to consider you sickly. Your father and I arranged this marriage so your future would be secure. But nothing is certain until Lord Haverford officially offers for you, and the papers are signed."

"I know, Mama. And I do appreciate the fact that you and Papa have managed to give me such a wonderful opportunity."

Henrietta sniffed in agreement. "Indeed, Lord Haverford is quite an eligible parti and would have been far above your reach had his father not been a childhood friend of your papa's. You should be very grateful."

"I am, Mama. Lord Haverford will make a fine husband."

"And he's young and attractive. You might have ended up married to someone much older and less agreeable." Pursing her lips, Henrietta pushed aside one dress after another, mumbling to herself about hair and pearls.

Anna seized on her mother's distraction to get her own emotions under control. She had always known she would become Lady Haverford, but lately everything seemed to be moving along rather quickly. The betrothal had always seemed something that would happen in the distant future. Suddenly that future had become the present, and she faced the reality of an engagement happening before the year was out. Perhaps even before the Season's end.

"You will be receiving callers with me this morning," her mother said, pulling a pale blue morning dress from the wardrobe. "I must say, your idea to travel to London was an excellent one. How clever of you to consider how you would appear to Society when you become a countess when you've never even had a London Season! I won't have it said my daughter is a country bumpkin. No, I certainly will not."

"I thought it might help," Anna murmured. Though at the time she had meant it would help in the search for the truth about Anthony's death, not help her to become a more polished wife for Lord Haverford.

"Where is that wretched Lizzie?" Henrietta asked in exasperation. "We can expect callers quite early, and you are not ready."

"I'll be ready, Mama. I promise."

Henrietta made a sound of impatience. "I will send Lizzie to you right away. And she can bring a cold compress for your eyes."

"Heavens, are they very red?" Anna turned to study her face in the mirror.

"Not very." Her mother came over and laid a

hand on her shoulder, meeting her gaze in the mirror. "I miss him, too."

Rendered mute by the emotion that clogged her throat, Anna squeezed her mother's hand in a rare moment of mutual understanding. Then Henrietta turned and left the room, leaving her daughter alone with her thoughts.

Where the devil had Peter gotten to?

Rome stepped out of his carriage with a curt nod to the servant holding the door open for him. He stalked up the steps to his mother's home and rapped the door knocker, frustration sharpening his every movement.

The harmless fencing club had changed before his eyes into something that could well prove dangerous. This morning he'd visited all Peter's haunts and paid a call on his aunt. No one had heard from him all night. After the incident at Vauxhall, he was certain Peter had gone into hiding along with his cronies, and when Rome found him, the boy's ears would bleed from the lecture he would receive.

As he waited for someone to come to the door, unanswered questions nagged at Rome like harping fishwives. Who was the swordsman who'd interrupted their party the night before and what was his connection to the fencing society? Where had Peter disappeared afterward? He wanted answers, and not just about Peter's activities.

The fact that the alluring Rose had slipped away from him and disappeared without a trace did not improve his disposition.

The door opened, reminding him of the reason he was not still out searching. "Ah, Mr. Devereaux." The butler stepped aside and motioned him to enter. "Your mother and Mrs. Emberly are waiting for you in the parlor."

"Thank you, Hinton." Rome stepped inside. In the few moments necessary to remove his hat and gloves and hand them to Hinton, he wrestled for control of his simmering emotions, forcing his annoyance and worry to the back of his mind. His mother was ever a fragile female, and his black temper would certainly ruin her evening.

When he had himself under control, he entered the parlor. His sister Lavinia sprang to her feet. "Rome!" she cried, throwing her arms wide to embrace her brother.

The last of his vexation melted away. "Have a care for my cravat, Vin."

"So you value your elegant neckcloth more than your sister?" Lavinia fixed him with the same infectious grin she had worn as a child, her hazel eyes sparkling.

"Let us just say that you are both of equal value to me." He squeezed his sister in an embrace that made her giggle.

"Roman, really." From the settee, Eleanor Devereaux sent them an indulgent smile that underscored the gentle scolding in her voice. "Lavinia, do remember you are a grown woman."

"As if I can forget, Mama." Vin gave him another beaming smile. "Congratulations, brother. I am about to make you an uncle."

"What's this?" Roman said, releasing her. "You and Emberly have finally decided to do your duty to the family line?"

"Roman!" his mother exclaimed.

"I'm simply shocked," Rome said as he made his way over to kiss his mother on the cheek. "You and I know Vin has never done anything she is supposed to."

Lavinia made faces at him, and Eleanor swatted him away with a playful wave. "Roman, you say the most scandalous things! I am thrilled for them both." She sent him a sidelong glance. "It's about time one of you made me a grandmother."

"Better Vin than I. I'm in no hurry to carry on this family's name." Rome heard the bitterness in his voice even as he saw the distress flicker across his mother's face. "Mother, I'm sorry."

Eleanor gave a sigh, her soft green eyes glowing with remembered pain. "You have every right to feel that way, I suppose."

"Don't let my foul temper spoil things," Rome said. He took her by the hands and pulled her from the settee so he could admire her evening dress. "Look at you. You're ravishing!"

The compliment drew a blush from her. "Now,

Roman, don't think you're going to distract me that easily."

"Tonight is not the night for unpleasant memories." Rome held his hand out to Lavinia. "I am escorting the two most beautiful women in London to dinner. Clearly, I am the luckiest of men."

"How clever of you to finally notice," Lavinia quipped, clasping his hand.

"Neither of you will stop me from saying what I intend to say," Eleanor said, putting a halt to the banter. "Roman, I worry that you'll let your anger at your father keep you from living your life."

"My anger? I've given up being angry at him. I'm more concerned with what he did to you."

Eleanor gave an elegant shrug. "I've learned to live with it."

"You shouldn't have had to."

"I agree with Rome," Lavinia said.

"Well, that's certainly a first," Rome said, with a roll of his eyes. Lavinia slapped his arm with her fan.

"Will you please both of you control yourselves?" Eleanor pressed a hand to her forehead. "I swear the two of you will give me vapors with your constant warring."

"He started it," Lavinia said, but a stern look from her mother silenced her. With a pointed sigh, she returned to her seat on the sofa.

Ignoring her daughter's pout, Eleanor laid a hand on her son's arm. "Roman, I know what the scandal did to you, and I'm sorry for it."

Rome patted the back of her hand. "Don't trouble yourself."

"But I must. Even from the grave, he still hurts you."

He couldn't think of a glib reply and settled for truth. "Mother, our father ruined his reputation and the reputations of all of us with it. But you will notice I have not let it destroy me."

"Right or wrong, he was still your father, and you must accept that. He wasn't a bad man."

"No, just a foolish and selfish one."

Eleanor shut her eyes and shook her head in defeat. "You must put that behind you and think about a family of your own."

"In good time. I've only just resigned my commission, Mother," he said, brushing a kiss over her forehead. "First I must secure some way to increase my fortunes."

"Henry tells me you're seeking a position with Edgar Vaughn," Lavinia said.

Rome raised a brow. "Gossip spreads quickly through the government offices, I see. Yes, I plan to speak to Mr. Vaughn about a position."

"That's splendid!" Eleanor exclaimed, clapping her hands together. "Will you move in the diplomatic circles, Roman?"

"It all depends on Mr. Vaughn. At least he didn't slam the door in my face the instant he heard my name."

"Devereaux is a fine name, an old name," Eleanor reminded him. "And you do it proud."

"Not all people associate the name Devereaux with scandal and gossip," Lavinia pointed out, earning a look of astonishment from both mother and brother. "Well, they don't! Roman has had to work harder than anyone else to atone for Papa's sins, and he's restored honor to the Devereaux name."

The clock chimed the hour, and Rome seized on the distraction. "Ladies, I am neglectful of my duties. If we don't leave straightaway, we will be late for dinner with Haverford."

Lavinia gave a squeal of alarm. "Henry will be so very vexed if I am late to an earl's dinner!"

"And where is Emberly this evening?"

"His presence was required at a political gathering with the Duke of Wellington." Lavinia flashed him a saucy grin. "Which is why you must be my escort this evening, dear brother."

"Will my labors never cease?" Rome groaned. "Fetch your wrap, brat."

Giggling, Lavinia hurried from the room, calling for Hinton. Rome turned back to his mother and offered his arm. "You do realize that any plans Haverford has for a peaceful evening have just been ruined? Vin will chatter incessantly to anyone with the bad luck to be seated near her."

"I, for one, plan to enjoy myself thoroughly." Eleanor slipped her hand into the crook of his elbow. "I haven't been to an elegant gathering in ages."

Because Father's scandal ruined that for you. Rome

forced a smile. "Come, Mother. The carriage awaits."

Marcus Devereaux, Earl of Haverford, always appeared charming and well-spoken. A tall man of thirty years, he handled himself with a quiet maturity that belied his youth. His dark hair contrasted with calm gray eyes behind his spectacles, and his face was handsome enough with no pimples or pockmarks to mar it. His clothing was simple yet well tailored, such as the basic black evening clothes he wore tonight.

All in all, he didn't make a bad potential husband.

Anna stood quietly beside her parents as her father engaged Lord Haverford in conversation. Having no interest in the state of the wool market in Yorkshire, she let her mind drift.

She had known her entire life that she was destined to become Lady Haverford. Her parents had reminded her again and again how lucky she was, that if it hadn't been for her papa's childhood friendship with Lord Haverford's father, she, the daughter of a mere naval officer, would never have been able to look so far above herself for a husband.

She had accepted her lot. She knew her parents were trying to secure the best possible future for her, and so she had never dared dream beyond what she knew she would receive.

They had tried to secure Anthony's future as

well, urging him to join the navy like Papa. Of course Anthony had had his own dreams, and he and Papa had fought incessantly about the direction his future would take. How many times had she advised her twin to just accept his lot in life as she had? At the time, she had found it comforting to know her future had been secured.

And yet now that her betrothal loomed on the horizon, she couldn't help but wonder what more life might have offered if she'd been able to choose her own destiny.

Between the deaths of Haverford's father and Anna's brother, the betrothal had been delayed over two years. Now here she stood, nearly twenty-one years of age, finally at the side of the man who would be her husband.

And she didn't feel so complacent after all.

The impending marriage was *there*, right in front of her. Papa had made no secret of the fact that he wanted to finalize the arrangements as soon as possible. She studied the young earl, whom she had only met twice before over the years, and tried to imagine living her life beside this man, managing his home, acting as his social hostess.

Bearing his children.

That last brought her up short. Of course he would want children. He was an earl and needed heirs, and as his wife, she would be expected to provide them. But she wasn't as naïve as she had once been. She knew some of what occurred between man and woman.

Memories from the night before flooded her mind—sight, sensation, and sound. She grew breathless just thinking about it.

Would Lord Haverford expect to kiss her like that? Touch her like that? Only years of practice allowed her to keep her expression serene as her mind exploded with panic.

She found Lord Haverford pleasant enough, but the thought of him undressing her, kissing her, slipping his hand between her thighs . . . She tried to envision it, tried to feel enthusiastic about it. But every time she formed the images in her mind, Lord Haverford's bespectacled face blurred and became the hawklike features of a stranger.

Rome.

Heat swept over her. She could still feel his hands holding her close, his lips on her skin, the pleasure that had coursed through her at his touch.

Dear God, he was a complete stranger, and yet she could not forget their encounter.

She should push it from her mind, pretend it never happened. She was not Rose, the poor soul forced by financial circumstances to seek her living on the streets. She was Miss Anna Rosewood, daughter of Admiral Quentin Rosewood, a gentle and well-bred lady who would soon become betrothed to an earl.

She had no business even thinking about another man, much less the scandalous intimacies "Rose" had shared with him.

"Are you cold, Miss Rosewood?"

Had she shivered with the memory? Dear Lord, she had.

Anna met Lord Haverford's gaze, able to keep her voice steady only from arduous hours spent learning the skill of self-control. "Not at all, my lord. Do continue with your story."

The earl launched back into his tale. An imperceptible nod of approval from her father and the surreptitious pat on her arm from her mother told her she had said the right thing. Thank goodness for that, as she hadn't been attending to the conversation at all!

The butler stepped into the room. "Lady Florington," he announced, then moved aside. A tiny elderly woman with a monstrous purple turban appeared in the doorway.

"Excuse me," Haverford said, stopping dead in the middle of his story. He went over to the lady and kissed her cheek, then exchanged a few words.

"That's the earl's great-aunt," Henrietta whispered to Anna. "She's a bit mad, but he dotes on her, so do have a care what you say to her."

"Yes, Mama." Anna pasted a welcoming smile on her face as Lord Haverford brought his aunt to meet them.

"Admiral Rosewood, Mrs. Rosewood, Miss Rosewood, I would like to introduce to you Lady Florington, my dear aunt."

The pleasantries were exchanged, and Lady

Florington produced a quizzing glass, which she used to examine Anna from head to toe. "This is the one, then?"

"Yes, Aunt Phyllis. This is Miss Rosewood. You've heard me speak of her."

"Pretty enough, I suppose." She dropped the quizzing glass and let it dangle from its ribbon. "Be sure you get an heir on her."

"My aunt is rather blunt," Lord Haverford said, with an embarrassed little laugh. Secretly appalled, Anna managed a nod and a smile.

"Skinny," Lady Florington added.

The earl closed his eyes briefly as if seeking patience, then cast Anna a flattering smile. "Miss Rosewood is a lovely woman, Aunt Phyllis."

Lady Florington gave a snort in reply, but said nothing more as she turned and found herself a chair.

The butler entered the room again. "Mr. Roman Devereaux, Mrs. Oliver Devereaux, and Mrs. Henry Emberly."

"Ah, here is the rest of my family." Lord Haverford turned to her father as a trio of people walked through the doors to the drawing room. "My cousin Rome has just resigned his commission, Admiral, and is newly returned from the Continent."

"Indeed?" The admiral looked on the new arrivals with interest, while Anna's insides seemed to freeze.

Had he just called his cousin *Rome*?

No, it was impossible.

Lord Haverford went to welcome the newcomers, two women and a man. Anna watched the exchange of greetings without revealing any save the most mundane interest, but her heart pounded like a rabbit's. That tall, dark-haired man . . . Those broad shoulders. That blade of a nose. How many men could there be named Rome?

Then again, what were the odds that Lord Haverford's cousin was the type of man to frequent a place such as Vauxhall? In her experience, most military men were Spartans at heart, disdaining the careless decadence of Society's pastimes.

Over the heads of the ladies, Mr. Devereaux looked up and scanned the room with casual interest. Anna stopped breathing and shrank back a step behind her mother.

It was *him*.

The earl returned with the newly arrived guests in tow. As he performed the introductions, Anna kept her eyes demurely lowered, panic screaming through her mind. It was him. Dear God, it was him, and her secret would be exposed!

"And may I also present Miss Anna Rosewood. Miss Rosewood, this is my aunt, Mrs. Devereaux, and my cousins, Mrs. Lavinia Emberly and Mr. Roman Devereaux."

Forced by good manners to look up, Anna first acknowledged Rome's mother, a woman about her own mother's age with kind green eyes. Then she greeted Lavinia, a young woman with an infectious grin and bouncing dark curls. Finally, pulse skittering, she looked into the face of Mr. Roman Devereaux.

And saw familiar green eyes that held no recognition at all.

Chapter 3

Rome had always enjoyed the food prepared by the Haverford chef, and this evening was no exception. As he ate heartily, he listened with interest to Admiral Rosewood expound on his views of the newly restored king of France and the ex-emperor, Napoleon Bonaparte.

The admiral paused for a breath, and Rome glanced down the table at his mother. She conversed with Mrs. Rosewood, and her laughter carried to him at the opposite end of the table. He couldn't help but smile as he watched her. His mother hadn't laughed nearly enough in the last ten years.

Lavinia was chattering away at Marc. Aunt Phyllis had fallen asleep at the table, and Miss Rosewood stared only at her plate, moving the food about with her fork, though not a bite of it passed her lips.

This was the woman Marc intended to marry? This quiet mouse who dared not meet anyone's eyes?

Society would eat her alive.

She glanced up at him and caught him studying her. For a long moment she held his gaze. He had expected shyness to be lurking in her wide doe eyes, but instead he saw intelligence and a hint of feminine awareness that took him by surprise. Then she looked away, her cheeks pinkening.

Good Lord, was she *flirting* with him?

He frowned. This woman was going to be his cousin's wife, so he doubted she was trying to capture his attention. Perhaps he had misread her expression.

Then she glanced back at him, a very feline look in her soft brown eyes, as if she knew his every secret desire and wanted to make them all come true. It was the look Eve must have worn when she held out the apple, and he could no more resist than Adam. His blood quickened despite the impropriety of the situation. Then Miss Rosewood cast down her eyes and once more moved food around her plate with her fork, biting her lower lip.

Dear Lord, that mouth.

Marc laughed at something Lavinia said, jerking him away from his lusty musings. What was the matter with him? Miss Rosewood was his cousin's fiancée—or very nearly so—and he had no business thinking about her as anything more than a potential cousin.

But she seemed to have no such compunction. She kept sneaking glances his way. Whenever he caught her at it, she turned away quickly, blushing. The light played over her curling hair, accenting the exotic-looking structure of her cheekbones. Her lush mouth drew his attention again and again.

Damn it, this was his cousin's woman! He loved and respected his cousin too much to ever cause him sorrow. Marc didn't deserve that.

He wasn't his father, blast it. There would be no more gossip about a Devereaux stealing another man's bride.

But what if the bride was trying to attract *him*?

There was no doubt about it—she kept looking his way, and the gleam in her eyes was far too knowledgeable for the schoolroom miss she was purported to be. What sort of female *was* Anna Rosewood? On the outside she looked to be a demure and proper lady, but no society maiden had ever looked at him like she was starving, and he was a sweet pastry.

None that were innocents, at any rate.

Damn it all! Had Marc attached himself to some sort of wanton? Did the jade only want to marry Marc for his money and title? Was she so immoral that she would flirt with her promised husband's cousin right at Marc's own dinner table?

Well, she had picked the wrong man if she thought to exercise her womanly wiles. He wasn't about to stand aside while she cuckolded Marc before they were even wed.

And he would make sure she knew it.

Dinner seemed to drag on forever.

Her mother sent her frantic signals, mouthing silent suggestions and nodding imperceptibly toward Lord Haverford. The admiral regarded her sternly from beneath his thick brows, clearly displeased that she didn't converse with the earl. But even though Anna knew she would bear the brunt of her parents' displeasure later, she didn't dare try and attract Lord Haverford's attention. Not with Rome sitting right there.

She tightened her fingers around her fork to stop their trembling. He was regarding her with a considering eye. Did he recognize her? She hadn't removed her mask, so she'd thought herself safe. But why else would he watch her so closely? Would he declare her a harlot in front of her family? Or would he pursue her further, hold his knowledge hostage in exchange for the favors she'd denied him the night before?

Her heartbeat thundered in her ears. She ate nothing, heard none of the conversation going on around her. Even if her parents threatened to lock her in her room for the next month with nothing more than bread and water, there was no way she could possibly attempt to comport herself normally. By some miracle, Roman Devereaux had not recognized her. Why betray herself by speaking and perhaps sparking some memory in him?

Finally, the meal ended. Lady Florington awoke as the ladies rose from their seats. "What's that? Is it time to depart?"

"No, Aunt Phyllis," Haverford said, assisting the elderly lady from her chair. "It's time to retire to the drawing room."

"The ladies?"

"Everyone. We're such a small party, I decided to forgo the formality of sending the ladies ahead."

"Scandalous," Lady Florington declared as her great-nephew escorted her from the room. "That was the worst dinner I've ever eaten. You must sack the chef, Haverford."

"Yes, Aunt."

Anna rose slowly. So, there would be no sanctuary for her in retiring with the ladies. No way to escape Rome. He lingered near the doorway, ostensibly to see to the comfort of his mother and sister, but his gaze never left Anna for more than a moment. The longer his gaze rested on her, the more difficult it became to breathe. Her stomach sank as dread swept through her. Why did he stare so? Had he actually recognized her?

As the admiral followed the earl from the

room, Henrietta descended on her like the wrath of Zeus. "What is the matter with you tonight, Anna?" she hissed in a low tone. "You haven't spoken more than two words to Lord Haverford all evening!"

"There was no opportunity."

"Nonsense. This is the perfect time to engage his lordship in conversation." Mrs. Rosewood took Anna by the arm and fairly dragged her toward the exit—and Rome. "This is your chance to show your future husband what an excellent hostess you will be."

They reached the doorway and paused while Rome's sister passed through the portal. Rome cast Anna one last, enigmatic glance before offering his arm to his mother and escorting her through. Anna and her mother followed.

In the drawing room, a card table had been set out. Lady Florington had dozed off again beside the fire, while Anna's father and Lord Haverford stood by two of the four empty chairs.

"Be charming, dearest," her mother murmured. She sat in the chair her husband pulled out for her and gave Anna a pointed, sidelong look. With a mental sigh—for she was a very bad cardplayer—Anna resigned herself to taking the last chair.

"Oh, it's been ages since I played!" Before Anna could take a step, Lavinia had slipped into the fourth chair.

Henrietta frowned, as did Lord Haverford. Anna

just stood near the table, relieved and yet uncomfortable in the face of her mother's displeasure.

"Vin." Rome approached the card table, having escorted his own mother to a chair by the fire. "Perhaps Marc would rather play with Miss Rosewood."

"Oh! How cloddish of me!" Flushing, Lavinia jumped from the chair. "Do sit down, Miss Rosewood."

"Nonsense. My daughter hasn't the head for cards," the admiral stated gruffly. "Do you, Mrs. Emberly?"

"Roman taught me to play," Lavinia admitted shyly. "But I haven't really done so since my marriage."

Rome gave a bark of laughter. "Don't be fooled, Admiral. My sister is very nearly a Captain Sharp."

"Indeed?" Anna's father raised a brow in interest. "Then do take the fourth chair, Mrs. Emberly. I've a mind for a good hand of cards this evening."

Lavinia glanced in question at Anna.

Regardless of her mother's look of warning, Anna waved a hand at the table. "Do play, Mrs. Emberly. I assure you I shall be more comfortable as a spectator."

"You're most gracious, Miss Rosewood." Lavinia sat down at the table, a grin sweeping her face as Admiral Rosewood began to shuffle the deck.

"Sit by the fire with me, Miss Rosewood," Mrs. Devereaux invited. "We shall have a lovely coze."

"Thank you." Stepping away from the card table and out of her mother's range of vision, Anna made her way to the sofa, more than conscious of Rome's towering presence as he trailed along behind her. She sat down beside his mother on the sofa with a respectful smile.

"Have you been in London long?" Mrs. Devereaux asked by way of starting a conversation.

"Not at all." Anna grew momentarily distracted as Rome seated himself in the chair across from them, his expression forbidding.

"And what sights have you seen?" Rome's mother asked. Anna forced her gaze away from the distracting man and managed to formulate a coherent answer to Mrs. Devereaux's question. Soon the two of them fell into the familiar rhythm of polite conversation.

But it took all her concentration. Anna gave the correct replies by rote, her every sense alive with Rome. What was the matter with her? The man she was supposed to marry sat just on the other side of the room, yet she hadn't given him a second thought since Rome appeared.

She had to get ahold of herself. Her entire future lay with Lord Haverford, not with Roman Devereaux. She must forget their encounter and pretend nothing had happened. She should be focusing on finding out the truth about Anthony's death. If she could just make it through this evening, then she would make it a point to avoid Roman Devereaux until the day she was finally wed to his cousin.

Provided he didn't blurt out her secret before then.

"Miss Rosewood?" Mrs. Devereaux touched her hand. "Are you quite all right?"

"Yes." She pasted a polite smile on her face. "I'm sorry. I grew a bit light-headed for a moment. Perhaps it's the proximity to the fire."

"Oh dear. We should move to the settee."

"No, no." Anna held up a hand when the older lady made to rise. "Please, don't. I'm fine now. Do continue your story."

"Are you certain?" Rome's deep rumble sent a shiver down her spine. She turned to look at him, meeting his piercing green eyes with much more serenity than she felt.

"I am quite certain, Mr. Devereaux. Thank you for your concern."

Trying to pretend he was just another piece of furniture, she attempted to block him from her mind and turned her attention back to his mother.

Rome seethed with annoyance as Miss Anna Rosewood so neatly dismissed him.

She sat there with her spine so straight it looked to crack, her hands folded demurely in her lap as she conversed with his mother. To anyone else, she looked like the perfect lady.

But not to him. There was something about her, a secrecy that set his every instinct to full awareness. What was it? He watched the firelight flicker in her hair, and a hint of recognition swept over him, so fleeting that he could barely grab the thought. Frowning, he studied her, the curling brown hair with its glimmers of blond, the big brown eyes. She laughed, and an elusive dimple peeked briefly from beside her mouth. Where had he seen . . . ?

She turned her head, and the light fell on an angle, casting a brief shadow across the upper half of her face. Almost like a mask . . .

Rose.

He struggled with the incredulity of it. The innocent debutante chatting with his mother could not possibly be the bold and worldly beauty. Rose was a young woman whose circumstances had so degenerated that she'd had to resort to the oldest trade in order to survive. She had possessed a fire that had drawn him irrevocably toward her and driven him mad with frustration when she had slipped from his grasp.

Anna Rosewood might be a flirt, but no young lady of her station would ever be caught dead masquerading as a courtesan, even in jest. It would mean the end of her social standing, and in Anna's case, the end of her betrothal as well.

He could not imagine any situation that would cause Anna to take such a risk. It was not possible. There was no way the two women could be the same person.

Because if she *were* Rose . . . He recalled how he'd touched her, the intimacy they're forged between them when he'd made her climax so easily, how he wanted her. The desire still burned like hell's fire. He glanced at the woman seated primly before him. If it were true, then he had taken liberties with the woman Marc was courting. It was too horrible to contemplate.

But what if he had?

The notion refused to be dismissed. Even their names were similar . . . Rosewood . . . Rose.

Dear God, what kind of wanton was Marc shackling himself to?

He must get her alone and speak to her. At first he'd thought she was just a schoolroom miss with a wild streak. Now he didn't know what to believe. Was she an adventuress of some sort? Had she masqueraded as a doxy for a bet or a dare? Or just for the sheer excitement of tasting the forbidden?

He studied the well-bred young lady across from him. Every hair was in place, every button buttoned, every mannerism and expression the product of years of proper teaching. Miss Anna Rosewood appeared a lady.

But he remembered a woman. Such a woman. His mouth went dry at the memories.

Something didn't fit, and he meant to discover what. If not tonight, then soon.

He would not stand by while she made a laughingstock of the Earl of Haverford. The Devereaux name had suffered enough in past years, and Marc didn't deserve the embarrassment. He was a good man, a fair man—and the only member of the family who would open his doors to Rome and his mother and sister after the scandal.

History would *not* repeat itself. As the son of the man who had once stolen a Haverford bride, Rome would see to it there was no more scandal brought upon the Haverford family.

She would have to see him again.

Anna accepted her wrap from the butler and followed her parents outside to their waiting carriage, lost in thought. What if Rome was a member of the secret society? What if he'd had a part in Anthony's death? She would have to see him again, perhaps more than once, in order to determine what he knew about her brother's last days. The knowledge dismayed her.

She had let him touch her, take liberties no man had ever taken. And she'd reveled in the desire he ignited. Much to her chagrin, she wanted more.

Wanton girl! She was spoken for, all but betrothed, and this man could well have had a part in her brother's death. Yet still her flesh sang when she remembered their encounter. Still she wanted to move closer to him, to revel in the deep rumble of his voice as he whispered passionate endearments. She wanted his hands and mouth on her again, longed to feel that devastating pleasure that had left her innocence shattered forever.

Even if he was the enemy.

"Well," her mother said in icy tones as the carriage lurched into motion, "I am *most* displeased with you, Anna."

She jerked her gaze to her mother's face. "Mama?"

"You are not doing your part to secure your betrothal," Henrietta said. Her mouth a grim line, she shook her head in disappointment. "You had all the charm of a potted plant this evening. Why, if Mrs. Emberly were not already wed, I'd swear you would have lost Lord Haverford to her."

"Oh, let the girl alone," her father said. "The thing's all but done. Just need to sign some papers."

"And I won't be satisfied until those settlements *are* signed," Henrietta snapped. "In the meantime, Lord Haverford might well come across a young lady who might possess enough charm and beauty to lure him away from our Anna. She must secure his affections, agreement or not."

"Haverford's an honorable man," the admiral said. "He won't be dismissing a promise made by his father."

"I refuse to depend on that. Anna is nearly twenty-one, and Haverford has yet to make an offer. If he is so keen to keep his father's promise, what's keeping the man?"

"He'll come up to scratch and do what's right. Invited the Devereaux bunch, didn't he? And he had no reason to, none at all."

Henrietta made a sound of exasperation. "They're his family."

"Lady Florington didn't say a word to them, did you notice? Not a single word. They're her family, too, but she doesn't even acknowledge their presence." The admiral shifted his position on the narrow seat.

"What do you mean, Papa?" Anna asked.

"'Tis not a tale for a young girl's ears," Henrietta declared with a disapproving sniff.

"Then why are you talking about it in front of me?" Anna asked. "Really, if you want to keep such things secret, you shouldn't discuss them openly."

"What cheek!" Henrietta gasped.

The admiral laughed. "Shorten sail, Henrietta. The girl's got a point."

"Disrespectful," her mother mumbled, but she turned her gaze to the scenery outside the window.

"She's marrying into this family. She's got a right to know." He turned to his daughter. "Roman Devereaux's father caused a scandal a while back, so his wife, son, and daughter are now no longer received in many circles."

"What happened?" Anna asked, fascinated.

"Really, Quentin," Henrietta interjected. "The details are not in any way a proper subject for a girl of Anna's age to hear."

"She needs to know," her father insisted.

"Not all of it." Her very posture declaring her displeasure, Henrietta returned her attention to the scenery outside.

"Fine then." The admiral gave a sigh, and said, "About ten-odd years ago, Oliver Devereaux ran off with Alicia Sefton, who was to marry the old earl. It was quite the scandal."

Anna's mouth dropped open. "I should say so!"

"Deplorable conduct," her mother asserted.

"Quite so," her father agreed. "Suffice it to say that young Haverford holds no ill will toward the family of the man who humiliated his father. Honorable man, Haverford. He'll make you a fine husband."

"If the betrothal ever comes to pass," her mother grumbled. "Anna, the next time we are in Lord Haverford's company, you really must be more amusing to keep his attention focused on you."

"Yes, Mama."

"I believe we are to accompany Lord Haverford to the theater on Thursday," Henrietta said. "You should perhaps wear blue to remind Lord Haverford of the Devereaux sapphire . . ."

Anna tuned out her mother's strategies. She would wear what her mother wanted her to; she always did. Honestly, Mama seemed to enjoy

Anna's London activities more than Anna herself did. Henrietta plotted and planned each stage of the pursuit of Lord Haverford with the ruthlessness of a general.

No wonder she and Papa got along so well.

While she knew she should be trying to placate Mama by thinking of ways to attract Lord Haverford, another gentleman preoccupied her thoughts. Roman Devereaux just would not be dismissed.

She would have to learn more about him, about his friends and the places he frequented. Perhaps she could learn the identity of the young man who'd accompanied him to the dinner at Vauxhall. One of them *must* know something about the society and maybe even about Anthony's death.

She would obtain the information she needed, even if it meant she had to spend time alone with a man who preoccupied her thoughts far more than he should.

Chapter 4

At precisely half past nine the next morning, Rome strode up to the door of the rooms frequented by Peter Brantley, curled his hand into a fist, and pounded. Then he paused to listen. A moan came from within the domicile, followed by a soft thud and the sound of something being dragged.

A small smile curved his lips. Good. The lad was at home.

He raised his fist and rapped again—solid thumps, designed to vibrate through the skull of a young man still in his cups—little caring that the racket would rouse not only Peter, but his neighbors as well.

There was a crash, a groan. The slow shuffling

of reluctant feet. And, finally, the click of the door latch.

Peter peered through the crack in the door, squinting against the morning sunlight. "Who the devil—"

"Good morning, Peter." Shoving the portal wide, Rome strode inside.

Peter clung to the latch as if to remain upright, staring at him with bleary eyes reddened by a night's worth of drinking. "Devereaux," he said. "What the devil are you doing here?"

"Waking the dead, it seems." Casting a disparaging look over the lad, Rome shook his head. He easily wrested the door from Peter's tenuous grip and slammed it closed.

Peter winced and pressed his palms to either side of his head. "Have a bit of compassion, won't you?"

"Where have you been? Don't answer. I can tell by the look of you—and by the stench—what you have been doing."

Peter glared at him. "Shove off, Devereaux. You're not my father."

"No, I'm not." Rome grabbed the younger man by the front of his wrinkled shirt—slept in, from the look of it—and dragged him up on tiptoe. "But I promised your brother that I would look after you, and by God, I will do just that, with or without your cooperation." He released his grip so suddenly that Peter staggered. "Now, we're going to have a talk, beginning with where you disappeared to that night at Vauxhall."

Peter sent him a baleful look as he smoothed the front of his shirt. "I went out with friends is all."

"And would those 'friends' include the swordsman who disrupted the party?"

Peter paled. "No."

"Let's talk about the swordsman." Rome shoved a crumpled coat off a chair and sat down. "Do you know who he was?"

"It's none of your affair." The bravado faded from his voice with the last word.

"On the contrary, Peter. Your brother made it my affair."

"When will you stop hanging that over my head?" Peter swiped a hand over his face. "I'm a grown man. My life is my own."

"Is it?" Rome rose and gripped Peter's hand, the hand that wore a ring with a black rose crossed with a sword. "Or does it belong to them?"

"You don't know anything!" Peter wrenched his hand away. "And I don't want you to know. This is my business. Mine."

The boy turned away, practically sobbing.

"Peter," Rome said quietly, "have they threatened you?"

Peter froze for an instant, then nodded. He sank down on a chair, shoulders hunched, head bent, shuddering. "I want to get out," he whispered.

"Get out?" Rome came over, laid a hand on his shoulder. "Get out of what?"

"The Black Rose Society." The words erupted, strangled, from Peter's throat. "I thought it would be fun, an adventure. And I would end up rich."

"Tell me."

Peter looked up at him, misery in his eyes. "I'm afraid, Rome."

Rome squeezed his shoulder. "I'm watching your back. Now tell me what's going on."

Peter sighed, as if all the strength had left his body. "Very well. I was approached by a friend who had joined the society. He encouraged me to become a member. It sounded exciting."

"I imagine he made it appear so."

Peter shrugged. "All the members are matched in secret duels. The person who wins the duel moves to the next level, and the one who loses must start all over again from the beginning level."

"I see. Do you pay some sort of fee to join?"

Peter nodded. "And if you start all over, you have to pay again."

Rome's jaw clenched. "Greedy bastards, aren't they? How did they threaten you?"

"The society is supposed to be completely secret." Peter held up his hand. "We all wear these rings to identify us as members."

Rome took the lad's hand and studied the symbol with close interest. "Everyone wears these?"

"Yes. Though the members of the Triad have rubies in theirs where the rosebud should be."

"What's the Triad?" He released the boy's hand.

"The top three duelists in the society. If you win against all your other matches, you have the chance to battle the members of the Triad. If you beat even one of them, you assume his position."

"And these three men—they are the members in charge of the whole society?"

"Yes, and they are the judges at the matches."

"I believe I am forming an accurate picture. Go on."

"That night at Vauxhall, it was a member of the Triad who disrupted the party." Peter dropped his gaze to the floor. "He was angry because we were all socializing together. We had betrayed the secrecy of the society."

"And that is why they threatened you?"

Peter nodded. "The swordsman found me at Vauxhall after he had appeared at the dinner party and told me that if I ever betrayed the secrecy of the society again, it might mean my life." He cast Rome a look of shame. "When you first asked where I went after Vauxhall, I lied about being with my friends. I hid alone at a tavern that night, like a scared child."

"It seems to me like you exercised good sense." Rome sat down in a comfortable chair. "And now that you've told me about it, you have no more reason to fear. I won't let anything happen to you, Peter. Now tell me what else you know about this Black Rose Society."

Peter sat back in his chair with a sigh of relief and told him.

Anna knocked on the door of the modest but attractive town house, accompanied by her maid, Lizzie. An elderly butler opened the door, studying them with somber eyes.

"I am paying a call on Mrs. Emberly," Anna said, producing her calling card. "Is she at home?"

"Madame is indeed receiving this morning," he said, accepting the card. "Do come in, and I will announce you."

Anna stepped into the house and handed her bonnet and wrap to the butler. He stowed both hers and Lizzie's belongings, then led them down the hall to a sunny parlor.

"Miss Rosewood," he intoned, then stepped back and led her maid away to the servants' kitchen.

As she entered the room, Anna took a moment to study the décor. Tidy, she decided. Nothing terribly expensive or ostentatious, but good solid furnishings that gleamed from meticulous care. Her hostess sat alone on the sofa, a teacup and some plain biscuits on the table beside her.

Mrs. Emberly stood. "Miss Rosewood, what a delightful surprise!"

"Good morning, Mrs. Emberly." Anna blinked in astonishment as the vivacious lady clasped both her hands in greeting.

"Please, do call me Lavinia. Or Vin. Why, we are all but family, aren't we?" Lavinia led her to the sofa. "Would you care for some tea? I keep the stuff nearby at all times since I discovered that I am increasing."

"Ah . . . congratulations." Uncertain how to react to such a candid statement—her mother would have been horrified that such a topic had been mentioned even in passing in the unwed Anna's presence—she sat down on the sofa. "Yes, tea would be lovely."

Lavinia rang for a servant. The same elderly man responded and was told to bring a tea tray. "And lots of biscuits," Lavinia added as the butler turned away. She gave Anna a mischievous smile. "I do love biscuits."

Anna smiled. "So do I."

"Something in common!" Lavinia giggled and reached for her tea. "I'm sorry, Miss Rosewood. I must appear appallingly familiar with you, but I feel as if I have known you my entire life, what with your arrangement with Haverford and all."

"If I am to call you Lavinia, then you must call me Anna. And the arrangement is yet informal."

Lavinia waved a dismissive hand. "Never fear, dear Anna. Haverford is nothing if not honorable. He will fulfill his father's promise."

"I'm certain he will."

"And then we will be cousins."

"So we will."

Their conversation was interrupted by the arrival of the tea tray. The few minutes necessary to pour and fix her tea allowed Anna a chance to think about how she should best broach the subject that had brought her here.

Once the butler left the room, Anna took a sip of her tea and began, "Did your mother enjoy the evening last night?"

"She did," Lavinia confirmed. "Mama rarely goes out anymore."

"I'm sorry to hear that." She took another careful sip of tea. "And your brother? How did he fare?"

"Rome is Rome." Lavinia gave a sigh of sisterly exasperation. "He only found out about my condition just before we left for Haverford's, and I swear he never took his eyes off me all night! As if I would shatter spontaneously or some such nonsense."

"Perhaps he's simply concerned for your health."

"Perhaps. However, I cannot thank you enough for giving up your seat at the card table. I do believe that was the first time during the entire evening that I didn't look up and find my brother glaring at me."

"I am a terrible cardplayer," Anna confessed. "It was a pleasure for me *not* to have to play."

"Instead you were the sacrifice to my brother's bad temper," Lavinia said, with a grin that held no hint of regret. "I hope you can forgive me."

"Of course." Anna reached for a biscuit. "I do

hope his ill humor doesn't overly affect you as of late."

"I just ignore him," Lavinia said, with a shrug. "I know he means well, but I am a married woman now."

Anna's lips curved at the bittersweet memory of her own brother. "I do understand."

"My goodness, do forgive me!" Lavinia's face reflected her dismay. "You just lost your brother recently. What a clod pate I am!"

"Please don't distress yourself. I take comfort in listening to you speak of your brother. It brings back good memories."

"But still . . ." Lavinia took a biscuit from her plate and plunked it onto Anna's. "There. Now you will understand how truly sorry I am."

"Indeed." Solemnly, Anna bit into the biscuit. "I do appreciate your sincere regret."

Lavinia giggled. "Oh, you are too delightful, Anna! I do hope Haverford speaks to your father soon so that we may be cousins that much earlier. Are you attending the theater with Haverford on Thursday?"

"Yes, as are my parents. Lord Haverford has invited us to share his box."

"I will be there, as well. I haven't been to the theater in ages!"

"And will your husband be attending?"

"I do hope so. His political parties frequently take him away, so I would hate for him to miss it." She reached for her last biscuit. "Mother does not enjoy the theater, and Roman may or may not attend, as the whim strikes him."

Anna strived to keep her tone casual. "Does he not enjoy the theater either?"

"I expect that he does, but business keeps him from such pleasure. He has just resigned his commission and has turned his attention toward a diplomatic position in the government."

"How exciting. I imagine he will travel frequently."

"It all depends if Edgar Vaughn will grant him the position. But Rome is determined to win the post, and I do not doubt that he will do so. Once Rome sets his mind to something he is relentless."

Rome's voice echoed through her mind. *This isn't over, Rose. I will find you, and we will finish what we've started.*

Anna choked on her tea.

"Goodness, are you all right?"

Anna dabbed her mouth with her napkin. "Yes, quite."

A knock sounded at the front door, echoing to them even in the tiny parlor. Anna glanced at the clock on the mantel and realized she had spent more than the proper allotted amount of time chatting with Lavinia. She set down her teacup. "Goodness, is that the time? Mama will be livid if I am late to my fitting at the dressmaker's."

"Must you go so soon?"

"Unfortunately, I must. I expect I shall see you Thursday night at the theater?"

"Indeed."

The butler appeared. "Mrs. Prudence Wentworth."

Lavinia wrinkled her nose, and whispered, "Gossiping old prune. But she is one of Henry's political allies."

Both young ladies stood as an older woman entered the room. Mrs. Wentworth steamed forward like a ship at full sail, her impressive bosom leading the way. "Mrs. Emberly, how well you look."

"Thank you, Mrs. Wentworth. Have you met Miss Rosewood?"

The daunting matron pulled out a quizzing glass and inspected Anna. "Admiral Rosewood's daughter, I presume?"

"Yes, Mrs. Wentworth."

"A pleasure to make your acquaintance. Ah, tea! Just the thing!"

"Allow me to pour you a cup," Lavinia said, doing so at once.

Mrs. Wentworth sank her substantial body into a chair. "Are you joining us, Miss Rosewood?"

"Unfortunately, no. I have an appointment I must keep."

"Good day to you then," Mrs. Wentworth said, then took the cup and saucer handed to her by Lavinia.

"Thank you for calling," Lavinia said. "Bagsley will see you out."

"Until Thursday." With a gracious nod at Mrs.

Wentworth, Anna left the room, shutting the doors behind her. She paused for a moment to gather her composure.

The Devereaux family was strangely lacking in pretense—or was it subtlety? Such candor, such open affection. These things didn't exist in Anna's world.

She glanced around for Bagsley. Finding the hallway deserted, she wondered if he might be fetching Lizzie.

"Bagsley?" she called. Footsteps sounded down the hallway, and she walked toward them. "Are you there?"

Silence. She gave a small huff of exasperation. She didn't fancy going back into the parlor and facing Mrs. Wentworth just so Lavinia could ring for the butler, but what choice did she have? She turned back toward the parlor, but something caught her eye in the room directly across the hall. Glancing about one more time for a servant and seeing none, she walked over and stepped into what looked to be Henry Emberly's office.

The painting that had so attracted her hung in a place of honor above the mantel. At first glimpse, she'd thought it was Rome, but now that she studied it more closely, she could see the differences between the man in the portrait and Roman Devereaux. She walked all the way into the room, her attention completely captured by the likeness. The striking, dark-haired man in the portrait had the same sharply attractive features as the man she knew, but he also had dark brown eyes—very different from Rome's piercing green—and a beauty mark near his ear.

Definitely a close relative.

"Good morning, Miss Rosewood."

Anna spun about with a squeak of surprise to find Rome himself standing behind her. "What are you doing here?"

He chuckled. "I came to call on my sister, but Mrs. Wentworth's presence inspired me to examine the library. What about you?" Amusement lurked in those mesmerizing eyes of his, as if he knew perfectly well she'd been indulging her curiosity.

She cleared her throat. "I've gotten a bit turned around," she fibbed.

"If you've come to call on Vin, I will be happy to escort you to the parlor."

"No!" She took a breath, willing her heart to stop its thundering. "That is, I was just leaving."

"The doorway to the street is not located in the library."

She blushed, caught. "I wanted to look more closely at this portrait. Who is he?"

Rome cast a hard glance at the painting. "My father."

"You look very like him."

"Unfortunately, there is nothing to be done about that." He took her arm and guided her away from the picture. "Vin hardly knew our father. Perhaps that is why she keeps his portrait when my mother demanded it be removed from her household."

The edge in his voice warned her not to trespass further.

"I shouldn't have intruded," Anna apologized. "I was simply drawn by the resemblance."

"Don't give it another thought. I find the situation much in my favor, as we did not have the opportunity to converse at Haverford's dinner party." He met her gaze for one, long, meaningful moment. "I thought we could renew our acquaintance beyond the masks of society."

Masks? Heaven help her, did he *know*?

Impossible. Shaken, she pulled her arm from his grasp. "I'm afraid I am late for an appointment. Some other time, perhaps."

"Surely you can spare me a moment. After all, we are practically family."

"I don't know—" She glanced toward the open door.

"Come now, Miss Rosewood," he coaxed. "I assure you we will leave the door ajar."

"Very well." Afraid that protesting further might arouse his suspicions, she ignored the instinct that urged her to flee and instead edged just out of touching range. "But only a moment, Mr. Devereaux. My mother expects me directly."

He gave a nod. "Message received, Miss Rosewood. I will do nothing to inconvenience your mama."

His persuasive smile shook her to her bones and spurred her to move immediately to the opposite side of the room, where two great leather chairs sat beneath the window overlooking the tiny garden. She smoothed one hand over the dark leather chair back and gazed out the window.

It was all she could do to maintain a calm expression. Inside, her intuition demanded that she run. But she didn't dare. If she left too quickly, it would only feed his suspicions. Yet if she lingered, she took the chance of betraying herself.

Watching her, Rome struggled to sort out his tangled emotions. When he'd seen her alone in the library, he hadn't been able to resist joining her. He told himself he just wanted to find out if she was toying with his family. That he needed to make certain she was not trying to play Marc for a fool. But her resemblance to the woman he had met at Vauxhall—and the possibility that they could be one and the same—stirred other, more disturbing feelings.

Her lush mouth haunted him, and the husky timbre of her voice played along his nerve endings just like the one in his memories. His body stirred just at the remembrance of holding that sweet female body in his arms, and he couldn't stop himself from taking a brief, frank appraisal of her physical charms.

She turned an inquiring glance his way, and he stifled his passionate thoughts with the chokehold of strong will.

Marc's intended. Forbidden.

He lingered near Henry's desk. Better to keep space between them, especially since his wits all but failed him in her presence. None of the usual social niceties came as easily to his normally glib tongue. He knew he wanted to find out the truth about her, but the delicate situation called for all his diplomatic skills.

If he was right, he might very well save Marc from marrying the wrong woman. And if he was mistaken, he would have deeply offended a lady who would soon be a member of his family. That was an insult even Marc would not overlook.

"What lovely roses," she said, sending him a nervous smile.

Roses? Was she mocking him? Or was she testing him?

"Roses are my favorite," he replied, watching her carefully. "No scent is sweeter."

Her eyes widened and her lips parted as if startled, but then she looked quickly away. Guilt? Or modesty?

The late-morning sunlight brought out the gold highlights in her brown hair and silhouetted her fair profile in orange, like a halo for the angel she appeared to be. Her dress was a pale green, quite appropriate for a young lady of her age and station, and yet he couldn't forget another green dress he had recently admired, a soft verdant satin that had adorned the slim body of the mysterious Rose.

Were the women one and the same? His intellect argued that such a thing was impossible, and yet he couldn't deny the evidence before his eyes. Anna Rosewood bore a certain remarkable resemblance to his Rose. If only he could kiss her, he might know for sure.

But one generally did not go about accusing gently born young ladies of masquerading as prostitutes.

She glanced at him again as the silence stretched on, her dark eyes wary. "Mr. Devereaux, you said you wanted to speak to me, and yet you say nothing. I should go."

She turned to do just that, and he stepped forward, cutting off her escape before she could move more than a pace. "Please wait."

"What do you want of me?" She took a step backward and gripped the top of the chair, her fingers creasing the leather.

"To get to know you better." He attempted a charming smile, but his head spun with the scent of her, the nearness of her. "Marc is my favorite cousin, and I am curious about his future bride."

"Not quite his bride," she corrected. "Nothing has been formalized."

"Does that mean you do not consider yourself betrothed to my cousin?" Drawn closer despite his resolution to remain aloof, he rested his hand on the back of the chair beside hers.

"There is an understanding between our two families." She inched her hand away from his.

"However, no formal settlements have been signed. Until that happens, I would not presume to call Lord Haverford my betrothed."

Did that mean she considered herself fair game for any available man? Was she the flirt he suspected? Or worse, was she the sort of woman who would pretend to be a doxy?

He moved a bit closer to her. Attar of roses teased his senses, bringing back the Vauxhall incident with vivid clarity. If he closed his eyes, he could almost imagine himself back there. She resembled Rose; she even appeared to be the same height. And heaven help him, she smelled the same. But that was still not enough to prove his outlandish theory. Many young ladies of quality wore the same scent.

"No doubt your parents are pleased that you are to make such a smart match," he murmured. "But how do *you* feel about the situation?"

She flicked him a cautious glance. "I am content."

"Are you? Marc is a good man, but his passion lies with his estate and his account books. Will you be happy married to such a fellow, I wonder?"

"Sir, you overstep." Pink swept into her cheeks, and she turned away from him.

She was right. "My apologies."

Her spine looked so stiff, he thought she would flounce away on the spot. Instead, she turned back. "I have no desire to insult a member of Lord Haverford's family, but I must tell you I find your questions most disturbing, Mr. Devereaux."

"And I find *you* most disturbing, Miss Rosewood. You seem very familiar to me. I cannot help but wonder if we have met before."

She paled. "I'm certain I would have remembered if we had met before the earl's dinner party."

"A gentleman fancies that a lady will find him more than merely memorable." Following an impulse, he took her hand and raised it to his lips, his eyes intent on her face.

He was testing her. Trying to trap her.

Anna's blood froze like ice in her veins. She willed her knees to stop shaking. "And are you a gentleman, sir?"

He gave her that charming grin again. "That's for the lady to decide."

Unsettled by the low, intimate tone, she yanked her hand from his grasp. "I think not. No gentleman would flirt so with a lady who was being courted by another."

Some fierce emotion flickered across his face, making her regret her rash rebuke. Her heart bumped awkwardly in her chest. Had he indeed guessed that she was Rose? How had she betrayed herself? Or had she?

"So loyal to Marc already? How admirable."

She tilted her chin at the goad in his voice. "We are not yet betrothed, but I can assure you that if I marry, I would be a loyal wife."

"Would you?" he murmured. "I wonder."

"You insult me," she snapped.

"My apologies," he said swiftly, so swiftly, she suspected he didn't mean a word of it. "I should have said, that where Marc is concerned, it is important to avoid even the appearance of disloyalty."

"Appearances can be deceiving."

He held her gaze a long moment. "Precisely."

She narrowed her eyes, tiring of his game. "And you, sir . . . what sort of loyalty to your cousin are you demonstrating by secluding me in this room and toying with me in such an outrageous manner? You should be ashamed of yourself."

His expression shuttered. "You're right. I apologize again."

She took in his penitent posture, the way he clenched his hands at his sides, and felt no pity. "If you will excuse me, I must take my leave."

"Allow me to escort you."

"I can find my way out," she insisted, heading for the open doorway.

"I will see you to the door." Brooking no argument, he caught up with her in two easy strides and slowed his pace to hers.

"You are a most stubborn individual, Mr. Devereaux." Anna swept out into the hallway, Roman behind her, just as the parlor door opened down the hall.

"Blast it!" Rome grabbed her arm and jerked her back into the library.

She let out a yelp of surprise as he shoved her

behind him and closed the door all but a crack. "What are you doing?" she hissed.

"Shhh. Mrs. Wentworth is out there. You don't want her seeing us alone together." He peered out into the hallway through the crack in the door.

"There would have been no chance of that had you not followed me in here." Knowing how precarious their position was, she kept her voice to the softest of whispers but gave him her most chilling look of disapproval, which she had practiced by watching her mother.

Clearly undaunted by The Look, he leaned closer to her. "Do you remember our discussion about loyalty, Miss Rosewood? Should my cousin hear from that busybody that we were alone together, even for a few minutes, your 'informal' betrothal to him would become nothing more than a fanciful dream."

"And you, of course, would suffer little if at all from society's interpretation of the incident," she scoffed.

His expression hardened, his lips thinning to a grim line. "Perhaps you simply do not value honor as much as I do, but I assure you that my good name means everything to me."

Belatedly, she remembered about his father. The shadow of his sire's scandal would surely have marked him. "Of course," she whispered. "Please forgive me."

"Stay quiet," he muttered, "and we shall both get out of this with our reputations intact."

She nodded, and he looked out at the events in the hallway, presenting her with a close view of his broad shoulders in a well-tailored, bottle green coat. She remembered how those shoulders had blotted out the light when he'd bent to kiss her.

She took a deep breath to control her thoughts, but she only succeeded in bringing his scent to her, the musky cologne that had lingered on her hands even after they'd parted company. A mere whiff sent her blood humming and her body tingling.

Dear Lord.

He was the most confusing, irritating man she had ever met. Yet as she stared at his back and shoulders, at the way his dark brown hair curled around his ears and nape, she wanted to touch him again, to tangle her fingers in that hair and hold him close as they kissed.

She nearly did it, had actually raised her hand to touch him, when Lavinia's muffled voice reminded her where she was. She snatched her hand away and curled her traitorous fingers into a fist. This was madness!

"Mrs. Wentworth is gone." Rome turned to her. "You can go now."

"I'm no longer your prisoner then?"

He arched a brow at her. "Do you want to be?"

She made a sound of frustration. "You are most vexing, Mr. Devereaux."

"I do what is necessary."

Pinned beneath that knowing green-eyed stare, she said, "Your concern for your cousin's welfare is most laudable. I assure you I will make him a good and loyal wife."

"I'm pleased to hear it, Miss Rosewood." Had she imagined it, or had he emphasized on the first syllable of her name?

She wasn't Rose, had never been Rose. That had just been a fantasy that had gone too far—and had felt too real.

She had to leave, to go meet her mother at the dressmaker's and be Anna Rosewood, soon-to-be-fiancée of Lord Haverford.

The sooner she escaped this house and this man, the better off they would all be.

Chapter 5

Rome closed the door behind Rose—Miss Rosewood—and resisted the urge to watch her from the window. The girl was gone, the danger past. Their names would not be bandied by gossiping tongues this night.

He rested his forehead against the door. What had possessed him to take such a chance with scandal? With the tantalizing memories of Vauxhall haunting him, he'd been unable to resist following her into the library. Had he really thought a few moments of privacy would coax Rose to emerge from the persona of the proper Miss Rosewood?

He'd flirted with her, nearly insulted her. He'd walked the edge of dishonor by his actions, and the lady had been right to call him no gentleman.

She was forbidden to him. He should stay away.

"Have you taken over Bagsley's duties, dear brother?"

Lavinia's voice jerked him from his thoughts. He glanced over to see her standing in the doorway of the parlor.

How long had she been there?

"I trust Miss Rosewood remembered to take her maid with her."

Blast. Too long.

"She did not," he realized, turning fully to face his sister.

"Really? How peculiar." Her voice was all innocence, but the sarcasm still sliced through.

"Drop the pretense, Vin," he said. "I know when you're displeased with me."

"Displeased!" Abandoning any semblance of calm, Lavinia advanced on him. "Try amazed! Are you *mad*? What possessed you to closet yourself alone with Miss Rosewood when that Wentworth woman was in the parlor?"

Guilt pinched like poorly made shoes. "'Tis none of your affair."

"It certainly is my affair! This is my house, Roman. If that woman had seen you sneaking about with Miss Rosewood, any shred of reputation you have managed to build for yourself would have been ruined, and probably mine with it."

"I'm aware of that." Casting a grim glance down the empty hall—where a servant might appear at any second—he jerked his head toward the parlor.

Vin heaved a long-suffering sigh and preceded him into the room. "Nothing you can say can explain this, brother."

"Hear me out." Once inside, he closed the door soundly behind them.

"You can be certain I am eager to listen." She folded her arms across her chest. "What happened just now between you and Anna?"

"I wanted to talk to her for a few moments."

"You could have done that just as well right here, in the acceptable company of your sister."

"With that gossiping Wentworth woman just salivating for a good *on dit*?" He gave a harsh bark of laughter. "I think not."

"True." She sighed. "She does seem to relish a juicy story, doesn't she?"

"She does. And since I but wanted to ascertain what sort of female Miss Rosewood was . . ."

"What sort of female? You nodcock, she's a perfectly acceptable lady. What more is there to discover?"

He shrugged. "I disagree. When we met last night, she seemed rather insipid. I wanted to make certain she was good enough for Marc."

"Good heavens, what a Banbury tale," she scoffed.

"Vin—"

She held up a hand, stopping his warning before he could finish. "Never mind. I know you will not share your motives with me."

"There was—"

"After all," she continued in a long-suffering tone, "I am just your sister."

He frowned. "Lavinia . . ."

"And the fact that your actions today could not only ruin your reputation but mine and by association, *my husband's*, should not disturb me at all."

He let out a long sigh, rubbing the bridge of his nose to soothe the headache that had suddenly bloomed behind his eyes. "Lavinia, you know I would do nothing to blacken your name or your husband's. Your marriage to Emberly is the only thing that keeps you from sharing the exile with the rest of the family."

"Then why would you do such a thing?" She spread her hands in entreaty. "Don't you remember how it was? You had barely reached your majority, and everyone treated you like you had committed the sin, not Father. Mother dared not show her face in polite circles. And I was a child, just turned ten, and I could not understand why my friends would no longer play with me."

"Of course I remember."

"Roman, you are so very close to leaving behind Father's dishonor and achieving your own success. Once you enter the diplomatic circles—"

"*If* I enter the diplomatic circles."

"*When* you enter your chosen position, your accomplishments will overshadow the scandal, and everything will change." She laid a hand on his cheek, forcing him to look at her. "Time has passed. Father died in that carriage accident with the woman he stole. You and I grew up and have made something of ourselves. We can end this curse."

Rome smiled, touched by her optimism, and pressed a kiss to her forehead. "You always make everything so simple."

"It is simple. I love you." She gave his cheek two sharp pats. "Now stay away from Anna Rosewood."

Her abrupt change of subject startled a laugh from him. "Vin, you were ever as tenacious as one of Haverford's hunting dogs."

"Only because I'm right." Her teasing smile faded. "I don't want any unkind gossip circulating about you."

He chuckled. "For heaven's sake, Vin, I was just talking to her. If it means that much to you, I promise to exercise better judgment from now on."

"I should hope so." She shook her head. "Such strange goings-on today."

"Now, Vin, it's not as bad as all that."

She blinked in surprise. "Heavens, I'd forgotten you didn't know. Mrs. Wentworth brought the latest news with her."

"Gossip is hardly news."

"This is more than gossip. Reginald Dalton was found dead this morning outside the Cock and Crown tavern."

"Reginald Dalton?" His attention sharpened as

he visualized the fellow. "Lord Huxley's cousin?"

"Yes." She pulled out her lacy handkerchief and delicately dabbed at her eyes. "I'm sorry. I have become a regular watering pot these days."

"It's understandable, Vin." As he pulled his still-sniffling sister into a comforting embrace, he visualized young Dalton, a blond, blue-eyed fellow who had a penchant for curricle racing and hunting. He'd barely reached his majority. "How did he die, Vin?"

"That's the oddest thing," she whispered, her voice muffled against his coat. "It looks as though he was killed with a sword."

She was late.

As the carriage came to a halt outside Madame Dauphine's, Anna almost didn't wait for the tiger to hop down and open the door for her. She had left Lavinia's without her maid, which was bad enough, but now she was nearly a quarter hour late for her appointment. Mama would be furious.

She hurried toward the entrance of the modiste's shop. She had tried to use the drive as an opportunity to calm her frazzled nerves, but it hadn't worked. Her conversation with Rome had left her tense and troubled.

She had a strong suspicion that he had guessed her secret, and he had seemed more than a little interested in her impending betrothal. If he did recognize her, perhaps he objected to her becoming Lord Haverford's wife? Her face heated. No man would want a wanton for a bride, and after her behavior at Vauxhall, she could guess what he thought of her.

Or, given the circumstances under which they had met, he might consider Rose some sort of threat to the mysterious society.

Since Rome was currently her only link to the group of men she believed responsible for her brother's death, she had no choice but to continue to see him. But she would have to be very careful. Roman Devereaux seemed very dangerous, and not just to her reputation.

She pushed open the door to Madame Dauphine's. Mama looked up from a conversation with Mrs. Bentley. "Good, you've arrived. Do go right into the back room, Anna. Madame Dauphine is waiting for you." She bent her head near Mrs. Bentley's and whispered in a low tone that her daughter couldn't make out.

Anna hesitated. She had expected a scolding and a lecture on responsibility, perhaps even an inquiry as to the whereabouts of her maid. But Mama was clearly completely oblivious to everything but her intense conversation with Mrs. Bentley. Puzzled, she made her way to the fitting room, where Madame Dauphine waited.

"At last, you have arrived!" The modiste snapped her fingers, and her two assistants, who had been sitting diligently sewing, leaped to their feet and took up the two dresses that Mama had ordered.

"I apologize for being late, madame," Anna said. She set down her reticule and untied the ribbons of her bonnet.

"*Ça ne fait rien*," Madame said, with a cluck of her tongue. She set about unfastening Anna's dress as Anna stripped off her gloves. "Your Maman, she is most insistent these be done today. We must hurry. *Vite, vite!*" she barked at her assistants. The two girls both came forward at the same time, each holding a half-sewn garment. As Anna skimmed off her own dress, Madame took a soft blue silk from one of the girls. The assistant took Anna's discarded dress, and Madame slipped the new one over Anna's head. "Ah, *bien*," the Frenchwoman sighed as the azure folds fell into place over Anna's body.

Anna regarded herself in the mirror as the dressmaker quickly nipped and tucked and pinned, but she barely noticed how well the pale blue silk complemented her complexion. There was a hum in the air, a tension that told her something had happened. Her mother made a habit of personally overseeing her daughter's wardrobe, especially when the new garb had been especially ordered for the purpose of charming Lord Haverford. Why, then, was she standing outside gossiping with Mrs. Bentley?

"Has my mother seen this lovely creation?" she asked Madame Dauphine.

"Yes, yes." The modiste shot an order in French to one of the girls, who scampered over with a small cushion bursting with pins. "She is here looking at this, telling me to fix this sleeve and straighten that hem." The dressmaker met Anna's gaze in the mirror, her dark eyes alive with indignation. "I am Madame Dauphine. I know a crooked hem when I see one."

"You are the best dressmaker in London," Anna said. "Please forgive my mother. She only wants what's best for me."

"*C'est vrai.*" Clearly mollified, the modiste dismissed her assistant with an impatient wave of her hand. "And then Madame Bentley, she comes into the shop, and the two of them, they are whispering together about the tragedy." She gave a quick laugh. "They think I do not know of this already? All the best gossip, it begins at Madame Dauphine's."

"What tragedy?"

The Frenchwoman paused in adjusting a sleeve. "You are young, Mademoiselle Rosewood. I do not know if I should tell you so distressing a tale."

"I will hear it anyway. Would you rather I say I did not hear it here first?" Once more their gazes met in the mirror, Anna's determined and the modiste's, hesitant. "Please, madame. I need to know."

She could see the struggle in the Frenchwoman's expressive face and knew the moment she had won.

"*D'accord.*" Madame Dauphine sighed. "It is a

sad tale, this one, but you are right that you will hear the story anyway, no?"

"Eventually," Anna agreed. "But if all the gossip begins at Madame Dauphine's, then of course, I must hear this *on dit* from you."

The dressmaker gave a quick laugh. "You are most clever, mademoiselle. Very well." Her expression sobered. "It is as I said, a tragedy. Monsieur Reginald Dalton, do you know him?"

"Slightly. He knew my brother."

"He is the *beau-frère* of Madame Dalton, whose dresses I make. This morning I am told to make many dresses for Madame Dalton, all in black. Monsieur Dalton, he is dead."

"Dead?" Anna exclaimed. Shock turned her insides to ice. "How? He's so young!"

The modiste nodded. "*Oui.* He is found last night, dead, outside the Cock and Crown. His brother swears revenge."

"Charles Dalton was an army man before he married his wealthy wife," Anna mused. "My father knows the Daltons; he and Charles's father were friends. Charles has always seemed to be the most calm and rational of men."

"But he believes his brother is murdered," Madame Dauphine said, lowering her voice. "He is killed with a sword through the heart."

"A sword!" Apprehension curled in her stomach. "How unusual."

"*Oui.* Swords are so old-fashioned. If it was a

duel, surely they would have used pistols. So Monsieur Dalton swears it is murder."

Cold had overtaken her heart, leaving her frozen inside. Just like Anthony, she thought, her mind numb with the shock of it. Two men dead by the sword. How many more might there be that they did not know about?

"Mademoiselle, are you all right? You have turned white like the snow."

"I am fine, madame. The news is disturbing, that is all."

"*C'est vrai.*" With a sigh, the dressmaker returned her attention to the sleeve that needed adjusting just as Anna's mother walked into the room.

"Ah, lovely!" Mrs. Rosewood exclaimed. "I see you have adjusted that hem, madame."

"*Oui.*" Madame Dauphine sent Anna a long-suffering look. "Just as Madame Rosewood suggested."

"Excellent! Allow me to tell you my ideas for the peach satin . . ."

The modiste rolled her eyes as Mama rattled on. At any other time, Anna would have found their exchange most amusing. Instead she let the scene fade to the back of her mind.

Someone in London was going about killing young men with a sword. Her brother's death had looked like the work of footpads, but Anna had never believed that. Footpads tended to use pistols or short, wide knives, not rapiers. Now it seemed that her instincts had been right— Anthony had been murdered, just like Reginald Dalton. And she had no doubt that the mysterious society and black-garbed swordsman from Vaux-hall were responsible.

And standing right in the middle of the mess was Roman Devereaux. What part did he play?

She wished she could confide in her mother, but her parents had made it perfectly clear that they wanted to hear no more theories about Anthony's death. They believed it was the work of thieves and had warned her that any further grief-stricken musings would only see her sent home to the country. And she desperately needed to be in London.

Madame Dauphine pushed Anna's arms up over her head as if she were a doll and removed the blue silk. Then Mama and the modiste slipped the peach satin over Anna's head, still debating about hems and trim and such. Anna barely noticed. Her mind had wandered far from the dress-maker's shop, to the docks and a well-known sailors' haunt called the Cock and Crown. Her father's cronies had often spoken of the area when they hadn't realized she could overhear them.

Maybe someone had seen something the night Reginald was killed. The spark of excitement ignited and spread through her body as the idea took shape. She had been unable to do anything about Anthony's death, and her insistence that her twin had been murdered had been dismissed by her well-meaning parents. But this time, there *was* something she could do. She could take her pin money and go down to the Cock and Crown and see if any of the locals had noticed something the night Reginald was killed.

Good heavens, could she do it? For a moment, common sense reared its head as she recalled the mess she had created the last time she went out in search of information. The Cock and Crown was located in a section of London to which no well-reared lady would ever go. Her presence in such an area, if discovered, could sully her reputation to the point that Haverford could not ignore it. Since he hadn't formally asked her to marry him yet, his honor would not be called into account by Society should he change his mind, and once the story of her activities got out, no one would blame him for his rejection.

No, it was impossible. She couldn't. If she were caught, it would destroy the future her parents had worked so hard to obtain for her. They deserved better from her. But so did Anthony.

What if this was her only chance to learn the identity of his killer? She was certain that Reginald's death was connected to Anthony's. How could she ignore this chance? Tracking down the truth was the reason she had convinced her parents to bring her to London for the Season.

Rose wouldn't hesitate.

The thought of her masquerade the other night

gave her pause. Rose was brave and smart and wouldn't think twice about going to the Cock and Crown and asking questions. But she was also a survivor. She would get the answers she needed, but she would do it in the most intelligent way possible.

Yes, this could be done, but only tonight. She could claim a headache and stay home from their dinner engagement with one of Papa's cronies this evening. Her parents would go without her; they never missed an event at Admiral Westerman's. And tomorrow night the three of them would attend the theater with Lord Haverford. Her mother would make certain she went to *that*, even if she were green with the ague.

Tonight was her only chance; she just prayed that intrepid Rose was up to the task.

"Explain yourself." Silhouetted in shadow, the leader of the Triad turned a cold gaze on his underling. The leader was dressed completely in black, and his costume caused him to blend in with the dark wood of the huge chair in which he sat. The ruby of his ring glittered like fresh blood in the scant candlelight, as did the green eyes of the black cat who lay in his lap. He stroked a hand over the animal, his movement lazy and relaxed, but his lieutenant wasn't fooled.

The man was furious.

"I did what had to be done." He held his rigid

stance, refusing to be cowed by his leader's anger. "The boy had come undone, was babbling about wanting to leave the group. He intended to go to his brother for help."

"So you killed him?" The words, when spoken in that silky tone, sounded pleasant to those who didn't know this man. Soothing, even.

But he knew better.

"Yes," he admitted. "He intended to violate the oath of secrecy."

"Which is what *you* did by leaving his body in so public a place!" The rebuke cracked like a whiplash.

He physically flinched. "He was a gamester. The boy was always in one scrape or another. I thought the Cock and Crown appropriate, that everyone would think he'd been in a brawl."

The cat jumped off the leader's lap and disappeared into the shadows. "Foolish of you to think we can afford so many deaths by the blade in London. Why didn't you follow procedure?"

"I thought—"

"It is not your place to *think*!" The leader lurched out of his chair and looked down on his shorter lieutenant. "Your blundering has risked exposure of the Society."

"He would have gone to his brother. Then Charles Dalton would ask questions."

"He's asking questions now!" the leader sneered. "Our policy is to dump the body in the countryside. Why go to the trouble to start rumors of the renegade bandit who kills his victims with a sword if my own man undermines my efforts? You had no right to do anything else."

"But Dalton—"

"Is mad with grief and swearing vengeance on his brother's killer. Bravo." He clapped his hands in scathing mockery. "Before, he would have been grief-stricken. Now he will not stop until we are disbanded."

The lieutenant opened his mouth to speak, but then closed it.

"Good," the leader said, noting his choice of silence. "Now you understand what you have done." He wandered over to the wall and perused the crossed swords that hung there. "Do you know the worst thing about this whole situation?"

The lieutenant cleared his throat. "Ah, no, sir."

The leader took down a sword and looked at it, then turned back to his underling. He swished the sword in the air with a practiced motion, each move perfectly graceful, perfectly executed.

Of course, he was perfect. He was the best swordsman in their society, the unchallenged leader of the Triad.

"The worst thing about this whole distasteful tangle is that Reginald Dalton did not die in a match as he should have." The leader came back toward his lieutenant, slicing the rapier through the air almost playfully. A hint of a smile touched his lips. "His purse is lost to us now. His pledged amount will no doubt go to his tailor or to cover his gambling vowels."

"He would have bolted," the lieutenant rasped, unable to tear his gaze from the blade.

"There is no way out." The leader lunged at an invisible adversary.

"Gone straight to his brother and exposed us," the lieutenant argued.

"You handled the matter poorly, and there is one less purse in the coffers of the Society." With a polished maneuver, the leader swung around and brought the point of the rapier to his lieutenant's throat. "But you will make up the difference out of your own winnings, won't you?"

The leader's eyes glittered with the light of battle, giving him an almost maniacal air. The lieutenant swallowed hard. Then he nodded.

There was no way out.

Chapter 6

⟨∽◦∽⟩

"**M**iss Rosewood, please, do let us go home. This place is simply wretched!" Lizzie peered out at the dim streets and shivered with revulsion. "This is no place for you, miss."

"I have no intention of getting out of this hack, Lizzie, so calm yourself." Anna glanced out the window and fought back the urge to echo the maid's shudder.

Papa's cronies had always spoken of the Cock and Crown with great affection, and while she knew it to be near the docks, she had still imagined a fairly harmless tavern, a welcoming place ready to serve seafaring patrons a hot meal and a healthy draught of ale. Instead, the neighborhood where the Cock and Crown resided was truly one of London's more unsavory ones, with drunken louts on street corners and doxies lingering in doorways. The building itself was a ramshackle pile of timber and brick that looked as if it would collapse with the next storm to blow in. Her instincts screamed at her to return to the warmth and safety of home.

But she couldn't. This might be her only chance to discover the truth about Anthony.

As instructed, the driver stopped a few doors down from the Cock and Crown. Anna tensed with expectation. She was here, mere feet away from where Reginald Dalton's body had been found. She was in disguise, garbed from head to toe in black with a veil over her face to hide her identity. Since she had no intention of leaving the coach, she had determined that she would pay the driver to ask questions of the locals.

Except the driver didn't want to cooperate.

"I drive a hack. I'm no Bow Street Runner," he called down when she asked him to make inquiries.

"But it's very important, and I dare not do this myself," Anna pleaded, arching her head out the window.

"Miss, you paid me to drive, and I drove. But if I leave this hack to go on some fool errand, my master'll hitch *me* to the traces!"

"Botheration!" Anna flounced back against the seat and frowned. "This is an unexpected wrinkle."

"May we go home now, miss?" Lizzie asked hopefully.

"No, I simply need a new plan."

With a forlorn sigh, Lizzie slumped in the seat.

Anna stared out the window, hoping an idea would occur to her. She had never imagined that the driver would refuse her offer of a few coins. To go herself was madness, social suicide.

But what were her choices?

A scantily clad woman, rouged and hard-faced, caught her eye. She leaned out the window. "You there!"

The woman glanced her way, sneered, then gazed in the opposite direction, where two sailors in naval uniform were stumbling down the street toward her.

"You there!" Anna called again.

The woman tossed her too-bright blond curls and glared at her. Anna held up her purse, and the prostitute's expression changed from annoyance to greed. She sauntered over to the carriage. "Ye talkin' to me?"

"Yes. I would like to hire you for an errand."

The woman smirked. "Never heard it called that before."

Anna ignored the crudeness. "I would like you to ask some questions for me."

"Me?" She cackled. "Them around here would soon as cuff me as talk to me."

"I'll pay you." She jangled the purse.

"Hmmm." The woman eyed the bulging pouch. "How much?"

"How's this?" Anna held up a gold piece.

"Right enough, long as that gold is real."

"Of course it's real!"

"Let me see it." She held out her hand.

Anna placed the gold coin in the woman's palm, then gaped as the prostitute turned and sauntered away. "Hey there!"

The woman ignored her, sidling up to the naval sailors and whispering in one's ear. They both laughed, and one grabbed her bottom in a fierce, one-handed grip as they turned down a dark alley.

"Very well then," she muttered.

"What, miss?" Lizzie looked over, then squealed in alarm as Anna pushed open the door to the hack. "Miss Rosewood, what are you doing?"

Anna paused before descending the steps and leaned close to her maid. "Lizzie, listen to me. Do not call me by my name. I do not want my presence known. If you must address me, call me Miss Rose."

The maid nodded frantically.

"Now let's go." Anna went to step down, and Lizzie cried out in alarm.

Anna swung back and grabbed the maid's wrist. "Lizzie, hush! Do not attract attention to us."

"But, miss, I can't go out there. And neither should you!"

"What are you talking about? Come on, Lizzie. We're just going to ask some questions."

The maid shook her head, a mulish look on her face. "You can sack me if you want, miss, but I'm not going out there."

"Of course I won't sack you."

Lizzie let out a relieved sigh. "Then let's go home, please? This is no place for either of us."

Anna sighed, then shook her head. "Fine, then. I'll go alone."

"But—"

"I know what I'm doing," Anna said, with a sharp look at the servant. "I'll stay within sight of the hack."

The maid wrung her hands and whimpered but said nothing more. Anna took a bracing breath and climbed down from the coach.

Immediately she felt exposed. Vulnerable.

She took another breath, the stench of the street filling her nostrils. The door to the Cock and Crown burst open, and two raucous males stumbled out, laughing and singing, with their arms wrapped around each other. Anna nearly climbed back into the coach, but she thought of Anthony and stood her ground. The two sots staggered past her as if she didn't even exist.

"Hmm." A cautious look around revealed several people watching her from windows and corners. A woman leaned against the wall in a nearby alley, her impressive bosom swelling above her scandalously low-cut bodice. Glaring, henna red hair fell in fat curls over her bared shoulders.

Another prostitute. But this time she would hold tight to her gold until the deed was done.

"What do you want?" the woman sneered, as Anna started toward her.

The threat in her tone made Anna falter. "I just want to speak to you."

"Do you now?" The slattern gave her a quick, head-to-toe study and curled her lip in distaste. "I don't tumble women, dearie. Go see Mary Fox near the Hawk and Hound. She's got what you want."

"I don't . . . Good heavens." Did women actually . . . how could that be done? Beneath the black veil, Anna's face burned. "I want to ask you some questions."

The harlot's face hardened. "Off wi' you now."

"I'll pay you," Anna hastened to add. "As long as you can tell me something about the body they found here the other night."

"The nob, eh?" The redhead chuckled. "You his woman then? Looking to see if he was nippin' out on you?"

"No. I just want to know what happened." She reached into her reticule and pulled out two silver coins, then held them up to the lamplight. "Please tell me."

Eyes gleaming with greed, the prostitute began to talk.

Nursing his ale at the Cock and Crown, Rome watched the two men at the next table. His inquiries had revealed that these fellows were the ones who had discovered Dalton's body. They seemed none the worse for their grisly experience, as both had imbibed copious amounts of liquor and were currently vying for the charms of the well-curved tavern wench.

Neither fellow seemed to be the type who belonged to the society.

Peter had told him that the Black Rose Society consisted of young men of means with adventurous spirits. These youths were approached by members higher up in the society and inducted into the group for a fee, then required to pledge an amount of money that they would stake on their first duel. Whoever won the duel would keep his stake and also win part of his opponent's.

The society had started out as a strategic game played by university students. However, recently a new element had reached the upper echelons, and Peter feared for his life.

The two at the next table did not look to be men of means by any stretch of the imagination, and their familiarity with the barmaid made it clear they were regular patrons of the establishment. It had probably been pure coincidence that they'd found the body.

Still, he got to his feet and lurched across the room as the very drunk were wont to do. He bumped the chair of one of the fellows, deliberately sloshing ale all over his chest.

"Bugger!" The bearded man leaped to his feet, his chair screeching backwards and tipping over. "Watch yourself!"

"Sorry." Pasting a simpleton's grin on his face, Rome took out his handkerchief and swiped at the ale staining the fellow's shirt. "Didn't see you there."

The bearded man's tall, thin friend stood up. "You spilled his ale," he accused. "Haven't you heard what we do to nobs around here?"

"Now, now." Rome turned to the tavern maid. "Fetch us ales, my pretty, all three of us."

The girl nodded and cast him a look of feminine appreciation before hurrying off to do as bid. Rome grabbed a chair from the table behind him and pulled it around.

"Give me a reason not to pound you into pulp," the wet man growled, ale dripping from his beard.

"Because I've just bought you a round. Sit, both of you." Dropping into the chair, Rome took a swig from his own tankard. "Please accept my abject apologies, gentlemen, in the form of the Cock and Crown's best."

The two fellows looked at each other in indecision. Finally, the tall one shrugged, and they both sat down again. The barmaid hurried over with three brimming tankards.

Rome pushed his empty one aside and lifted a new one in toast. "To this beautiful lady," he said, then drank. The barmaid giggled and hurried away as the two other men awkwardly followed suit.

"Meggie's a fair one, to be sure," the skinny one said.

"Best broadside I've ever seen." The bearded

fellow gazed after Meggie, then gave a lusty sigh and took a deep drink of ale. "I see you've a fine eye for the ladies, but what brings you to the Crown? It's clear as day you're not a regular."

"Is it?" Rome scowled. "I had thought to blend."

The skinny one gave a bark of laughter. "Not in that fancy coat."

"A friend of mine was killed the other night. I had hoped to find out what happened."

"The nob." The bearded one nodded, then gestured to his associate. "Reese and I found him, you know."

"You did?" Rome goggled. "Where? What happened? Did you see who did it?"

"Easy there." Reese sat back a bit, as if afraid such open emotion would contaminate him. "Let Birch tell you the way of it."

"We didn't see a bloody thing." Birch slurped at his ale, then wiped his mouth on his sleeve. "Reese and I come here every night. We have a pint or two, then head home."

"That night we stopped in the alley because Birch here had to . . . how do you nobs say it? Relieve himself, that's it."

"And I tripped over the dead bloke," Birch said. "Near pissed on him."

"He was just lying there?" Rome asked.

"Aye, just lying there," Birch confirmed with a nod. "Bleeding all over the street. Reese here checked his pockets—"

"To identify him," Reese quickly interjected.

"And then the watch came. We had witnesses who saw us here in the Crown all night, else they might have thought it was us who done him."

"But we didn't," Reese said. "We just found him."

Birch nodded sagely. "Poor blighter."

Rome took a quick swig of his ale, then slapped the tankard down on the table. "Show me," he said, his voice rough like a man trying to control his emotions. "Show me where you found my dear friend Dalton."

Birch awkwardly patted his arm. "Soon as we finish our ale, friend."

"Birch and Reese found him," the red-haired doxy was saying. It had taken another coin before Anna discovered her name was Maude. "Those two are at the Cock and Crown every night."

"I take it you know these men."

"O' course I do." Maude tossed her red curls and gave her a feline grin. "Gave 'em both a ride a time or two when they had the coin."

Grateful for the veil that hid her blushing cheeks from the other woman, Anna asked, "Do you think they had anything to do with killing him?"

"Birch and Reese?" The harlot gave a cackle. "They're harmless, those two. Apt to pinch a purse now and again if they get the chance, but that's just so they can buy more ale."

"And you didn't see anyone else around before the body was discovered?"

"I was busy, dearie." She winked. "I've got customers to see to."

"Of course." Anna cleared her throat. "Thank you for your time, Maude. I appreciate it." She held out a couple more silver coins.

"Easiest work I've ever done." The doxy snatched them from Anna's hand and tucked them away inside her bosom.

"I'm glad you feel that way. Perhaps—"

"Oh, I wasn't talking to you." Maude gave her a grin that suddenly seemed more calculating than friendly. "Was I, lover?"

"No, you weren't." A masculine hand clamped down on Anna's shoulder and spun her around. "What have we here?"

Anna got an impression of a big, brawny, dark-haired man with a pockmarked face silhouetted against the streetlamp. She tried to jerk from the man's hold, but his grip was like iron. "Let me go!"

"I'm betting we've got ourselves a virgin," Maude said, coming around to stand beside the man. "All them hoity-toity society ladies are virgins."

"That would be a nice stroke of luck." Holding Anna firmly by the arm, Maude's lover ran a huge hand over Anna's breasts and down along her waist to trace her hip. "Decent teats. If her face ain't half-bad, we could fetch a pretty price for her."

"Unhand me!" Anna struggled to free herself,

but she was pinned like a butterfly caught beneath a cat's paw.

Maude laughed. "Unhand her, do you hear that?"

"You'd best get used to a man's hands on you, wench," the man said with a chuckle. "Starting with mine."

"No!" Anna kicked hard at the man's shin, startling a bellow out of him, but it didn't make him release her.

Maude's expression hardened. "You shouldn't ought to have done that, you fool. Now you've made Graham cross."

Graham gave her a hard shake, nearly breaking her arm with his grip. "Maybe a beating will teach you to behave."

Anna looked around frantically, but no one on the streets made a move to help her. Most of them looked away, as if they didn't see what was going on. The door to the Cock and Crown opened, and three men strolled out. By some miracle, they headed toward the alley.

"Help!" she cried. "Please, help me!"

Graham cursed and yanked the veil away. "You'd better be worth my trouble, wench."

Maude gripped Anna's chin and tilted her face toward the light. "She's a pretty one."

"And look at that mouth. Blokes will line up to have a piece of that."

Anna looked her tormenters in the face, opened her mouth, and screamed.

"What the—"

"Shut your mouth, you—" Graham shook her again.

"What's going on over there?" The three men from the Crown broke into a run.

"Miss Rose!" Lizzie shoved open the door to the hack. "Hurry! Run!"

"You there!" The hack driver yanked a pistol from beneath the driver's seat and fired it into the air.

At the report of the pistol, Graham dropped his grip. "She's not worth dyin' for. Come on!" He and Maude raced away down the street.

Anna gathered her skirts and bolted past the three men charging to her rescue and toward the open door of the coach, where Lizzie beckoned.

She scrambled inside and flopped back against the seat, panting, her heart pounding. Lizzie slammed shut the door to the hack, and the coach lurched into motion.

Through the window she saw Roman Devereaux standing near the alley, staring after her with openmouthed astonishment.

The search of the alley had revealed nothing in the way of Dalton's death, but the presence of the lady named Rose had shaken him.

Dear God, could it really be Anna Rosewood?

Back in his rooms, Rome stripped off his coat and hung it in the wardrobe, then began to untie his cravat as he walked across the room to the brandy decanter. He paused beside the liquor and struggled with the knot in his neckcloth. It would be a hell of a lot easier to dress fashionably with a valet, but as a former soldier, he lived simply and saw to his own needs. Most of his blunt went to support his mother's comfortable home, and it pleased him to be able to provide for her.

He won the battle with the knot, and with the wrinkled cravat dangling from his neck, he poured himself a glass of brandy and pondered the situation.

The young girl in the hack tonight had looked like the maid Anna had forgotten at Lavinia's home. He had only caught a glimpse of the girl when Vin had arranged for her to be sent back to the Rosewood residence, and the light on the street had been dim. Yet the girl in the hack had called his mysterious lady "Miss Rose," and Miss Rose herself bore a striking resemblance to Anna Rosewood.

If it were any other woman, he would not be doubting his own eyes. But why would Anna Rosewood be in that part of town, in the company of a harlot and her partner?

He tossed back a swallow of the brandy and savored the taste on his tongue. The evidence didn't lie. He'd seen the lovely Rose up close, had kissed her and touched her.

Lord, had he touched her.

And if Rose and Anna were the same woman . . .

That meant he had played fast and loose with his cousin's future bride.

He groaned and sat down as the truth crashed over him. He hadn't wanted to believe it, had willed it to be untrue. How could it be that the one woman who had gotten him that sexually excited happened to be Haverford's future bride?

He'd known that night that she wasn't a common doxy. He'd sensed something unusual about her, recognized the hints of her breeding and dismissed them, never for one instant imagining that a lady would find herself in such a situation.

She hadn't corrected his assumption. She'd not rejected his advances, hadn't slapped his face soundly or screamed for help. No, instead she'd called herself by a different name. She'd responded to his kisses. She'd climaxed in his arms.

Bloody, bloody hell! What game did she play?

He squeezed his eyes shut in horror as his father's path stretched before him. Had she known who he was? Had she realized the irony of the situation?

Or perhaps that had been a thrill of her twisted game?

He reined in his wild imagination and forced himself to think logically.

The reason he had been at the Cock and Crown had been to investigate Dalton's death. What if Anna had been there for the same reason? After all, they had first met at Vauxhall at a dinner party hosted by members of the Black Rose Society.

Then he had seen her tonight near the Crown. Either Anna Rosewood was involved with the Black Rose Society in some capacity, or else she knew of their activities and was sticking her pretty nose where it didn't belong.

But why?

Whatever her reasons, she had dragged him into a situation he had secretly dreaded all his life, yet never expected to occur.

When his father, curse him, had run off with the old earl's fiancée twelve years ago, the incident had shamed his mother, had destroyed Vin's faith in men. As for him, he'd been forced to prove he was not his father's son. His cousin Marc had had every reason to cut off their branch of the family completely.

But Marc was a good man. An optimist, who believed in second chances. It had been his endorsement of Rome's family that had given Vin the social cachet needed to snare Emberly as a husband. His mother still dared not show her face in Society, but Marc still invited Eleanor to events. He'd paid for Rome's commission, giving him a chance to prove himself a man of honor in his own right. He owed Marc much.

Haverford had earned his respect and loyalty by supporting the family when no one else would. He must *never* find out what had happened at Vauxhall.

The consequences of exposure staggered him. Marc trusted no one since Rome's father had run off with his future stepmother. Another scandal would tear asunder the few shreds of dignity the family had left, and it would ruin Anna's family as well. Marc himself might retire completely from society and from the company of his own family, might even decide not to wed at all.

Which, ironically, would leave Rome as his heir.

And oh, what fun the gossips would have with that tidbit! No doubt they would accuse him of deliberately seducing Marc's fiancée in order to keep his status as heir. Marc might even believe it himself.

That thought pierced deeply, as nothing else had. Would Marc truly believe that Rome could act so dishonorably?

Dear God.

He swiped a hand over his face, blowing out a harsh breath. He couldn't let that happen, not any of it. Such disgrace would cost him the career in diplomacy that he so desired, but it was the emotional repercussions that ripped him apart.

History could not be allowed to repeat itself.

Rome tossed back the last dregs of brandy and set the glass aside. In order to avert disaster, he would have to get Anna alone and talk to her. He would make her confess her duplicity, then he would swear her to secrecy, with blackmail if necessary.

And after he got to the bottom of the Black Rose Society and made sure Peter was safe from harm, he would obtain a diplomatic position, no matter what the cost, and he would have himself assigned to a country far away from London.

And far away from the temptation of Anna.

Because the worst part of it was, even though he knew that she belonged to another, he still wanted her for himself. And the shame of that truth dishonored him far greater than anything Society had ever dealt him.

Chapter 7

~~~~⌒⌒⌒~~~~

Haverford's theater box had an excellent view of the theater and, in turn, the occupants of the theater had an excellent view of Anna, seated beside the earl. She watched as various members of the *ton* put their heads together, whispering, while they cast their speculative glances toward the Haverford box. Their pointed interest did little to ease Anna's nerves. Last night's near disaster haunted her still, and she found herself more than once stroking the familiar cameo of her newly repaired locket between her fingers in an old gesture of anxiety.

Would Roman Devereaux betray her?

She squirmed in her seat, only to earn a sharp look of rebuke from her mother. Forcing herself to stillness, she focused on breathing. The rising feeling of suffocation was more mental than physical, because of her sensitivity to the close confines of her surroundings. Though large enough to accommodate all the members of their party, the box seemed unusually crowded to Anna, no doubt due to the brooding presence of Roman Devereaux.

Rome had been watching her all evening. He wasn't obvious about it; that would have drawn inquiry. But since Anna had been watching *him* as well, she had noticed his intense study.

She had seen the look on his face outside the tavern. He'd clearly recognized her, but had he identified Anna Rosewood or Rose from Vauxhall Gardens? Either way, he suspected something.

But what would he do about it?

"Is something wrong with your locket?" Haverford's quiet inquiry jolted her back to the present.

"Not at all." She realized she was toying with the cameo again and dropped her hand to her lap, attempting a reassuring smile.

"Are comedies not to your liking?" He searched her expression, his gray eyes steady and earnest.

"On the contrary, I quite enjoy them." She glanced down at the play being enacted below. "Some of them are very clever."

"I picked this performance specifically because I thought you would enjoy it."

This time her smile was genuine. "And you were correct, my lord."

He winced. "Please, call me Haverford. Or even Marc."

Flustered, she glanced down at her hands as heat swept through her cheeks. "I could never be so bold as to use your Christian name."

"Haverford then." In a move so quick as to be invisible to anyone outside their box, he covered her hand with his own and squeezed it. Then he made a show of holding up his program with both hands for the benefit of the observing gossips below.

Staggered by so daring a gesture by a man considered impeccably proper, Anna turned her head slightly to glance at her mother, who sat behind and slightly to her right—the perfect angle to witness the earl's clandestine caress. Mrs. Rosewood kept her gaze fixed on the actors below, but a small, satisfied smile curved her lips. The admiral dozed in his chair beside her, and next to her parents, on the far right, Lavinia grinned at her, clearly having observed the brief gesture of affection across the seat that remained empty on Haverford's other side.

From beside Lavinia, with a clear view of everything, Rome glared at her, his program crumpled in his fist.

His displeasure hit her like a blow, and she swiftly turned her attention back to the play.

Bother Roman Devereaux and his foul humor! Haverford's actions illustrated his regard. No doubt he would offer soon, and they would be officially betrothed. For an instant she indulged herself and imagined the announcement in the *Times*, the banns being read at the church, the engagement ring she would be able to show to all her friends. What would her wedding dress look like? Where would they go on their honeymoon?

She thought of their wedding day, of walking down the aisle on her father's arm to meet her groom before the altar, of his green eyes glittering with passion as he bent to give her the kiss of peace . . .

Haverford's eyes were gray.

Good Lord. She clenched her fingers around her reticule, squeezing her eyes shut, wishing the image away. But it would not be banished.

The man she saw waiting for her at the altar was Rome.

It seemed as if an eternity passed before intermission.

Haverford had danced attendance on Anna throughout the whole first act. He had a right to do so; Anna was the woman he intended to wed. But Rome hated watching it.

Everyone else in their box clearly approved of Haverford's actions, seeing the courtship unfold as it should under normal circumstances. But these circumstances were *not* normal. Not with Anna's secret activities casting a shadow on the whole situation.

Not with Rome's own desires warring with his determination to do what was right.

The theater patrons began wandering to other boxes to greet their friends or to the lobby to seek refreshment. Mrs. Rosewood stood. "Quentin, do escort me to dear Sophia's box."

The admiral awoke with a harrumph. "What's that?"

She tapped him on the shoulder with her folded fan. "Do come with me, Quentin. Right now." She tilted her head ever so slightly toward Haverford and Anna, who were conversing quietly.

The admiral glanced over and hauled his bulk from the chair. "Indeed. Delighted to, my dear."

"Isn't it wonderful?" Lavinia whispered to Rome as the Rosewoods left the box. "Do you suppose they will fall in love? I do so adore a romance."

"It's an arranged marriage, Vin, not a love match."

Vin wrinkled her nose. "Really, Rome, you are such a cynic."

"Just a realist."

"Cynic," she insisted. "Now do be a dear and fetch me some lemonade. I will stay and chaperone."

He rolled his eyes even as he stood up. "Vin, Miss Rosewood is only a year younger than you are."

"But I am a married woman." Vin gave him that impish grin that always washed away his annoyance with her.

"Thank God for it," he muttered. "Let Emberly be your keeper then." She made a face at him, and he turned to leave just as a distinguished older man entered their box. The gentleman held himself with the bearing of a military man, and his silver hair and mustache made him look older than his youthful stride implied.

"Devereaux," he said with a polite nod. "I saw you from across the way."

"Mr. Vaughn." Surprised but pleased, Rome acknowledged the greeting.

Marc stood up. "Evening, Vaughn. I thought you didn't care for the comedies."

Edgar Vaughn made a face. "Tragedies or histories are more to my taste, my lord, but my wife enjoys these wretched farces."

"Ladies often do," Marc agreed. "May I present Miss Rosewood, daughter of Admiral Rosewood?"

"It's a pleasure to meet you, Mr. Vaughn," Anna said. "My father has spoken of you."

"Charmed to meet you, Miss Rosewood. Your father's a fine man," Vaughn said.

"And this is my sister, Mrs. Emberly," Rome said, indicating Lavinia.

"Henry Emberly's wife, eh?"

"Yes. I'm honored to meet you, Mr. Vaughn."

"The pleasure is mine, Mrs. Emberly." He turned back to Rome. "Well, Devereaux, I won't keep you from this delightful company. Just wanted to pay my respects. I expect I'll see you tomorrow at three o'clock?"

"Most definitely, sir."

"Excellent. Until then." Vaughn exited the box.

"Heavens, Rome!" Lavinia squealed. "*He singled you out*. He intends to offer you a position!"

"Perhaps," Rome said, still bemused by Vaughn's visit.

"Appears so to me." Marc clapped him on the shoulder. "You look like you need a drink, Rome. Come with me while I fetch some lemonade for Miss Rosewood."

"I need more than lemonade." Elation surged through him. "By God, it does look promising, doesn't it?"

"It does." Marc nodded, clearly pleased.

"This is so wonderful!" Vin squealed.

Anna smiled at him, her beautiful eyes luminous with happiness. "I'm certain you will secure the position."

Rome basked in the warmth of her approval, falling beneath the spell of her welcoming gaze. It was as if her soul reached out for his, beckoning him near. The world narrowed to just the two of them, heartbeat for heartbeat, breath for breath.

He knew when she, too, got caught up by the current of desire. Awareness flickered across her face and a moment of panic. But it was too late. She was trapped there with him, swept along by this unappeased hunger, a prisoner of forbidden desire.

"Lemonade, Lavinia?" Marc's voice jerked him free of the siren song.

"Yes, thank you."

"All right then. We'll be back once we've fought our way through the crowds." Marc grinned at the ladies. "And once we've located something stronger for Rome."

Rome glanced from Marc to Vin, but neither seemed to have noticed anything out of the ordinary. He peeked back at Anna, but she looked away, spine perfectly straight, hands folded properly in her lap.

For some reason her posture infuriated him.

How dare she act the part of the well-bred lady? She drove him mad with one smile, one glance. When she cast her attention his way, he forgot everything but how much he wanted her. Where was his pride, his sense of honor? How could his body betray him like this? *How could she betray Marc by looking at another man like that?*

She had been there that night at Vauxhall. She had climaxed in his arms, and she had enjoyed it. The scent of her pleasure had clung to his fingers hours after they'd parted ways.

His joy at Vaughn's acceptance of him faded in the face of the truth. Anna played a cruel game with him and with Marc, a game that could erupt into scandal and destroy everything he had worked so hard to achieve.

Tonight he would put a stop to that once and for all.

"I am so pleased I could burst," Lavinia said as soon as the men departed. "Rome has worked so hard, and now it seems as if his dream will come true!"

Anna smiled and nodded, unable to utter a civil word. Her blood thundered through her veins, practically deafening her. Her entire body trembled with the strain of controlling her unruly emotions. She clenched her shaking fingers around her fan, the stiff spines digging into her flesh and keeping her focused on the here and now.

What had just happened, and how could it have happened with Haverford standing right there?

Lavinia moved into Haverford's chair. "Father's scandal affected him the most," she confided in a low tone. "Mama was mortified, of course, and I was too young to know what had happened, just a child, really. But Rome had just finished his time at university. Suddenly the doors of Society closed in his face, as if everyone expected him to be as dishonorable as my father." She sighed, her normally vivacious mien giving way to a mature sobriety. "If it hadn't been for Haverford's buying his commission, I don't know what would have become of my brother."

"He was fortunate that the earl is a kind man," Anna managed, her heart aching for the outcast youth Rome had been.

Lavinia grinned and squeezed Anna's hand. "No, *you* are fortunate to be marrying such a decent sort."

"I'm not—"

"Now don't even begin with that nonsense that your betrothal is not yet official! I think we can all see what Haverford's intentions are."

Anna blushed. "I hate to presume."

Lavinia giggled. "Oh, Anna, you and Haverford are truly a perfect match."

Were they? With such traitorous feelings confounding her normal modesty, Anna had begun to wonder if she deserved so honorable a husband as Lord Haverford.

Lavinia leaned close. "I have the pressing need to refresh myself, Anna, yet I dare not leave you unchaperoned. Do come with me."

"Lavinia!" Scandalized at her friend's candor, Anna glanced about, hoping no one had overheard.

"Just come with me. Please, Anna!"

The urgency in Lavinia's voice prompted Anna to rise from her seat. "Very well."

"Thank you!" Lavinia hurried out of the box, clearly driven by the insistence of her body's needs. "We shall no doubt meet Haverford and Rome on the way back."

"No doubt." Anna trailed behind her friend and wondered with a hint of desperation when the impetuous Devereaux family would cease rattling her composure.

A bracing draught had done wonders to restore Rome's equanimity regarding Vaughn's possible approval, but his ire at Anna's subtle rejection still simmered.

Haverford preceded Rome back to the box, a glass of lemonade in each hand. The crowd parted for the earl like the Red Sea before Moses, and the deference only made him feel worse. Marc had used his influence to ensure that Rome had a chance to mold his own future, and here Rome stood on the brink of insulting his cousin beyond measure. He was disgusted with himself.

They reached the box, only to find it empty.

"How puzzling," Marc mused. "Where have the ladies gone?"

"Perhaps they are visiting another box."

"Perhaps." Frowning, Marc set down the two lemonades.

"I'm certain they're together, wherever they are. Would you like me to go look for them?"

"I'll come with you," Haverford said, but as they turned to leave, the Duke of Brimwald entered the box, his ruddy face fixed in a frown.

"Haverford, there you are! Want to have a word with you about that sheep debacle in Leicestershire," the duke commanded in his booming voice.

"Of course, Your Grace." Haverford glanced meaningfully at Rome.

"Good evening, Your Grace," Rome said, bowing to Brimwald.

The duke sent Rome a look of disapproval and did not reply.

"You remember my cousin, Roman Devereaux, don't you, Your Grace?" Haverford asked smoothly.

So challenged, the duke had no choice but to acknowledge Rome with a curt nod. "Devereaux."

Still easing his way, thought Roman. Where

would he be without his cousin's benevolence? Rome caught Haverford's gaze. "Shall I fetch the ladies?"

"Yes, please do."

Needing no more urging, Rome took his leave of the gentlemen and ducked out of the box. As he wandered through the crowd, he looked for Vin and Anna, his greater height allowing him to see over the heads of most people. Finally, he spotted them talking to a slender, dark-haired man.

Who the devil was that? Alarmed, he stepped up his pace. He couldn't see the fellow's face, as the ladies' companion had his back to him, but there was something familiar about that lean figure, something that sparked unease.

He reached the group and clapped the fellow on the shoulder—and found himself looking into the startled face of his brother-in-law. He quickly adjusted his hold so the warning grip he had intended became a quick squeeze of friendship. "Emberly, good to see you. I didn't think you enjoyed the theater."

"I don't." Henry Emberly gave them all a self-deprecating smile. "However, I accompanied Lord Wexley and his Russian guests. Apparently, Her Highness Princess Josefina is quite fond of the theater."

"Henry was just saying he would like to introduce me to Her Highness." Vin's eyes sparkled with excitement. "However, I didn't want to leave Anna alone."

"The box is quite full," Emberly said apologetically. "There is barely enough room for me and Lavinia."

"But now that you are here," Vin said, beaming at Rome, "you can escort Anna back to the box while I go with my husband to greet Russian royalty."

"That would work famously." Emberly turned his solemn dark eyes on Rome. "Can we count on your assistance, Devereaux?"

"Of course." Rome gave Anna a taunting smile. "I will be more than happy to escort Miss Rosewood back to her seat."

Anna suppressed a shiver at the tooth-baring grin he turned upon her. No doubt a tiger cast the same expression upon its prey minutes before devouring it. But as Lavinia happily went off on the arm of her husband, Anna found herself alone in the care of the very man she wanted to avoid.

"Shall we go back to the box? I'm certain Lord Haverford is looking for me."

"Let's do that." He indicated that she should precede him. A little hesitant to have him lurking behind her, she nonetheless gathered her courage and began walking.

She kept her eyes fixed forward, every nerve aware of his lean strength only a step behind. Could she really feel the heat of his body? No, that was her imagination. He wasn't that close. She glanced back just to be sure.

He was closer than she'd expected.

He raised an eyebrow at her, and she faced forward again, cheeks warming, pulse skittering.

She marched along like a soldier to an invisible drum, her gaze fixed on her path. As soon as she reached the Haverford box, everything would be fine. Rome would retreat to his place in the shadows, and she would be safe from him, surrounded by her parents and husband-to-be.

They turned a corner. He took her elbow and firmly steered her in the opposite direction, down a deserted hallway.

"What—?"

He clamped a hand over her mouth and dragged her back against him, arms pinned to her sides. She struggled in his grasp, but she was unable to loosen his firm grip. He staggered to a door and fumbled with the door latch, then managed to thrust it open. As she dug in her heels, he hauled her into the small, dusty broom closet and abruptly released her.

She stumbled forward, gasping for a decent breath. Behind her, she heard the door shut firmly.

"Now," he said. "We have some things to talk about . . . *Rose*."

Chapter 8

❝**A**re you *mad*?" Anna clasped a hand over her bosom to calm her pounding heart. Rose. He'd called her Rose! "Open that door at once!"

He leaned back against it, nearly blocking the light coming from the cracks. "Not until I get some answers."

She tried to reach past him for the latch, but he didn't budge. "You know what will happen if anyone finds us alone like this!"

He captured her gaze. "I do know. And since we don't have much time, let's not pretend any longer."

Her traitorous heart skipped a beat, but she let nothing of her inner turmoil show. "I don't know what you're talking about. If you have something to discuss with me, why don't you call on me tomorrow so we can converse like civilized people?"

He leaned down so his mouth hovered near her ear. "Because I don't feel very civilized when I'm around you . . . *Rose*."

Fear drained the blood from her face, and her stomach dropped with a lurch. "Mr. Devereaux—"

"Please, don't deny it," he told her, cynicism twisting his lips. "And cease this false formality. Even if you could somehow explain away the resemblance, there's this." He scooped up her cameo, his fingers warm against the skin of her throat. "I remember this bauble. I remember *you*."

Panic swept through her on an icy wave. "Please let me out."

"Oh, no, not until we've untangled this mess."

"A mess indeed if you will not open that door!" Her composure slipping, Anna tried to squeeze past him, but only managed to wedge her shoulder and arm behind him. She grabbed the door latch and tugged. Nothing happened.

"Not until you tell me the truth," he said, his expression unyielding.

She jerked herself out of the snug cocoon between his body and the door and turned away, unsettled by even so brief a contact. A gentleman would have recognized the impropriety of her shoulder pressed so intimately against his back, of her hip nestled so casually against his . . .

Well, a gentleman would never have closed them in a closet!

She tried to put distance between them, but their cramped quarters only allowed her a single pace. She wrapped her arms around herself, ashamed at her lack of control.

"I'm not opening this door until you answer some questions."

She glanced back at him. "Are you trying to trick me into an indiscretion?"

His expression hardened. "My dear Anna, don't be foolish. If anyone has been tricked, it is I."

"What?" She spun back toward him, unable to hide her astonishment. "You've locked us in this closet, knowing full well that your cousin will come seeking me, and you dare claim to be the victim?"

"Spare me the indignation of the innocent." He folded his arms and regarded her with unconcealed disgust. "What's your game, Anna?"

"I have no game!"

"Then why were you at Vauxhall Gardens that night, calling yourself Rose? Why did you allow me to think you a doxy?"

"This is outrageous!"

"Oh, come now." He advanced on her, forcing her backwards up against the closet wall. "You never denied my assumptions. You let me believe you a lightskirt, and I treated you accordingly."

Caught between the wall and his lean body, she couldn't escape the heat of him, the scent. One whiff of his cologne transported her back to that dark niche at Vauxhall, when he'd touched her so scandalously.

So deliciously.

She forced the feelings back and looked up into his eyes, unable to maintain her pretense of denial. "And what of you, sir? Do you make a habit of associating with that set?"

"What I was doing there makes no difference. I wasn't breaking every rule of society." He cast a searing glance over her body. "*I* am not promised to anyone."

Her pulse raced. She was trapped by the only other person in the world who knew her secret. Would he expose her? Would he confess his sins to Haverford, claiming ignorance as his petition for forgiveness?

"It was a private party. Only members of a certain organization were supposed to be present." She cocked her head to the side. "Are you a member?"

"A guest of one, actually." He leaned closer. "Now what were *you* doing there?"

"That's none of your affair."

"You made it my affair, Anna, when you allowed me to put my hands on you."

She closed her eyes on a wave of shame, remembering all too vividly how he'd made her feel. How wickedly wonderful . . .

"Would you have believed me if I'd told you the truth?" she whispered, looking at him again.

He studied her face. "I knew something was different about you."

"But would you have let me go? Or would you have continued to try and convince me to lie with you that night?"

"All I could think about was becoming your lover." He let out a deep breath. "God help me, I still think about it."

"Stop." She shook her head, fighting the sinful urges rising within her. "We can't. You know that."

"You should have told me the truth at Vauxhall," he murmured near her ear. "Before I knew how you feel in my arms."

"That night was a mistake, one I can't afford to make again." She touched his shoulder, drawing his gaze to hers. "Open the door, Rome."

"God." He sucked in a harsh breath and took a step back from her. "Just my name on your lips is enough to make me forget myself."

"I belong to Lord Haverford."

"And always have." His expression grew stony. "So why would you pass yourself off as a whore in Vauxhall Gardens, at a dinner party for a bunch of drunken young bloods?"

"My reasons are somewhat complicated."

"Simplify it for me. Why would you take such a chance with your future? What if one of those fools had forced you?"

"I tried to leave. You stopped me."

"Why, Anna?"

"I—"

"*Why*?" he demanded harshly. "I deserve the truth. Is someone paying you?"

"What?" Completely confused, she could only stare at him.

"Is someone paying you to ruin my family?" He took her by the shoulders. "Tell me who it is, damn it!"

"I don't know what you're talking about!"

He dragged her to her tiptoes. "You tricked me into betraying my cousin, Anna. *I will know why.*"

"I didn't—"

"If Marc finds out, we are all of us ruined." His hot breath swept the sensitive flesh of her ear, surprising a shiver from her. "If no one paid you, why did you do it? What was a sweet little virgin like you doing in a place like that?"

"I was looking for someone," she whispered, her body humming with a wild hunger that she couldn't control. The heat of his hands made her flesh prickle even through the silk of her dress. His scent surrounded her, and the maleness of him overwhelmed her in the tiny space. Her mouth watered to kiss him again.

"Who? A lover?"

"No." She shook her head wildly, dislodging a hairpin in the process.

"Who then?" he demanded.

She stared straight into his eyes, her lips an inch from his. "The man who killed my brother."

Of all the possibilities, here was one he had never entertained.

Rome straightened, ignoring the temptation of her mouth. "What do you mean? I thought your brother was killed by footpads."

"Everyone thinks that." She gave a mocking little smile. "Except me. I will find the true murderer, and I will prove that Anthony's death was no random act." Her eyes glittered with fervor, and a flush swept her cheeks. Her passionate loyalty touched him, and it was all he could do not to pull her back into his arms.

"You cannot continue to put yourself and your reputation in danger," Rome said.

"You're right. Open the door."

"In a moment. Anna, be reasonable. You're a woman. You can't investigate something like this."

"I can, and I have been." She tilted her chin in challenge.

"Don't forget what happened at Vauxhall. Had I been less a gentleman, you would have lost more than your locket."

"Which is why you have imprisoned us both in this closet. Because you're such a gentleman," she taunted.

He shoved her away. "Little fool. You have no idea the depth of my will."

She lost her footing for only an instant, then rallied. One curl had dislodged itself and curved along her cheek and neck. He wanted to twirl that lock of hair around his finger, inhale her sweet scent as her body moved beneath his . . .

"All I know," she whispered, watching him warily, "is that the next act will be starting, and I am here in a closet with you instead of sitting beside the earl."

The mention of Haverford helped him clamp down on his hunger. "I have no wish to give the gossips anything to chew."

"Then open the door, and we forget anything that has passed between us."

"Can you forget?"

Silence trembled between them. Finally, she said, "We must."

"I shall remember you warm and wanting in my arms until my last breath." He closed his eyes, struggling for discipline. Her scent seduced him in the close quarters, like some ancient enchantment. He knew what she felt like in his arms, how she kissed, the soft sounds she made as she found her pleasure. His body clamored to finish what they'd started that night at Vauxhall.

"Rome." Her whisper wrapped around him like an embrace. "I wasn't playing a game. I wasn't trying to hurt your family, but merely seeking the truth."

"I believe you."

"I'm just trying to find out who killed my brother." She touched his arm, and he opened his eyes to meet her earnest gaze. "Perhaps we can help each other."

His body surged to life at the soft words, and his primal urges strained the leash of his will. "What are you talking about?"

"My investigation. You can help me. You can go places I cannot, and you have a friend within the society."

"No. I will not help you put yourself in danger."

Her mouth thinned. "Then I will continue alone."

"I can't allow that."

She lifted her gaze, showing him the determination in her eyes. "You can't stop it."

A gauntlet, boldly thrown between them.

He hauled her into his arms and kissed her. He hadn't meant to. Knew it was wrong. But dear God, the taste of her . . .

She stood on her tiptoes and responded to his kiss, opening her mouth and pressing herself against him with an eagerness that stunned him. He caressed her cheek, her throat. His fingers brushed the chain of her locket, warm from her skin.

What was he doing?

He broke the kiss and stepped back so quickly that she swayed, off-balance. He put a hand on her shoulder to steady her.

"Oh, my God." Grasping his arm, she reached up and touched her lips with a trembling hand. Distress widened her eyes as she stared at him. "Why did you do that?"

"I shouldn't have. I'm sorry."

She took another breath, then noticed her hand still on his arm. She snatched it away. "Forget what I said. I think it's best we try to avoid each other."

He folded his arms, amused despite the grimness of the situation. "How do you propose we do that? Haverford is my cousin, and besides, we need to continue our conversation about your brother's killer."

"That conversation is over."

"No, it isn't." He'd seen the determination in her eyes. She would continue to search for her brother's killer, no matter what it cost her.

He couldn't allow that. Better to keep her close . . . and safe.

"I've decided your idea about becoming partners has merit," he said.

"Partners? For all I know, you're involved. Why else would you be at that dinner party?"

"If I were involved, you'd likely be dead by now." He ignored her look of stunned horror. "Oh, come now. I was there for the same reason you were."

"So you say." She tried to appear indifferent, but he caught her furtive glance at his hand, bare of any jewelry.

"I am not a member," he confirmed as she raised her gaze back to his.

She didn't even try to pretend. "Then what were you doing there?"

"Investigating." He arched his brows. "So many

questions. Are you certain you don't want to join forces?"

"I cannot trust you, sir." Blushing, she glanced away.

He sobered. "In this matter, you can. If you change your mind, send word through Lavinia. We can meet at her house to exchange information." He opened the door and extended his arm. "Now allow me to see you back to your seat."

"Insufferable man." She placed her hand on his arm with obvious reluctance.

He reached past her to close the door behind them and seized the moment to whisper in her ear, "You suffer me quite well, actually."

A glare was her only response.

Anna was shaking as they made their way back toward Haverford's box. Rome had made the connection between her and Rose. He'd claimed he was investigating the society as she was, that he wasn't a member and therefore wasn't party to Anthony's death. Dared she believe him? She wanted to.

But was the desire to trust him rooted in sound logic or the wild emotion spawned by his kiss?

And partners? Even if he was innocent as he claimed, this attraction to Rome could only lead to disaster. Yes, she had convinced her parents to bring her to London so she could investigate her brother's death, but she also wanted to be a dutiful daughter and marry Lord Haverford. Every moment she spent alone with Rome endangered that future.

She wished the earl would ask her to wed him and be done with it. Once she had his ring on her finger, she would surely be able to resist the lure of Roman Devereaux.

Which begged the question—why was Haverford hesitating?

"We're later than I thought," Rome said, bringing her back to the present.

She glanced around and realized he was right—many of the theatergoers had returned to their seats. "Dear Lord, we'll be missed!"

They stepped up their pace, rounding a corner near Haverford's box, then slowed, seeing the earl waiting for them. He was not alone; Dennis Fellhopper and his sister Charlotte were conversing with him. As alike as two peas, the fair-haired, blue-eyed duo had recently returned to London after several Seasons in the country.

"Be calm," Rome murmured. "No need to panic."

She shot him an incredulous glance, then smiled as Haverford looked up and saw them.

"There you are," the earl said. "I had just thought to look for you."

"My apologies. I was detained by an acquaintance." Anna removed her hand from Rome's arm and took her place beside her suitor.

"Well, you have arrived in the nick of time. The next act is set to begin." Clearing his throat, he turned to the man and woman waiting politely for introductions. "Mr. Fellhopper, Miss Fellhopper, this is Miss Rosewood," Marc said. "And this is my cousin, Mr. Devereaux."

"Charmed as always, Miss Rosewood," Fellhopper said. "Mr. Devereaux, a pleasure."

"You know each other?" the earl asked, glancing from Anna to the Fellhoppers.

"For many years," Charlotte said. "Anna and I made our debut together." The sweet-faced blonde cast a shy glance at Rome. "But I have not had the pleasure of Mr. Devereaux's company until now."

"Fellhopper. Miss Fellhopper. It is indeed an honor to meet you both." Rome acknowledged them with a quick bow. "If you will excuse me, however, my sister awaits my return."

"Of course," Haverford said.

"Another time," Fellhopper replied.

"Good evening, Mr. Devereaux," came Charlotte's soft reply.

He gave a polite nod and walked away. Anna's gaze lingered on his back until Haverford's voice returned her to the conversation.

"My cousin is just returned from the war," he was saying.

"How brave he must be," Charlotte breathed, also looking after Rome.

Haverford cleared his throat again, his face curiously flushed. "Indeed. I would have bought a commission myself had my responsibilities to my estates not taken precedence."

Charlotte turned her big blue eyes on the earl. "We all do our part, my lord."

His ears reddened. "Indeed, as you do your part to assist your brother."

"Charlotte is a wonderful hostess," Fellhopper said, with a fond smile.

"She is indeed," Haverford agreed. He looked at Anna. "Fellhopper and I have business dealings together, and I have spent many a comfortable evening at his home in Leicestershire."

"How lovely," Anna said. She found herself glancing over to where she'd last seen Rome, then, horrified, jerked her gaze back to her companions. Luckily, Lord Haverford was facing the Fellhoppers and had not noticed her blunder.

The signal sounded for the next act, and the Fellhoppers took their leave.

"Fine people," Haverford said, leading her back to his box.

"Indeed," Anna agreed, determined to finish the evening without further adventure.

They took their seats just as the curtain rose.

Anna's mother leaned close to her daughter. "You were gone quite a while, dear," she murmured.

Anna shrugged and smiled in apology, hoping that would be the end of it.

"And your hair is mussed," Henrietta continued, arching a brow.

Anna raised her hand to discover a lock of hair had indeed slipped from its pins and dangled from the back of her upswept curls. Anxiety rushed through her, and she searched her mother's expression for some hint of disapproval. "How curious."

"Not really." Mrs. Rosewood smiled fondly, her eyes darting to Lord Haverford, who sat enraptured in the performance. "I notice the earl is looking a bit flushed."

"Oh?" Baffled now, Anna cast a sidelong look at Haverford. He did appear a bit flustered, come to think of it.

Henrietta patted her daughter's arm. "As long as you are discreet, dear, I have no objection to anything you must do to secure his lordship's affections."

Anna gaped. Her mother thought she and Haverford had . . . "Mama!" she hissed, cheeks burning.

Henrietta merely gave her a nod of approval, then relaxed back in her seat to enjoy the rest of the play.

Despite her best intentions, Anna couldn't stop herself from glancing at Rome. His knowing look did nothing to help the situation.

She turned back to face the stage and suffered through the rest of the performance, wishing she'd never walked down that dark path at Vauxhall Gardens.

Chapter 9

On Friday at three o'clock, Rome arrived at the office of Edgar Vaughn. His heart pounded as if he were a schoolboy who had just received high compliments from his instructor. If he presented himself well at this meeting, his dreams of a career in diplomacy could become reality.

Upon stating his name and his business, he was directed to Rupert Pennyworthy, Vaughn's secretary.

"Mr. Devereaux," Pennyworthy said, with a pained smile as he rose from his desk. "I know you have an appointment today with Mr. Vaughn, but he has been unexpectedly called out of town."

At the news, Rome's heart plummeted to his stomach. Had Vaughn changed his mind about hiring the son of Oliver Devereaux?

He should have expected this.

He forced a polite smile to his lips. "How unfortunate. I would, of course, like to schedule for another day."

"You'll need to speak to Mr. Vaughn about that."

"Of course." It had been problematic enough obtaining the first appointment, as Edgar Vaughn was notoriously difficult to contact. Securing a second appointment might prove challenging, if not impossible.

He thought briefly of asking for Marc's assistance, then immediately rejected the idea. He would obtain this position on his own merits, without trading upon his connection to the earl.

The slender young man came around the desk. "Mr. Vaughn can only see you for a few minutes, as he must leave London shortly. This way, Mr. Devereaux."

"Vaughn is here?" he blurted, unable to hide his surprise.

"I'm sorry, perhaps I gave you the wrong impression." Again that pained smile. "Mr. Vaughn will see you, but you must keep the visit very brief."

A huge smile spread across Rome's face. "I appreciate his making time for me."

Pennyworthy led the way to Vaughn's office, announced Rome, then took himself off as discreetly as a whiff of smoke.

"Devereaux! Come in. My apologies, but I only have a few minutes." Edgar Vaughn shuffled through papers on his massive desk, shoving some into a satchel and others into his desk drawer.

"Your secretary told me." Rome closed the door, glancing around at the elegant splendor of the décor. "Quite a handsome office, sir."

Vaughn gave a short bark of laughter. "Impresses foreign dignitaries. I'd be happy enough in something less opulent."

Rome grinned. "I understand."

"You would, I'd imagine. Do sit down, Devereaux." As Rome took a seat in one of the plush leather chairs in front of the desk, Vaughn gave him a short, piercing look that seemed to sum up Rome's character in mere moments. "Military man, weren't you?"

"Yes. I recently returned home from the Peninsula."

"Not easily shaken, then. Good quality to have in this position." Vaughn shuffled more papers, sorting them into two piles. "I've read the reports, of course. Your commanding officers speak very highly of you."

"It was an honor to serve under them."

Vaughn gave a bark of laughter. "Very diplomatic answer, Devereaux."

"No, just the truth."

"Even better." Vaughn yanked open another drawer and grabbed a small velvet bag, which he tossed on the desk. The strings had not been pulled closed, and the contents spilled across the surface with a clatter. "Botheration!" Vaughn exclaimed as gold coins scattered over the solid mahogany.

"Allow me to assist," Rome said, bending down to scoop up the few coins that had fallen on the carpet.

"Not necessary," Vaughn insisted as he gathered coins back into the bag.

"Too late." Rome straightened, but his smile faded as he came within a nose length of a gold ring sitting on the edge of the desk.

A rose crossed with a sword within a circle, and the rose was a bloodred ruby.

The back of his neck prickled. What was Vaughn doing with a Triad ring?

"Blast it all," Vaughn muttered, scooping the ring and remaining coins out of Rome's view and into the bag. "Why is it these things always happen when a man is in a hurry?"

"I wish I knew," Rome replied. He stood and handed the coins over to Vaughn. As the older man deposited them into his pouch and pulled the strings tightly, Rome glanced around the office again.

Swords, everywhere. Why hadn't he noticed before?

Jeweled broadswords, crossed rapiers, elegant fencing foils. All graced the walls like artwork in the Louvre.

He turned his attention back to the other man, the muscles in his chest and stomach tense with battle readiness. "You fancy swords, Mr. Vaughn?"

"A hobby of mine. I collect them." He shoved the purse of gold in with his papers and closed the satchel. "Not to be rude, Devereaux, but I do have an urgent matter to attend to outside London and no time to spare. I would like to reschedule our appointment for Tuesday at ten o'clock. Is that convenient?"

"Quite convenient."

"Excellent. Until Tuesday then." Vaughn thrust out his hand.

Managing to hide his aversion, Rome shook it. "I look forward to it."

"Excellent. Pennyworthy will see you out."

Anna sat at the writing desk in her room, a stack of unposted letters to various friends at her elbow. She was right in the middle of a lengthy missive to her cousin Melanie when the door to her bedroom swung open. Her mother stood there, her well-endowed chest heaving, her lips thin with anger.

"I have just heard the most amazing account," she announced, "of a certain young lady sneaking out of this house at night and taking a hack to the docks."

The pen dropped from her suddenly nerveless fingers. "What?"

"You heard me." Henrietta closed the door firmly behind her. "The housekeeper noticed that Lizzie was nowhere to be found on Wednesday night. She had to threaten to sack her, but finally the girl confessed the whole story."

"Mrs. Nivens is most persistent," Anna mumbled.

"How could you?" Henrietta demanded. "How could you have the audacity to sneak out of this house and venture to that part of London? Do you have any idea how much you risked by doing such a foolish thing?"

"I can explain."

"I don't need your explanation." Henrietta loomed over Anna and pointed a finger at her. "I know what you were doing."

"But don't you want to hear—"

"No!" Henrietta made a slicing motion with her hand. "From now on, I forbid you to do leave the house without my express permission."

"But, Mama—"

"Hush." Her mother held up a hand, and Anna fell silent. "I know this has to do with Anthony. Good God, Anna, but I thought you had dispensed with that nonsense when we came to London. I'm most disappointed to discover this is not the case."

"He was murdered," Anna broke in. "And—"

"By footpads," Henrietta interrupted. "Let it lie, Anna. There is nothing you can do for your brother except marry well and live a life of happiness."

"I can't be happy unless I find out the truth."

"Bah! Haven't you heard me? This ends *now*, my girl."

Anna glanced down at her half-written letter. The words swam before her stinging eyes, and she blinked back tears. "Yes, Mama," she whispered.

Henrietta patted her on the shoulder. "You will see I am right in this, Anna. When you are wed to the earl and live the rest of your life in comfort and security, you will thank me." She moved to the wardrobe. "Now, let's see what you have to wear to the Lorrington soirée this evening."

Anna said nothing as her mother began to sort through her dresses, but her mind raced. How could she possibly continue her investigation with Mama watching her like a hawk?

"Perhaps the blue silk, Anna?"

"The Melton ball." She fingered the edge of her stationery. Words danced along her peripheral vision. *Mrs. Emberly . . . the earl's cousin . . . may become good friends . . .*

"Oh, that's right. You can't wear that again because the Lorringtons are cousins to the Meltons. Perhaps the ivory satin?"

"I don't believe I've worn that yet." Anna stared at Lavinia's name on the page, an idea formulating in her mind.

"And flowers in your hair," Henrietta continued. "You'll look like a fresh young bride, and perhaps his lordship will be inspired to offer."

Anna turned to look at her mother, who held up the ivory satin, studying it with a critical eye. "Mama, I was supposed to call on Mrs. Emberly today."

Henrietta cast her a glance askance as she hung the evening dress back in the wardrobe. "I just told you that you cannot leave this house without my permission."

"Then may I have your permission to go?"

"I don't know, Anna." Tapping her foot, her mother studied the other dresses in the wardrobe. "Has that peach satin been delivered from Madame Dauphine's yet?"

"I believe it's supposed to arrive today," Anna replied, getting to her feet. "Mama, I promised Mrs. Emberly I would call. Since she is Lord Haverford's cousin, I should hate to slight her."

"Oh." The mention of the earl broke Henrietta away from her contemplation of fashion. "That's right, we would not want to offend his lordship's family. Unfortunately, I am to call on Admiral Whiting's wife today, which is very important to your father. And you cannot go alone to Mrs. Emberly's."

"Lizzie—"

"That girl!" Henrietta gave an exasperated huff. "She is lucky I did not turn her out without a reference for going along with that half-witted plan of yours! No, you will not take Lizzie anywhere, Anna."

"Then who can accompany me, Mama? If you are otherwise engaged, and Lizzie is not allowed to go . . ."

"Bliss shall go!" Satisfied with her solution, her mother turned back to the wardrobe.

"Bliss?" Anna echoed weakly. She sank back into her chair. Her mother's maid never smiled, rarely spoke, and tolerated no nonsense of any sort. She was a completely humorless creature who was totally devoted to Henrietta.

"It is the perfect solution. Bliss will be certain that you indeed arrive at Mrs. Emberly's home and do not, shall we say, 'divert' down any unscheduled paths." Henrietta gave her a hard look. "It's the best offer you will get from me, my girl."

Anna sighed. "Very well."

"What time are you expected at Mrs. Emberly's?"

"About four o'clock. She has asked me to tea."

"How lovely. Now what will you wear to that, I wonder?"

As Henrietta flipped through the dresses again, Anna set aside the letter to her cousin and pulled forth a fresh sheet of paper. Since she had just manufactured the appointment for tea out of thin air, she needed to let Lavinia know that she was coming and also to make certain that Rome joined them.

This turn of events had forced her hand. She only hoped that Rome still wanted to be her partner.

Having received a note from his sister to present himself before four o'clock, Rome arrived on Lavinia's doorstep in a state of annoyed disbelief. Fate had dealt him a rotten hand in the past twenty-four hours, and he didn't know if he should bet or fold.

First, his suspicions about Rose's true identity

had been verified, confirming that he had indeed made improper advances to his cousin's woman. That he hadn't known her real name at the time was irrelevant; if the truth came out, his relationship with Marc, as well as everything he had worked for, would be irrevocably damaged.

His best opportunity to overcome the shadow of his father's scandal had appeared to be a position in Edgar Vaughn's office. But now he didn't know what to think about Vaughn. What was he doing with a ring that belonged to the Black Rose Society? Was he a member? Peter had said that only members of the society wore such rings, and that the ones worn by the elite members of the Triad had rubies where the rose should be.

Just like the one in Vaughn's office.

Before Vaughn had entered the diplomatic arena, he had been a military man, well-known for acting honorably even in the most horrific of circumstances. As he had carried on his duties as a diplomat, he had earned a reputation for being a stickler for propriety and decorum.

Which had made his willingness to consider the son of Oliver Devereaux for a position in his office even more of a miracle.

Coldness dragged at his shoulders and knotted his guts. He respected Vaughn, had even looked upon him as a role model. Now he wondered if he'd been mistaken in his admiration.

Bagsley admitted him and showed him to the parlor.

"Rome, there you are." Lavinia greeted him from the sofa, her smile inviting but not quite as vivacious as usual.

"Hallo, Vin. Are you all right? You look a bit too pale, if I may take a brother's prerogative and say so."

She shook her head. "Brother or not, you always say what you think, Rome. And yes, I imagine I resemble day-old porridge, if how I feel is any comparison."

Rome came to sit beside her and covered her cold hand with his. "I'm surprised you summoned me here if you are not feeling quite the thing."

"It came on rather suddenly. Normally I nibble on a bit of bread to settle my stomach in the mornings, but even that makes me ill to think of it."

"Shall I summon the physician?"

"No, silly. It's just the child. Mama told me to expect such things."

"Oh. Well, then if that is what our mother said . . ." Uncomfortable with the talk of such feminine mysteries, Rome shifted and patted her hand. "You should follow her advice."

Vin gave a little laugh. "Very well, I shall take pity on you and change the subject. How was your interview with Mr. Vaughn?"

"Very short." Rome rose, still disturbed by the ring in Vaughn's possession. "He had to leave town unexpectedly."

"Oh, dear. Does this mean you did not secure the position?"

"No, we rescheduled the appointment." Rome prowled the room.

"Then what's wrong?"

He stopped near the mantel and tried to smile at her. "Nothing's wrong. I'm just disappointed that the interview did not go as expected."

"Are you certain there's nothing else?"

He came to his sister and kissed her cheek. "I have no intention of burdening you with my troubles, Vin. 'Tis nothing dire, I promise you."

"You always do this," she scolded. "You're clearly worried about something, and yet you won't tell me what's wrong."

"Just being in your presence is enough to cheer me," he said, completely sincere. "It's just some business matters that need decisions. Don't fret."

"How can I not fret when you won't confide in me? I'm a grown woman, Rome." She patted her belly. "Or had you forgotten?"

"Vin!" His face flushed. "You are far too outspoken for a lady."

"So I've been told. But I'm a married woman now, and once in a while I will speak my mind. I do wish you would talk to me honestly."

He shook his head slowly. "I'm sorry, Vin."

Hurt flickered across her face. "Very well. By the way, Anna Rosewood sent a note around that she would be calling today."

He couldn't mask his surprise. "Really?"

"She asked if I would invite you as well. Rome, what's going on?"

"I don't know what you mean."

Vin pounded the cushion of the settee with one small, clenched fist. "There you go again, keeping secrets! Just tell me this isn't what it looks like."

He stiffened. "That depends on what it looks like."

Concern shadowed her hazel eyes. "An affair."

"You know better than that."

"I should, but I also know other things. Such as the way you closeted yourself in the library with her the other day. The fact that she asked questions about you the last time she visited me. And now she is coming to call and asked me specifically to invite you here."

He let out a deep sigh. "I am not intent on stealing Haverford's bride, Vin."

"Then what *are* you doing? Because whatever it is, Marc will think the worst if he gets wind of it. You know how he is about loyalty."

"I know." He rubbed the back of his neck. "Anna has information I need for an investigation I am conducting. And no, sweet sister, I am not going to tell you about it."

"How can Anna be involved in an investigation? I thought her reputation was impeccable?"

Rome sent her a look. "Didn't I just say I am not going to tell you about it?"

"It's my house, and if Anna is involved with something that could possibly hurt Marc—"

"It's nothing like that. Her brother was involved, not Anna. She is a perfectly acceptable female. And that is all I am going to tell you, brat."

Lavinia pouted, but only for a moment. "Very well. Just take note that I have no intention of playing Friar Lawrence for you, dear brother."

"I understand. But since this is the only place Anna and I can meet to discuss our business that would cause no gossip . . ."

She sighed. "Oh, very well, as long as this is not a romantic rendezvous, you may meet here."

"Of course it's not." Unable to look her in the eye, he said, "I have no romantic interest in Anna Rosewood."

Before Lavinia could say anything more, Bagsley entered the room. Rome and Lavinia looked up expectantly.

"The Earl of Haverford," Bagsley said, then stepped aside.

Marc entered, his polite smile widening. "Good afternoon, Lavinia. Rome, a pleasant surprise."

"Good afternoon," Rome echoed, stunned. What was Marc doing here, when Anna was due any moment? He turned away, staring out the window until he could get his guilt under control.

"Good afternoon, Marc." Lavinia flicked a concerned glance at Rome, then turned a wan smile on her cousin. "Do sit down."

A frown wrinkled the earl's brow as he settled into a chair. "Lavinia, you seem rather pale. Are you ill?"

She cleared her throat. "I must look worse than I had imagined."

"Don't let her fool you," Rome remarked from the window. "She's not feeling well at all."

"I'm very sorry to hear that." Marc tapped his fingers on the arm of the chair, lips pursed in thought.

"Is something wrong?" Lavinia asked. "It's unusual for you to call unannounced, though I am always happy to see you, of course."

"I have been summoned to Leicestershire to assist with a business matter for Mr. Fellhopper. I had thought to have you come with me, Lavinia, as you are acquainted with Mr. Fellhopper's sister."

Lavinia brightened. "Dear Charlotte? I recall her well. She had barely made her debut when her parents died."

"A tragedy, that," Rome remarked. "Old Fellhopper had gotten himself into some deep waters financially."

"I remember." Vin shook her head. "Charlotte had to cut her Season short and return home while her brother tried to recoup the family fortunes."

"Which he has done admirably," Marc reminded them.

"Quite so," Rome said. He came away from the window, comfortable that he had recovered from the surprise of Marc's visit. "I thought they were in Town for the marriage mart. Isn't that right, Marc?"

Haverford cleared his throat. "Mr. Fellhopper has indeed brought his sister to London for the purpose of finding a husband for her."

"I imagine she would have any number of suitors already," Lavinia said, reaching for her tea.

"I have no doubt of it," Rome agreed. "Miss Fellhopper is a lovely woman."

Marc shot him a quick glance. "Do you have interests there, cousin?"

Rome blinked at the edge behind the polite words. "Not at all."

"Oh. Very well then." Marc turned his attention back to Lavinia, once more his usual urbane self. "Fellhopper has requested my assistance with this matter, and I thought you and Emberly might want to join the party to keep Miss Fellhopper entertained. I am certain she will miss the delights of London."

"That's very kind of you," Lavinia said. "However, I must decline the invitation. Henry's schedule is quite full, and I cannot believe the motion of a carriage for all that time will improve my state."

Marc flushed from neck to brow. "Of course. I apologize for being so insensitive to your condition."

"What about Miss Rosewood?" Even as he said the words, Rome could hardly believe it. But if Anna were with Marc in the country, she would be protected, and he could see to the Black Rose Society without having to worry about her safety. "As I recall, she and Miss Fellhopper are acquainted."

"Ah . . . I had thought of that." Marc's eyes darted away. "But it is improper for her to accompany me alone, and I know her parents have many engagements in the city."

"Nothing they would not cancel for an earl's request," Rome said, his lips twisting in a brief, cynical smile.

"Rome!" Lavinia gave a sigh of exasperation.

Marc frowned. "Even if that were true, I would never ask such a thing."

"Of course not," Lavinia agreed, with a quelling glance at her brother. "It's a lovely idea, Marc, but surely Miss Fellhopper has friends in the country. After all, she has only arrived in Town quite recently."

"I suppose you're right."

"When do you leave?" Rome asked.

"In the morning. I don't expect the matter to take more than a day or two."

"Oh, then dear Charlotte will be fine," Lavinia asserted with a dismissive wave of her hand. "Certainly there are activities to keep her entertained—riding, visiting with friends?"

"True." Marc's smile reached his eyes. "She's a very skilled rider from what I understand."

"Then everything is settled."

"Quite." Marc stood. "I have other appointments today, so I had best take my leave."

They all looked up as Bagsley stepped into the room. "Miss Rosewood," he announced.

Chapter 10

❧

Anna stepped into Lavinia's parlor, her focus on Rome. She almost didn't notice Lord Haverford until he turned toward her. "Miss Rosewood, how unexpected!" He came over, took her hand, and brushed a kiss across her knuckles.

Shocked at his presence, she slowly lowered her hand to her side, her fingers secretly clenching. "Good afternoon, Lord Haverford." Confused, her eyes sought her hostess's. Vin gave a nearly imperceptible shrug. She glanced at Rome, met his fierce gaze for one blistering moment, and hurriedly turned her attention back to her suitor. "Ah . . . are you joining us for tea?"

"Unfortunately, no. Though had I known you

were coming to visit Lavinia, I would certainly have changed my schedule. Alas, I am leaving for Leicestershire tomorrow."

"Oh?"

"Mr. Fellhopper needs my assistance with a business matter. I should only be gone two days or so."

"I'm sorry you cannot stay." Anna forced a smile, more than aware of Rome's intense regard from across the room. "Do have a good trip, my lord."

"Thank you. I expect I shall see you at Severley's ball." He gave a little bow, then turned to his cousins. "Lavinia, I shall call on you when I get back. Rome, are you staying?"

"Yes, for a while."

Something flickered across Haverford's face—confusion or distress, Anna wasn't sure. "Very well then. I'll bid you all good afternoon."

He left the parlor. His muffled voice echoed back to them from the hall as he spoke to Bagsley. The three of them stayed frozen in place—Lavinia on the sofa, Rome standing just to the side of her, Anna just inside the room—until they heard the front door close behind the earl.

Lavinia let out a huge breath. "I am not of the proper disposition for such dramatics!"

"I wouldn't say that," Rome quipped.

"Hush, you wicked thing. Anna, do sit down."

Anna gratefully took a seat beside Lavinia, her

knees weak from the bone-thrumming tension. "I had not expected to see his lordship here."

"Leave it to Marc to choose today of all days to call unexpectedly," Lavinia said. "I thought I would succumb to the vapors when he walked in."

"Not dramatic?" Rome teased with a grin.

"Be quiet, Rome."

Anna watched the byplay between the two. A bittersweet smile touched her lips as she recalled similar banter with her own brother. "Thank you for allowing me to invite myself here," Anna said. "I realize it was somewhat rude . . ."

"Not at all." Lavinia waved a hand. "Do not think on it for another moment."

"But certainly you must wonder why I did such a thing—"

"I've explained that we have a business matter to discuss," Rome interrupted, his green eyes so intently focused on her that it stole her breath. "That is why you've come here?"

"Yes." The word slipped from her lips before she'd barely formulated the answer.

"Good. Vin—"

"I'm not leaving."

He let out a huge sigh. "Lavinia . . ."

"No." She set her chin stubbornly. "This whole situation is already too close to scandalous. I will sit right here on the sofa, and you can discuss your business on the other side of the room, where I can see you." She gave him a saucy grin. "You can whisper."

"Fine." Rome stood and gestured for Anna to precede him. They walked together to the far side of the room and stopped in a corner.

"I cannot stay long," Anna said, pitching her voice low. "Mama has confined me to the house."

"How is it that you are here, then?"

Anna wrinkled her nose. "She sent her maid with me, but Bliss is a stickler for the proprieties and will come fetch me when the proper time for tea has passed. She's a veritable dragon of a chaperone."

Her exasperated tone brought a smile to his face. "Why are you confined to the house?"

Unnerved by the warmth in his eyes, she dropped her gaze. "Mama found out about my investigation."

She had expected him to laugh at her. Instead, he said, very seriously, "I'm glad to hear you will no longer be putting yourself in danger."

She didn't bother to hide her annoyance. "I did what was necessary, and I would do it again if given the choice."

"So fierce." His smile grew tender. "I admire your loyalty, Anna. Your brother is lucky to have you standing up for him."

Something in the vicinity of her heart seemed to melt. "Thank you."

"But I doubt he would be happy about some of the things you have done in his name. Vauxhall for one. The Cock and Crown for another."

"No one else would do it."

"If it were Lavinia," he said, his voice taking on a stern edge, "I know I would be most displeased."

"And if it were you," she shot back, "would you leave her murder unavenged?"

His face settled into the hard lines of a warrior. "Never."

His sudden transformation startled her, and she nearly retreated a step. This, then, must be the Roman Devereaux the enemy had seen on the battlefield. "So you understand."

"I do understand. But you don't." His expression eased, but the echo of the soldier remained in his eyes. "The world you need to walk in to discover the truth about your brother is not one that is safe or appropriate for a woman. Your desire to take the risks is admirable, but you're not alone anymore. You have me."

"I do need you," she admitted, then wanted to call back the imprudent words immediately. She glanced up at him, noticing the way his jaw clenched. "I'm sorry; that wasn't well said."

"I know what you meant," he bit out. His chest rose sharply and fell again.

She could practically feel the tension rolling off him, a sudden sexual heat that lapped at her like the ocean at the shore. This was the reason she hadn't wanted him for a partner—this uncontrollable hunger that seized both of them when they were together.

"Is everything all right?" Lavinia called.

Her voice broke the spell, and they both took a

step back, putting more space between them.

"We're fine, Vin," Rome said. Dear God, where was his control?

Anna stood with her head bowed, and when she raised her eyes, she couldn't hide the desire that lingered in those dark depths. His body tightened all over again in response. Sweet, brave girl, trying to do what was right to honor her dead brother. Such faithfulness was rare, and for a moment, he envied Anthony Rosewood. What would it be like to have that love and loyalty directed at him instead?

His heart ached just imagining it.

"I've come to take you up on your offer to be partners," she said.

"So I assumed. But how can we work together if you are confined to quarters?"

She opened her reticule and pulled out a sheaf of folded papers. "This will be my contribution."

"What's this?" He took the proffered papers and unfolded them.

"This is my research," she said, craning her neck to view her own neat writing. "I have kept notes on every death by sword in the past year. Gossip, it seems, is a fertile source of information."

"Amazing." His admiration for her grew as he flipped through the sheets of carefully laid-out notes. He shuffled back to the first page, and his gaze lit on one name at the top: Anthony Rosewood. "You've done a lot of work."

"I thought perhaps you could take this information and use it, maybe visit the sites where the men were found—that sort of thing."

"I could indeed." He squeezed her hand. "Thank you, Anna."

She blushed and snatched her hand away. "Now that Mama is haunting my every moment, I'm trusting you to follow these clues, Rome, and help me find the man who killed my brother."

"I will." He folded up the papers and tucked them in the pocket of his coat. "I will have Vin send a note around when I have some results."

"Contact me even if you've found nothing. The waiting will drive me mad."

"No, it's best if we don't have too much contact."

"But—"

"No." He held her gaze, his implacable. "Together we will find your brother's killer and disband the Black Rose Society, but after that, we should stay away from each other." He glanced at her full, lush mouth, then flicked his gaze back to hers. "You know why."

Her pupils had dilated, and she nodded, biting her lower lip.

He sucked in a harsh breath. Damn it, but she aroused him like no other woman ever had. Her body, her heart, her fierce loyalty. He wanted them for himself.

"Business only," he said, talking to himself as much as her.

"Business only," she echoed. "I understand."

The parlor door opened and Bagsley appeared. "Miss Rosewood's chaperone indicates it is time for the lady to depart."

Anna sighed. "Tell her I will be out directly, if you please."

"Very good, miss." The butler withdrew.

"Anna," Lavinia said, as they approached her sofa, "did your maid just order you home?"

"It's my mother's maid, and she has her orders." Anna pressed Lavinia's hand. "Thank you, Lavinia."

"You are always welcome here."

Bagsley came back into the room. "Miss, your companion is most insistent."

"I'm coming. Good-bye, Rome."

"Anna." He gave a little bow, but couldn't stop a grin. "I wish you luck taming the dragon."

She grinned back, a dimple flashing in her cheek. "Thank you. I look forward to hearing the results of our business transaction."

"As soon as I know, you will know."

Bliss appeared in the hallway behind Bagsley and cleared her throat loudly. The indomitable woman was taller than the aged butler, her graying dark hair pulled ruthlessly back in a braided coronet, her clothing stark black. Over the butler's head, she fixed Anna with a look of warning.

With a sigh, Anna turned and left the room.

Rome watched her go, the papers in his pocket a testament to the love she bore her brother.

Would she demonstrate the same devotion for her husband?

"Are you certain you know what you're doing?"

Lavinia's quiet question drew his attention away from Anna's departing form. "I told you, Vin, this is just a business matter."

She sighed, toying with the swirling design of her teacup handle. "You don't look at her like a business associate."

"And how do I look at her?"

Lavinia met his gaze. "Like she's your last chance for happiness."

Struck dumb by this evidence that he had failed to conceal his true feelings, Rome didn't reply.

After a long moment of silence, Lavinia said, "Just be careful, Rome. There are more hearts than yours at stake."

"En garde!" Slashing swords drowned out the sharp command. In the moonlit clearing, the two young men parried and thrust, weapons gleaming in the silvery light.

On the side of the clearing, three masked figures dressed in black watched the battle silently. One of them shifted a bulging purse from one hand to the other, the rapid clink of coins lost in the scrape of steel upon steel. A second man fingered two pieces of white paper.

The leader held out a hand, snapped his fingers. The second-in-command handed over the notes. "Both of them?" the leader asked without taking his eyes from the duel.

"Yes. We've been more careful these past months since we lost that one."

"Reassuring." He folded the letters and slipped them into his pocket, then watched the swordplay with his companions and waited for the victor to be revealed.

Chapter 11

⌒◯◯⌒

"**I** do not understand his hesitation," Henrietta Rosewood said as she tied the ribbons of her bonnet. "Lord Haverford is an honorable man. Why does he not satisfy his family obligation and speak to your father?"

Already dressed for their outing, Anna gathered up the books she needed to return to the lending library. "I don't know, Mama."

"You've been all that is amiable, Anna. Anyone can see you are the perfect wife for him." Henrietta emphasized her words with grand gestures, and one waving hand nearly hit the footman in the nose as he went to open the front door for the two of them. She didn't even notice the near miss as she paraded down the stairs to their carriage.

"Perhaps he feels the need for a certain amount of courtship," Anna offered, hurrying after her parent.

"Nonsense!" Mrs. Rosewood clambered into the carriage with a loud creaking of springs. "There is no uncertainty here. He knows what must be done."

Anna handed her books to a footman to be stowed, then climbed into the carriage herself. "I don't know why he hasn't made an offer, Mama," she said bluntly. "He does not confide in me."

"Men never volunteer information, daughter. This is the first thing you must learn as a wife." Henrietta pondered the subject as the footmen shut the carriage door and the driver set the horses in motion. "A woman must learn a man's thoughts by observation and assumption."

"Lord Haverford has always behaved quite correctly in my presence, so I can only assume that he is a gentleman," Anna said, with a grin.

"Indeed?" her mother asked slyly. "He seemed very attentive at the theater on Thursday."

Warmth swept her cheeks. "Mama, that was four days ago."

"Nonetheless, it is rather encouraging," Henrietta said with a smug smile. "Observation and assumption, Anna!"

"I *observe* that Lord Haverford has not come to call," Anna retorted. "Though he is out of Town, so I suppose that does not signify."

"I *observed* him squeezing your hand," her

mother challenged, "and so I *assume* he finds you pleasing!"

"I cannot comment on his lordship's feelings toward me." Anna turned her attention to the passing scenery, hoping to put an end to the discussion.

"I also *observed* your dishabille when you returned to the box, Anna Eugenie Catherine," Henrietta said pointedly. "And I *assume* that something of a romantic nature occurred between you and his lordship."

"Mama!"

"Do not try to deny it," Henrietta said, raising a staying hand. "I know what I observed, and I forgive you the transgression. I was the one who told you to encourage the earl."

"You are making much of nothing." Anna glanced away again before her mother could see the panic in her eyes. Henrietta was an astute woman, and she had a way of seeing through the mildest of deceptions.

For the night at the theater had indeed lingered in Anna's thoughts, but not because of the earl.

"It is quite puzzling that he did not call on you before he left," Henrietta mused.

Rome hadn't contacted her either.

"I was certain after the theater that he would be on our doorstep the following day," her mother persisted.

Had she been wrong to trust him?

"I certainly hope any . . . romantic interludes . . . between you did not change his opinion of you. Men can lose all sense of civility if a lady acts even the slightest bit forward. I declare I do not understand the phenomenon."

The first time she'd asked him for help, he'd refused.

"Can you recall anything you did or said that would make Lord Haverford less enthusiastic in his courtship?" Henrietta waited, watching her daughter with keen expectation.

Anna scrambled for something to say that would placate her mother. "When I saw him at Mrs. Emberly's, his lordship did comment that he would attend Lord Severley's ball."

"Did he?" Henrietta's expression brightened. "How gratifying. We, too, have received an invitation. I will accept at once. You must wear the peach silk, Anna."

"Yes, Mama." As her mother droned on about possible wardrobe accessories, Anna let her thoughts return to more pressing matters.

She had trusted Rome when he'd told her that he wasn't a member of the society. What if he'd lied?

He hadn't contacted her as he'd said he would. He also hadn't really explained why he was at the dinner party that night. What if he'd simply been trying to get her to admit that *she* had been there? There had been no obvious connection between Rose and Anna Rosewood, yet somehow he had put the two together and even gotten her to admit the truth.

Had she signed her own death warrant?

A chill rippled down her spine. She glanced at

her mother, desperate to confide her fear. Mama continued to wax on about the wardrobe choices that would best ensnare Lord Haverford, oblivious to her daughter's distress.

Anna pressed her lips closed and turned away to watch the passing scenery without really noticing any of it.

At least she had realized her own danger. She had only Rome's word that he had no ties to the society, but a ring was an easy thing to remove and slip into a pocket. What if he was playing some game with her to see what she knew? Had she completely betrayed herself? She had spoken Anthony's name, had not denied that she had passed herself off as a doxy named Rose. She had handed him all her careful research. And yet somehow, when she thought back on their conversations, Rome had managed to give her vague answers to every question she had put to him. He had assured her he would take care of everything.

What if that, too, was a lie? What if he had gleaned the information he sought from her and even now planned to remove her from the scene?

Tears stung her eyes. *Anthony, Anthony, I need you so right now!*

She blinked the moisture back, not wanting to attract her mother's attention. Anthony was dead. He would not come to rescue her as he had so many times in the past. She was utterly alone, with only her wits and instinct to guide her.

And she didn't want to die.

She could stop her search for the truth, marry Haverford, and retire to the country to bear babies. She could pretend that she believed the Banbury tale of Anthony's death at the hands of footpads. She could act as if she had never met Rome Devereaux.

She could do all that to remain safe—and she would betray Anthony in the process. To remain safe, all she need do was bury suspicions with her murdered brother. All she need do was leave his death unpunished.

Or she could keep going and uncover the secrets of the Black Rose society at the risk of her own life. And she might save others. She would find a way around her mother's strictures and do what needed to be done. There would be no more bodies found in alleyways, no more mysterious deaths by sword, unexplainable to shocked families. She would finally be able to properly grieve for her brother.

Or she would join him.

Either way, she knew she could not give up. Walking away took more courage than she had.

Rome slipped through the throng clogging the doorway to the lending library. The crowd hummed with an appalling excitement that he had seen over and over again on the battlefield— and never been able to explain.

The *ton*—indeed, people in general—treated death as one more act in a macabre circus that equally outraged and titillated.

And now Robert Chambers graced the center ring.

"Dead—"

"Found him at the side of the road—"

"—bloody footpads! A man's not safe in his own carriage—"

"His mother took to her bed—"

Leaving the buzzing crowd behind, Rome slipped into the relative quiet of the lending library, but the gossip had already taken hold. Through the tangle of bonnets and skirts, he saw Mrs. Rosewood deep in conversation with three other ladies and, behind her, Anna, her dark eyes wide and stricken in her pale face.

She saw him.

He froze, struck into immobility by the sheer destitution of her expression.

She held his gaze, accusation and devastation warring in her eyes. Her lips quivered, but she pressed them together firmly and stood tall, as if daring anyone to put a name to her obvious suffering. With an imperceptible tilt of her head, she indicated a row of bookshelves to her left. Then she inched away from her oblivious parent, eventually slipping out of sight between the huge wooden cases.

Rome went in the opposite direction and worked his way around the back aisle of the shelves until he came upon Anna in the far corner, behind a rack of ancient history texts. A stack of the thick, dusty tomes rested on a table in front of her, rendering her nearly invisible to anyone passing. As he stepped into the cozy niche of table and shelves, she stood with neck bowed, a lacy handkerchief clutched in her hand. Her exposed nape lent a vulnerability that made his heart ache. Her head came up as she became aware of his presence, and she quickly crumpled the dainty bit of cloth in her fist and faced him.

"Anna." He reached out a hand, but she flinched away.

"Don't."

"Sorry." He dropped his hand to his side. "I had forgotten where we were."

"I suppose you've heard the news already." Her misty, reddened eyes broke his heart. "Robert Chambers was found dead on a country road. Killed by a sword."

"I know. I wanted to tell you myself. I just missed you at home."

"So you followed me here?"

"Yes. I was hoping the news had not yet spread."

"I knew him, you know." She stretched out the wrinkled bit of lace again. Twisting it in her fingers, she murmured, "He declared his undying love to me when we were nine."

"Oh, Anna." Heart aching for her, he had to glance away for a moment. "I'm so sorry."

"Did you kill him?"

Her whisper jerked his head back around. "What did you say?"

"Did you kill him?" Pale as a marble statue, she waited, utterly still, for his answer.

"Of course not." He scrambled for rational thought. "How could you think that?"

"You told me that night in Vauxhall that you had killed men."

He nodded slowly. "It's true. But I was a soldier, Anna. I killed men in battle, not in cold blood."

"Are you part of the society?"

"No."

"How can I believe you?" Her agitation brought color back to her cheeks, flags of red signaling a bull about to charge. "How can I take your word when men are being murdered all around us?"

"I can only tell you the truth, Anna. I can't force you to believe me."

"I thought I was brave. I thought I knew what path to take, whom to trust. But I don't know anything."

"You can trust me."

"Can I?" The longing in her voice conflicted with the wariness of her expression. "I still don't understand your part in all this. You have not confided in me, though you expect my confidence. Are you even conducting an investigation? Or was this all an elaborate ruse to find out what I know?"

"Of course there's an investigation." He held her gaze, desperate to chase that haunted look from her eyes. "Someone I care about is involved in the society. I want to keep him safe."

"Who?"

"The brother of a friend."

"I meant, what is his name? I want to talk to him."

"No."

"No?" The word jumped an octave in volume, but luckily not loudly enough to be heard over the steady rumble of gossip at the front of the room. She dropped to a whisper again. "If we are on the same side in this, you must tell me."

"We are on the same side, but I'll not put you in danger."

Her mouth fell open. "How can you keep so vital a piece of information from me?"

He shook his head. "I'm sorry, but I will not endanger him or you by speaking his name."

"And you want me to trust you?" Her eyes flashed fire. "I will do better alone, I think."

"No, you wouldn't." He stepped closer, both to make his point and to inhale the forbidden scent of her. "You need me, remember?"

She narrowed her eyes and held her ground. "Rome, learning the truth about Anthony's death is the only thing that kept me from Bedlam this past year."

"Our deal was that I will do the actual investigating, and I will keep you apprised."

"And I haven't heard from you in three days!"

"Because there is nothing to report. I was going down your list and validating the facts."

"Validating!"

"Yes," he said. "You admitted that much of your

information came from gossip, and I am verifying all the facts. Hearsay can be misconstrued."

"I've done a fine job of investigating," she hissed.

"And taken your reputation in your hands with each escapade. For *both* our sakes, allow me to be the one to travel to the more unsavory parts of town while you turn your clever brain to untangling the new clues I uncover."

Her angry posture relaxed. "Clues like the name of the member you refuse to tell me?"

"See? Clever."

Her lips curved just a bit at the edges, as if her high dudgeon disallowed a true expression of pleasure. "I shall take that as a compliment, though I doubt you meant it that way."

"Believe me, this whole situation would be easier if you weren't so intelligent." He touched a curl peeping from her bonnet. "Or so beautiful."

"No." She leaned away from him, smile fading and caution flickering across her face. "Ours is a business partnership, Mr. Devereaux."

He took a step back. "You are correct, of course."

"We must remember ourselves at all times," she whispered, "and forget the night at Vauxhall."

"I will never forget that night." Just the memory stirred his blood.

"Then if you cannot forget, take the incident to the grave with you. But in any circumstance, it must not happen again."

"I know." He wanted to touch her again, but instead stroked the heavy leather binding of a tome on the table. "You belong to Marc."

"Indeed." She frowned. "Though Mama fears he has lost interest."

If only that were true.

"He returned from Leicestershire just today," Rome said. "I imagine he will call on you soon."

"Mama will be relieved."

"Are you?" Even as he said the words, he wanted to call them back.

"I must return to my mother," she said quickly, ignoring the question.

He noted the tremble in her voice. "Yes, I suppose you must. I will contact you when I have information to relay."

"I want to talk to your friend."

"I cannot allow that."

She arched her brows in haughty command. "I suggest you reconsider."

"And I suggest you return to your mama before she calls Bow Street."

"Very well, but I have not given up."

"Neither have I."

She threw him a look of exasperation before she swept past him to return to the front of the library.

He stayed where he was a few moments longer, both to prevent gossip and to give his body the chance to settle down. Another few minutes, and he might have taken her right there on top of— what was it? He glanced at the book on the table. *Philosophers of Ancient Greece.*

He traced the embossed letters of the title, reliving the past few minutes in his mind. His heart had melted at the tears in her eyes, and he'd wanted nothing more than to console her. But taking her in his arms, even in comfort, was not his right. Better to focus on the mystery and treat her as a colleague.

But no colleague of his had ever smelled of attar of roses.

Damn, damn, damn! He slapped his hand against the book, struggling to push aside the vision of her big dark eyes and seductive mouth. The woman tied him in knots. His hunger for her grew every time he saw her, and though she had directed him to forget the incident at Vauxhall, he could not.

But neither could he afford to forget that she belonged to Haverford.

The Black Rose Society deserved his full attention, women be damned. The best course of action was to continue the investigation and forget about Anna Rosewood except in the most peripheral sense.

The sooner Haverford offered for her, the safer they would all be.

Anna shut the door to her bedroom and leaned back against it, sagging with relief at finally being alone.

She had returned home from the lending library without a single book to justify her visit.

Her mother had fussed about Robert Chambers's death the entire way home, and her constant reminders of the tragedy only served to keep Anna's already precarious emotions on edge. Claiming distress over the incident, Anna had escaped to her room upon their return, waving aside her mother's suggestions for comfort.

All she wanted now was silence to calm the chaos within her.

She took a deep breath and let it out, then moved away from the door with the slow steps of an elderly woman. Her entire body ached as if she'd been run over by a carriage, but the bruising existed on the inside, not the outside. The events of today had pummeled her like the physical blows of Fate.

Robert Chambers, dead.

Rome, still a nearly irresistible temptation.

She sank down on the chair before her vanity mirror. Death and desire, all in one day. And of the two, desire grabbed her by the throat and shook her until she could barely breathe.

How could she possibly be so attracted to a man who might be using her?

Because she was an imprudent, bedazzled country mouse. The man was handsome, certainly, and charming, and sophisticated beyond anyone else of her acquaintance. She wanted to believe him when he claimed that he wasn't a member of the society, that he was trying to help a friend. But who was this friend? Where was he? Did he even exist?

Despite the doubts, her body longed for his touch.

Wicked, wicked girl. One evening in his embrace, and you can think of nothing else! What about Anthony? What about poor Robert? Men are dying, and all you can think about is the sinful pleasure to be found in the arms of a man you cannot have!

She looked at her reflection. The young woman in the mirror appeared to be a true English lady, gently bred and proper in every way, but inside a hunger roared that shocked even her. That night at Vauxhall, she had gotten a brief glimpse of heaven, and every time Rome Devereaux came near her, she could think of nothing else.

He'd called her clever. "Foolish" would be a better word. Shameless, even. Her parents had secured her an excellent future with Haverford, and she couldn't seem to dredge up the fortitude to forgo the joy of Rome's attentions in order to preserve it.

She wished things had remained simple. She wished she had never heard of the Black Rose Society, that she had never gone to Vauxhall that night.

That Anthony was still alive.

She touched her locket, shoulders slumping as grief pressed down on her. How many more young men would die? How many would she know personally? And would she be able to stop it?

Her actions to uncover the mystery of the society certainly put her relationship with Haverford in jeopardy, especially with the added complication of Rome. But ceasing the investigation now was not an option. She would simply hope that Rome was telling her the truth, that he would indeed help her. As a man, he could go places she could not. Once he brought his findings to her, they could combine forces to unlock the puzzle.

And such an arrangement would assure that they remained separated for extended amounts of time, leaving her to do her duty by Haverford. There would be no chance for unexpected encounters.

She had risen above her parents' patronizing disbelief in her theories about Anthony's death. She had managed to conquer her grief and do what needed to be done. Now she simply must gather the strength to resist the seductive lure of Rome Devereaux long enough to accomplish her goal.

She met her own eyes in the mirror. She had always accomplished every task she set out to do.

Resisting Rome Devereaux's rakish charm would be no different.

Rome returned to his rooms, his feet dragging as if bound in iron. He had thought that staying away from Anna would soothe the ache in his heart, but today's encounter had proven him completely wrong. The attraction hadn't dimmed a whit; if anything, it had only grown stronger in the short time he hadn't seen her. He couldn't forget her taste or the feel of her in his arms. Curse him for a fool, but he wanted her even though she belonged to another man.

The best thing to do was to stick to their new bargain. Her notes had proven invaluable, and he was starting to get a good picture of the Black Rose Society by using them as the basis for his own investigation. He would have to share some of his findings with her, he decided, stopping before the door to his rooms. Certainly not everything, but definitely enough that she felt he was keeping her involved.

He would keep her safe, no matter what.

The matter of Edgar Vaughn, for instance. How could a man so steeped in honor and tradition turn colors so quickly? His second appointment with Vaughn was scheduled for tomorrow, and he would use that time to discover what he could about Vaughn's connection to the society.

He entered his rooms. She had been right earlier when she'd said the attraction between them must not be encouraged. He was not his father, to be sniffing after another man's woman. The first time had been an accident; he hadn't known her true identity. Anything after that, however, he could not excuse.

He slammed the door, both the physical one to his rooms and the mental one marked "Anna Rosewood."

A movement in the darkness claimed his attention. He froze, already formulating how to get to the desk drawer where his pistol lay. "Who's there?"

"It is I. Peter."

His tense muscles relaxed. "Peter, what are you doing sitting here in the dark?" He moved to the table to light the lamp.

"I need your help, Roman."

Hearing the tremble in the boy's voice, Rome quickly lit the lamp and turned to look at him. "Dear God, Peter, what happened?"

His clothes stained and dirty, his hair uncombed, Peter watched him with the eyes of a condemned man. "I don't know what to do."

"About what?" As Rome came closer, the stench of the lad hit him like a board in the face. "Bloody hell, boy! What the devil have you been about?"

"I haven't been home." He swiped a hand over his unshaven cheeks. "Apparently I spent the night asleep on the table in a taproom."

"Or inside a wine bottle."

"Roman, please." He spread shaking hands in supplication. "I need help. I don't know what to do."

"Just tell me what the problem is."

Peter gazed at him with torment in his bloodshot eyes. "I killed a man last night."

Chapter 12

“**W**hat did you say?”

“I killed a man. Oh, God.” Peter stumbled back a step, fell back into his seat. His pale face resembled a Greek mask, eyes huge and dark with the shock of truth. “I didn't want to. It was supposed to be a game.”

Cold to his bones, Rome sank down on the edge of a chair. “Tell me what happened.”

“I didn't expect it. I thought it was a game.”

“Peter!”

The young man flinched. “Sorry. Sorry. What was the question?”

Rome jerked to his feet and went to his brandy decanter. “What happened?”

“I got called.”

“Called? By the society?” Sloshing a healthy

amount into a glass, Rome turned back to Peter and pressed the drink into his lax fingers.

The boy wrapped both hands around the goblet, as if he didn't trust his own grip. "Yes. I got called." He lifted the glass to his lips, teeth chattering against the rim as he managed a swallow.

"You probably don't need any more alcohol," Rome said, folding his arms, "but it will steady you long enough to tell me the way of it."

Peter licked drops of brandy from his lips and nodded. "Yes, thank you."

"You're not the only man who's come to me after his first killing," Rome said quietly. "It's quite common on the battlefield."

"Richard told me," Peter agreed. Then his face crumpled. "I wish he were here. I wish he could tell me what to do."

"Easy, soldier." Rome squeezed his shoulder once, then guided the glass back to his lips. "I'm here in his stead. Remember, he asked me to guide you since he couldn't be here to do it himself."

The boy nodded, one tear escaping his welling eyes as he took another sniffling sip of the brandy. He lowered the glass and swiped a hand across his cheek to obliterate the telltale track of moisture. "What was I saying?"

"You got called by the society."

"Yes. My first match." He gave a hollow laugh. "I was excited. Yes, yes, I know. I was supposed to tell you when I got called. You didn't trust the society." He laughed again, higher pitched and tinged with hysteria. "You were right. Damn it, Roman, you were right."

Rome sighed. "I wish I hadn't been."

"The note with the symbol arrived in the post three days before the match."

"With directions to the duel, I assume."

"Actually, no. When you receive the note with the symbol, you are to go to the agreed-upon place and wait for further instructions."

"What place is that?"

"A posting house just outside London. They told me when I joined the society that when I received the symbol, I was to go there and wait for contact."

"And since there are no words on the note you receive, they do not betray themselves. Which posting house was it?"

"The Vernon Crossing Inn."

"Do you still have the note?"

"No." At Rome's exasperated look, the boy straightened defensively. "We have to bring it with us! It's part of the instructions."

"Convenient."

Peter let out a weary sigh. "I heard that some-one lost his letter once, and there was a big fuss about the secrecy of the society being compro-mised. So now we all have to bring them."

"Fine. So you received a letter with a symbol that meant you were to go to the Vernon Crossing Inn. I assume the duel was not at the posting house."

"No, one of the Triad picked me up in a carriage."

Rome nodded. "Clever. I take it the carriage took you to the site of the match."

Peter nodded. "He blindfolded me before we left so I wouldn't know where we were going."

"Clever again, curse it! They make it impossible to retrace your steps." Rome began to pace. "Continue your story, Peter."

"We arrived at the site—it was a clearing near some backcountry road. The other members of the Triad were there waiting for us, along with my opponent. I guess they picked him up at a different posting inn. Everyone wears masks, even the duelists."

"So there can be no accusations at Almack's or Bond Street or anywhere else outside the battleground," Rome said, shaking his head at the ingenuity of it. "The secret society remains utterly secret."

"Everything was fine at first," Peter continued, staring down into the dregs of his drink. "It was a good duel. I drew first blood. I thought I had won."

He fell silent and rotated the glass in his hand as if it were his only world. Then he threw back the last mouthful of liquor in one, desperate swallow.

Rome closed his eyes for a moment, knowing without hearing it what had happened next. But Peter needed to speak of it, needed to accept what he'd done. "And then?"

"And then I killed him." His voice broke, and he sagged forward as if unable to cope with the weight of his monstrous deed. He cradled the goblet to his chest like an infant. "God save me, but I killed him."

"Just like that?" Rome kept his voice steady, his tone practical. "You drew first blood, then you decided to kill him?"

"No!" the boy gasped. He sat up, indignant. "I wouldn't do that!"

"So what happened then?"

"The Triad. They said it wasn't over, that we would fight to the death."

"Ah." Rome nodded, unsurprised.

"I refused! Roman, I swear by all that's holy, I refused!"

"And your opponent?"

"He didn't want to do it either, at first." He slumped against the chair back, the empty glass nearly tipping from his fingers. "But then they said they would kill both of us if we didn't do what they said."

"And they were three to your two."

"Plus the two carriage drivers. They had pistols."

"Five to two, then."

"Five to two," Peter agreed. "The other fellow, he started at me like a madman. Guess he was afraid." He frowned, as if working the situation out in his mind. "Nothing I said would stop him. I had to defend myself."

"Of course you did. You were outnumbered, and you were being attacked."

"We fought, but in the end I killed him." He shook his head and placed his empty glass on the table. "I keep saying it, but it seems too fantastic to be true. I killed a man, Roman."

"I know."

"I stood there staring at him, bleeding on the ground. Even when they handed me the purse, I could barely believe—"

"Wait." Rome raised a hand, narrowing his eyes in suspicion. "What purse?"

"My winnings. Even with the society's cut, I won quite a bit. But it wasn't worth it. I took that purse to the nearest tavern and got stone drunk."

"You mentioned a membership fee. You never said that you were dueling for money." Though his tone remained calm, anger clenched his gut and burned its way through his veins, boiling hotter than a blacksmith's fire.

Someone was getting rich off the lives of unsuspecting innocents.

He longed to vent his rage, punch something, fight someone, but the lad needed comfort and direction, not a demonstration of temper. He forced his wrath beneath iron control, knowing he would pay the price later for suppressing such consuming emotion.

"It's true that when you join the society, you have to pay a membership fee," Peter was explaining. "But then you have to provide a stake. Every time you fight a match, you win half your opponent's stake. The other half goes to the society."

"How much is this stake?"

"Mine was three hundred pounds."

"Three hundred pounds! Good God, Peter, that's nearly a month's allowance!"

"Allowance," Peter sneered. "I'm two-and-twenty—a grown man! And yet I cannot control my own fortunes until I reach the age of twenty-five. Why Richard set such a ridiculous condition, I shall never understand."

"How can you not understand?" Rome cast him a look of disdain, fury pressing to escape the boundary of his will. "Look at the mess in which you have landed yourself. Richard was wise to set such a condition, else you would certainly have found yourself in Fleet prison by now!"

"It's *because* of the restriction that I joined the society!" Peter jumped to his feet. "I want to control my own money, not have it doled out to me as if I were still in short pants. The society promised me a sound return on my initial investment."

"Yes," Rome snapped back. "And all you had to do was kill for it."

"I didn't know that at the time!" Peter spun away, rubbing his head. "Damn, but I'm starting to feel that brandy."

Rome grabbed his arm and yanked him back around. "Be glad you won this time, boy," he said, leaning in until their noses practically touched. "Or else I'd be planning your funeral right now."

Peter jerked away from Rome's hold. "I know. I'm sorry. I didn't mean any of that."

"Yes, you did." He waved an impatient hand to dismiss any further apologies. "Right now we need to decide what to do with you."

"What do you mean?" Panic sharpened his words. "You don't expect me to go to the magistrate?"

"And swing for a death you were forced to cause? Hardly. That would serve no purpose, especially since you have no way to prove your tale."

"Thank God." Peter let out a long breath.

"You'll have to leave the country."

"What!" he squeaked.

"There's no other way." Rome planted his feet and folded his arms. "You were foolish to become involved in this thing, Peter, but you must accept the facts. You killed a man. That's a crime punishable by death."

"Perhaps the magistrate will listen to reason."

"I doubt it. Imagine the look on the judge's face as you try to explain about a secret society of duelists. If they don't hang you, they'll cast you in Bedlam."

"Oh, my God." Peter sank weakly into his chair. "You're right, I must leave. If I stay, the society will expect me to do this again."

"True. Could you do it, Peter? Could you kill for money again?"

Revulsion flickered across his face. "No. Never."

"Which means if you stay, you will die, for they will surely kill you if you refuse to fight to the death."

"I have to leave England."

"You have to leave England," Rome agreed. "Under normal circumstances, I would insist you board the first ship out of the country, but these are not normal circumstances."

"I don't understand."

"Usually duels take place in front of witnesses, forcing the victor to flee immediately if a death occurs. But this time the secret society works in our favor."

Understanding dawned on Peter's face. "Oh, I see. No one knows about the match except the Triad."

"And they would hardly run to the magistrate," Rome said with a curt nod. "Why don't you go home and pack some belongings? Have a bag ready to go, then just go about your normal business until I contact you."

"What are you going to do?"

"Arrange passage for you so we can slip you out of England safely and secretly."

Peter's whole body sagged with relief. He grabbed Rome's hand and shook it. "Thank you, Roman. You've arrived at the perfect answer."

"Just be careful, Peter. The society may have spies, and if they think you are getting ready to flee, they may try and stop you. Do nothing differently, and be ready to go at my word."

"I will." Peter took a deep breath and let it out again. "Thank you again, Roman. Richard could not have come up with a better arrangement.

Rome gave a tight-lipped smile. "I'm flattered. Now off with you."

"I'll be waiting for your signal."

Rome rolled his eyes. "This isn't espionage, just an escape plan."

Peter grinned, for an instant looking like the carefree young man he used to be, then headed for the door. "I'll still wait to hear from you."

"Oh, Peter."

The boy paused with his hand on the door latch. "Yes?"

"Take a bath, will you?"

Peter chuckled, then ducked out the door, shutting it behind him.

Left alone, Rome let the smile fade from his face.

The Black Rose Society had changed in his estimation from merely a dangerous group of hotheaded young bloods to a most despicable sort of organization. Clearly this was no game of strategy created by students, but a manipulative deception controlled by adults whose greed fed off the lives and fortunes of gullible young men longing for adventure.

The mere notion of it sickened him.

How many times had he witnessed this sort of

exploitation during the war? People stealing from the bodies of the dead, women abused by soldiers fevered by battle, brother betraying brother for the price of a few pounds. To find something so contemptible here, in England . . .

The bastards. How dared they force a green youth like Peter to murder?

Taking a life sank into a man's heart and soul, marred it like a rotted spot on an apple. Some people were made of stern stuff, able to handle the bone-deep changes that came about after such an experience. Others could never honestly cope with such an invasion of self, and they lived day after day with misery and guilt as their constant companions.

Peter would never be the same.

That knowledge, certain and irreversible, burned like hot coals in his gut. He couldn't turn back time for Peter and undo his heinous act. He couldn't fight the villain who had lured the unsuspecting lad into the trap. He couldn't change the law so that Peter could stay in England.

But he could track down the leaders of the Black Rose Society and ensure that they paid for their crimes.

And he would start with his only living lead—Edgar Vaughn.

Anna would want to know about this. She would want to be with him every step of the way to watch the society crumble.

He couldn't allow that. Peter's tale had convinced him that these were ruthless men who killed without mercy, and he would do everything in his power to protect her from that.

No matter what it cost him.

Chapter 13

❦

Days later, Anna stood with her mother at
the Severley ball, searching the crowd for a
familiar tall figure. She had expected to hear from
Rome before now. Surely he had been able to uncover some sort of clue about the Robert Chambers murder. Rome's conduct confirmed her fear
that his promise to include her was merely a way
to keep her from exposing his involvement

"Anna," her mother murmured, "I know you
are excited to see the earl, but do not make a cake
of yourself by appearing too eager."

Anna flushed and came down from her tiptoes.
"I'm sorry, Mama."

"I appreciate your enthusiasm, dear, but we
must not give the impression you are fast."

"Of course not." She fluttered her fan near her heated cheeks. If her mother only knew!

Henrietta took her by the arm and guided her behind a potted palm for a moment of privacy. "Listen to me," she whispered. "You must charm an offer from his lordship very soon. The Season is nearly finished, and we cannot afford another. This is your only chance, Anna."

"Yes, Mama."

Henrietta smiled and adjusted the lace on Anna's sleeve. "You are a good daughter, Anna. You do the family proud."

Anna's stomach clenched with a healthy dose of guilt. What would her mother's reaction be if she knew about Rome?

Henrietta stepped out from behind the palm tree. Anna followed, then halted as she caught sight of Rome entering the ballroom with his sister and her husband. His tall, lean figure looked absolutely dashing in black evening clothes, and his dangerous attractiveness drew the gaze of every female in the room. The air of scandal about him only added to his appeal.

He glanced her way. Her breath caught in her lungs; her heart skipped wildly, then steadied into a strong, rapid beat. She held his gaze, heat curling low in her belly as they communicated in hot, hungry silence.

Then he broke contact and walked in the opposite direction, as if he hadn't seen her at all.

What in the world . . . ? For a long moment, she stared at his back, willing him to turn back to her. They were supposed to be partners, weren't they? Why hadn't he so much as said hello?

"Anna," her mother whispered. "Lord Haverford has just emerged from the card room."

Haverford. Yes. Anna forced her gaze away from Rome's retreating back and focused on Haverford wending his way through the crowd. This was the man who should have her attention. This was the man who held her future in his hands.

But Rome held the key to the truth.

"Good evening, my lord," Henrietta said.

"Good evening, Mrs. Rosewood. Miss Rosewood." Haverford bowed, then turned a polite smile on Anna. "Miss Rosewood, I would be honored if you would save me the waltz."

Anna colored. "I cannot, my lord."

"Anna has not yet been given license to dance the waltz by the patronesses of Almack's," her mother hurried to say. "Perhaps the minuet?"

"Of course." Haverford took Anna's dance card and scribbled his name for the first minuet. "Until then, Miss Rosewood."

"Until then, my lord."

As Haverford took his leave, Henrietta snapped open her fan. "We must obtain permission for you to waltz," she hissed. "I do not understand why you have not been granted it. Many other ladies are allowed to waltz."

"Calm yourself, Mama. Lord Haverford has secured a minuet. It would have been much worse if he had not asked at all."

"Bite your tongue, daughter!" Henrietta fanned even faster. "Of course he asked. You have an understanding."

"Then we must be content."

"Do not be content, Anna, until the Devereaux sapphire is on your finger." She snapped the fan closed and pointed it at her daughter. "You must charm the earl into declaring himself. We are running out of time."

With this pronouncement, she turned away to engage a crony in conversation.

Anna let out a deep sigh. She was indeed running out of time. Haverford aside, it seemed nearly impossible that she could discover the secret behind her brother's murder in the few weeks she had left. Her only chance lay with the man who moments ago had acted as if she were invisible.

It looked as if she would be tasked with charming *two* Devereaux men tonight.

"Rome, do try to enjoy yourself," Lavinia pleaded.

Rome continued to scowl at the crowd. "I am enjoying myself," he lied.

"Yes, I have always been partial to the way your eyebrows come together when you smile," Vin said, with sweet sarcasm. "I understand you are upset that your second appointment with Mr. Vaughn was rescheduled, but I am certain it is not personal."

"I'm not so certain."

"Rome, really." Vin rolled her eyes. "If Mr. Vaughn held the scandal against you, he would not have been willing to consider you for the position to begin with. He is a busy man. I'm certain this is all a matter of bad timing."

"Perhaps." Rome tried to smile for his sister, but inside he had his doubts. Had Vaughn noticed his interest in the ring? Rome had tried to hide it, but Edgar Vaughn had not ascended to his current status by accident. The diplomat had always been known for canny intellect and keen observation.

"Would you like me to have Henry make inquiries?" Vin glanced around for her errant husband. "He can be very discreet."

"Absolutely not." He caught his sister's stubborn gaze. "Let it go, Vin."

"I worry about you," she said. "I'm certain Henry wouldn't mind."

"*I* would mind. I'm a grown man, Vin. Save your mothering for your babe."

Hurt flickered across her face, and her lower lip slowly protruded in a familiar pout. "I was just trying to help."

"I know." He ignored the twinge of guilt and turned gratefully as Dennis Fellhopper called his name.

"Devereaux," Fellhopper greeted him. "Good to see you again."

"Fellhopper." Rome nodded to Charlotte. "Miss Fellhopper, charming to see you again. I believe you both know my sister, Mrs. Henry Emberly."

"Mrs. Emberly," Fellhopper said with a nod. "A pleasure."

"Goodness, Lavinia!" Charlotte exclaimed. "It's been an age!" Then she flushed. "I'm sorry, it's Mrs. Emberly now, isn't it?"

"Vin is fine," Lavinia said with a smile. "I understand my cousin recently visited your country home."

"Yes, Lord Haverford traveled to Leicestershire to assist my brother with a business matter."

"No doubt sheep were involved," Rome said with a chuckle. "Marc does love the wool market."

"Exactly so," Fellhopper confirmed, with a grin.

"Oh, yes," Charlotte chimed in with a little giggle. "Everything revolves around sheep in Leicestershire!"

They were still laughing when Marc joined them.

"Good evening," He said, sending a smile around to all of them. "Miss Fellhopper, Lavinia, you are both visions this evening."

"Thank you," Lavinia said with a pleased smile.

"Thank you, my lord," Charlotte murmured, glancing away in maidenly modesty.

"We were just discussing your recent visit to my estate," Fellhopper said.

"Ah yes, I do hope all is well," Marc said.

"Quite," Fellhopper assured him, a wide grin spreading across his handsome face. "Your cousin was also commenting on the wool market."

Marc glanced at Rome. "I didn't know you followed the market."

"Actually, we were discussing sheep," Charlotte said, with another giggle. "Mr. Devereaux is quite a wit."

"Yes, Rome is quite entertaining," Marc said, his expression utterly polite. "Miss Fellhopper, would you do me the honor of saving me a dance?"

She beamed. "Why certainly, Lord Haverford." She extended her dance card.

"I would request one as well, Miss Fellhopper," Rome said.

Marc flicked a glance at Rome, then smiled at Charlotte. "Do you waltz?"

"Why yes, I have been granted permission to do so."

"Then the waltz it must be." He scribbled his name on her card, then handed the small pencil to Rome.

Vin raised her eyebrows but said nothing. Rome stepped forward and scrawled his name beside the minuet.

"Until the waltz," Marc said, bowing to Charlotte. He nodded at the rest of the group. "Fellhopper, Rome, Lavinia."

"And we must greet some acquaintances who

have just arrived," Dennis said, as the earl strode away. "Good evening to you both."

"Fellhopper," Rome said with a nod. He bowed over Charlotte's hand. "Miss Fellhopper, I look forward to our dance."

She gave him a sweet smile, her blue eyes shining with pleasure. "I will see you then, Mr. Devereaux."

The Fellhoppers moved away, and Rome turned back to see Lavinia staring after them with a contemplative expression on her face.

"I know that look," Rome said. "What is it?"

"Nothing." She smiled at him, but he wasn't fooled.

"Lavinia." He drew out her name and fixed her with his most intimidating stare.

She rolled her eyes. "Do not attempt to freeze me with your impressive glare, Roman Devereaux. As your sister, I am immune."

"You are up to something. I want to know what it is."

She gave an impatient huff. "Fine. I was just thinking that Marc was acting odd around the Fellhoppers. Did you notice anything?"

"Not at all. He seems quite friendly with them, actually."

"Exactly. If he weren't courting Miss Rosewood, I would think he had an interest in Miss Fellhopper."

"But he *is* courting Miss Rosewood." The words

felt like sawdust in his mouth. "They are practically engaged."

"I know," Vin said with a dismissive wave. "I just thought he acted odd just now."

"You are imagining things."

"Perhaps." Vin stared after the earl, her lips pursed in thought. "We will see."

"I see Mrs. Emberly," Anna said to her mother. "I am going to go speak to her."

Deep in conversation with an acquaintance, Henrietta nodded and waved a dismissive hand.

Anna made her way across the room, her gaze fixed on Rome's broad shoulders as he stood talking to his sister. With every step closer, her heart beat faster.

Business, she reminded herself. She was approaching him for business reasons, not personal ones.

He looked up as she reached them, and his animated expression faded to a practiced air of polite inquiry.

"Good evening, Lavinia, Ro—ah, Mr. Devereaux."

"Anna!" Lavinia exclaimed, her face lighting with pleasure. "We were just speaking of you."

"Were you?" She darted a glance at Rome. His impassive expression did not reassure.

"We were speaking of Haverford," he said, "and therefore your name was mentioned."

Vin sent her brother a look of annoyance. "Pay

no attention to him, Anna. His appointment with Mr. Vaughn has been rescheduled, and he is out of sorts about it."

"Vin," Rome warned with a glower.

"Don't bother fixing your famous glare on me, Roman. I already told you it doesn't work."

He stiffened. "I dislike you advertising my personal business to all and sundry."

"Anna is practically family," Vin protested, clearly becoming irritated with her brother.

"She's not family yet."

Anna jerked as if from a physical blow.

"Rome!" Lavinia gasped, clearly appalled at her brother's conduct.

Anna lifted her gaze to his. The indifference in his eyes transformed him from the ardent lover she had met at Vauxhall to a man she did not know.

She sucked in a much-needed breath, fighting for composure. Perhaps it was best to be rid of him. Their history together had proven that they were a dangerous combination.

But how could she accomplish her goal without him?

Lavinia's husband joined them at that moment. "Good evening, all," he said, his joviality breaking the chilly silence.

"Henry, there you are." Lavinia's relief came through in her voice. "Have you met Miss Rosewood?"

"Not formally." Emberly smiled at her, his dark

brown eyes full of warmth and good nature. "How do you do, Miss Rosewood?"

"Very well, thank you, Mr. Emberly," Anna lied.

"If you will all excuse me," Rome said suddenly. He gave them a bow and stalked away.

Emberly cast his departing brother-in-law a puzzled look. "Gad, Lavinia, what's the matter with your brother?"

"I have no idea," she replied. "He was unconscionably rude to Miss Rosewood."

"How odd." Emberly smiled at Anna. "I hope you will forgive Roman, Miss Rosewood. He does have something of a temper, I'm afraid."

"And I would like to apologize for him as well," Lavinia said. "Pray do not hold his bad manners against the rest of us!"

"Of course not," Anna said.

"Roman spent quite a bit of time in the battlefield," Emberly said. "That sort of thing tends to change a man. I am certain the next time you see him, he will apologize for his behavior."

Anna forced a smile. "I'm sure you are right."

Lavinia reached out and touched her hand. "Do call on me tomorrow, Anna. Even though my brother is clearly a clodpole, I quite enjoy your company."

"Thank you, Lavinia. I will do just that."

"In the meantime," Emberly said, "I have come to claim my wife for the next dance."

"How lovely!" Lavinia squealed.

"I know how you love to dance, my dear," Emberly said, gently touching his wife's cheek.

"Yes, and I intend to take full advantage before my confinement. Anna, will you excuse us?"

"Of course." Anna watched the couple head for the dance floor and wondered if she would ever find such happiness.

One thing was certain; she would never find contentment until she discovered the truth behind Anthony's death. If Rome had decided not to help her, then she would take matters into her own hands.

Mama might have confined her to the house, but there were other ways she could help. The ring, perhaps. She would bring Anthony's note with her and make discreet inquiries of all the jewelers to see if someone knew where the rings came from. Even Mama could not object to a shopping trip!

Once the Black Rose Society was exposed for what it truly was, only then would her brother's soul find peace.

Only then would the nightmares stop.

Rome watched Anna from the other side of the room. The hurt expression on her face had squeezed his heart like a wine grape, but he knew he was doing the right thing by pushing her away. The Black Rose Society was more than a club of duelists that had gotten out of hand; the organization condoned murder for money, which meant that the men behind it would kill to protect their secret.

He couldn't allow Anna to put her life in danger.

As Emberly claimed Vin for a dance, Anna slowly made her way back to her mother. Rome ached to wipe the sorrowful look from her face, to take her in his arms and make everything right. But he couldn't do that.

She wasn't his woman, and the farther away he stayed, the better it was for both of them.

"Miss Rosewood, I believe I have this dance," Haverford said.

Anna looked up from her conversation with one of her father's cronies and smiled at the earl. "I believe you are correct, my lord." She excused herself from Captain Raymond and took the earl's proffered arm.

"I trust you are enjoying yourself this evening," Haverford said, as they took their places for the set.

"It has been most entertaining," Anna assured him. "I especially like the Grecian theme."

"Indeed," the earl replied.

"Hello again!" Charlotte Fellhopper said, taking a place next to them for the minuet. Rome accompanied her, moving to the spot across from Charlotte. His green eyes glittered like cold gemstones, and Anna nearly shivered.

"Miss Fellhopper," Haverford said with a nod. He slanted a sharp look at Rome. "Cousin."

"Marc," Rome acknowledged. His tone utterly bland, he glanced at Anna. "Miss Rosewood."

The orchestra launched into the minuet before Anna could respond. She stepped into the dance by rote, exquisitely conscious of Rome so close by. He smiled at Charlotte and made her laugh with murmured witticisms while he treated her, Anna, with a disdain she did not understand. What had she done to earn his enmity?

Caught up in her furtive glances at the other couple, she moved into the next pattern of the dance, only to crash into Lord Haverford. "Oh! My apologies, my lord!"

"Nonsense. Entirely my doing." Haverford recovered himself and fell back into step. He sent a dark look at Charlotte and Rome, then mustered a smile for Anna. "All is well."

Anna turned in time with the music, passing near enough to Rome to almost touch him. She gritted her teeth and determined not to look at him. Lord Haverford was her concern, and the displeasure she spied on her mother's face from across the room only drove home that point.

Lord Haverford stepped on her toe. She winced and looked at him, only to see him jerk his gaze away from Rome and Charlotte. "Apologies, Miss Rosewood! I fear I am not a very good dancer."

Despite her throbbing toe, Anna managed to form her lips into a smile. "No one is good at everything, my lord."

"Except my cousin." Haverford sent another look Rome's way. Rome was moving with Charlotte in perfect time, clearly a superior dancer. "I have been . . . er . . . watching him to try and match his steps."

"I see." Puzzled, for she had never before observed any problem with the earl's dancing ability, Anna lapsed into silence. Haverford made no attempt at further conversation and focused on his movements with a single-mindedness that should have flattered her.

How was she supposed to attract a man intent on silence?

By the time the orchestra played the last note, she felt as if she had run for miles. Her heart pounded, and moisture misted her forehead.

Haverford escorted her back to her mother's side and made a very correct bow, then walked off. Anna watched as Rome did the same with Charlotte, returning her to the company of her brother with a flourish. His duty dispatched, he then headed for the French doors, disappearing through them to the moonlit gardens.

Haverford appeared almost immediately before Charlotte, offering his arm to lead her back to the dance floor as the first strains of the waltz filled the room. The couple took the traditional position, then swept across the floor in a graceful whirl.

"It's just not fair," her mother grumbled. "You

should be dancing the waltz with Lord Haverford instead of Miss Fellhopper!"

"We danced the minuet." She watched the French doors, but Rome did not reappear.

Henrietta sighed. "And his lordship is such an accomplished dancer. I do wish it were you out there, Anna."

Anna turned her attention to Haverford and Charlotte. Indeed, they moved together as if reading each other's minds. Never once did the earl stumble or tread on Charlotte's toes. He swept her around the floor with the grace of a dance master, his face animated as he conversed. Charlotte smiled and listened, her expression rapt.

"Perhaps he only knows the waltz," Anna mused. "He certainly seems more confident now."

"I shall see about obtaining permission for you to waltz." Henrietta snapped open her fan. "By tomorrow, I daresay. If it is the waltz that Lord Haverford wants, then it is the waltz he shall have. With *you*, my girl."

"Yes, Mama." Anna caught sight of Lavinia across the room. "Would it be all right if I went to speak with Mrs. Emberly?"

"You should probably remain close by in case his lordship wishes to dance with you again."

"That is a sensible idea." She paused, pursing her lips. "Or I could engage his cousin, Mrs. Emberly, in conversation. He is bound to pay his respects to her."

A crafty smile curved her mother's lips. "An excellent notion, daughter. Yes, do go speak to our dear friend, Mrs. Emberly. I'm glad to see you are finally taking an interest in your future."

"I am very interested in the future," Anna said, then began to make her way to the other side of the room where Lavinia stood. Just as she got there, Mr. Emberly appeared and coaxed his wife to the floor a second time.

Just as well, Anna thought, and slipped through the French doors in pursuit of her real prey.

Chapter 14

A lone with the night, Rome puffed on a slender cheroot he had taken from a hidden pocket. The flavor of the pungent tobacco lingered on his tongue as he blew out the smoke in a slow, steady stream.

He shouldn't be out here, smoking in the garden. The intimate grottoes were designed for lovers, not for solitary fools like him. Smoking was normally limited to exclusive male venues such as gentlemen's clubs or a man's study. It was particularly bad form to be seen smoking in public.

But he didn't care. He needed to do something to maintain control, and the cheroot had seemed a damned good idea at the time.

He heard the scrape of a shoe behind him. With a

muttered curse, he tossed the cigar into the bushes and turned around, a polite smile on his lips.

The smile vanished when he saw who was there.

"Were you smoking?" Anna asked.

He narrowed his eyes. "What are you doing out here alone?"

"I'm not alone. You're here. Were you just smoking?" She sniffed the air. "I thought I smelled cigar smoke."

"Go back inside," he said, turning away again.

"No." Her shoes made a soft shuffle as she crossed the stone terrace. "I want to talk to you."

"I have nothing to say to you." He went down the stairs and began to follow a flower-lined pathway.

She scurried after him. "You will not escape me so easily, Roman Devereaux."

"Go back to your mama," he said over his shoulder.

"I will not."

He stopped and faced her. She skidded to a halt just in time to avoid crashing into him. "Go. Back. Inside."

Her lips tightened in mutiny. "No."

She stood so close, he could smell her scent, even above the fragrance of the flowers surrounding them. He squeezed his eyes shut for an instant as he fought for control. Then he opened them again and looked at her, so soft and beautiful in the moonlight. The shimmering peach silk dress clung to her every curve, and her skin glowed like rich cream. Her locket glimmered in the moonlight.

"I will speak with you, Rome," she said, with a stubborn lift of her chin.

The challenge in her stance roused the sleeping beast he kept so tightly leashed. He reached for her, his hands closing on her supple, silk-clad shoulders. A gasp escaped her lips as he dragged her to him, pressing those sweet curves against his greedy body.

He lowered his mouth to her ear. "Don't you know bad things happen to innocent girls in the dark?"

"You don't frighten me." Her voice trembled, as did her body. But when she turned her gaze to his, it was not fear he saw, but passion.

"Damn it, Anna." He rubbed his cheek against her elegantly arranged curls, the scent of roses making him drunk with wanting her. "Why couldn't you leave it be?"

"What have I done," she whispered, "that you would treat me so hatefully?"

"You know what you've done." He straightened, breathing hard. "You made me want you. And I shouldn't."

"It was an accident." She leaned away, resisting his possessive hold. "We agreed to forget that night at Vauxhall, to work together as partners to solve the murders."

"I cannot be your partner, Anna." He forced his

fingers to release her. "Not in the way you mean."

"But why?" She took a step back, putting space between them. "I can't do this without you."

"Because it's dangerous."

"I don't care."

"I do." He traced her cheek with his thumb. "I don't want you hurt."

Her breath caught at his touch. "I won't get hurt."

"You might." He made himself drop his hand and back away. "These are dangerous men. Killers. They must not discover you know of their existence."

"I'm not a fool."

He gave a short, harsh laugh. "I am."

"My brother deserves the truth."

"You already know what happened."

"No, I don't." She looked like an Amazon queen in the moonlight, her body delicate and her will indomitable. "I have suspicions, but no facts. Anthony was not just my brother but my twin, Rome. A part of him lives in me and cries out for justice."

"I can't let anything happen to you. I won't."

"For pity's sake!"

"No, for *your* sake."

"You said you would help me." She jutted out her chin, eyes gleaming with ire. "You are breaking your word."

He shrugged. "Your life is worth that."

"My life is *nothing* unless I discover the truth."

"No." He shook his head. "You don't know what you're asking."

"I'm asking to be treated like a grown woman. Like a business partner."

He laughed again, the edge of desperation clear even to him. "No man would ever call you a business partner, Anna." He slanted her a hungry look. "And don't tempt me to treat you like a grown woman. My control is thin."

"There is more to this than your passions, Rome. Lives are at stake."

"My point exactly. Your life is at stake if you remain involved, so I am not giving you the option. Stay away from the Black Rose Society, Anna."

"I can't." Her doelike eyes begged him to understand. "I'm sorry, Rome."

He saw the determination in her stance, the stubbornness of her mouth. "Damn you."

She flinched. "This is the way it has to be."

"This is not the way it has to be! I doubt your brother would want you to endanger your life to help him."

She paled. "That may be so, but he was a part of me, and I can't give up on him." She clicked open the locket with trembling fingers. "Can you see him? The man he was? The adventurous young man who was kind to children? The born seaman who longed to captain his own ship? The loyal brother, the tenderhearted son?" Her voice grew hoarse as her eyes glistened with tears. "The world will never know Anthony now, and I *will* find out who took him from this life, even if I die trying."

He studied the image of the young man, barely visible in the moonlight, then lifted his gaze to her tearful one. His heart rolled over in his chest.

When this woman loved, she loved completely.

"You're an amazing woman," he murmured, then placed his hand over hers to close the locket. He allowed his fingers to linger against her scented skin, the thud of her heart steady against his flesh.

"I can't give up on him, Rome." The tears trickled like liquid diamonds down her cheeks. "No one else will listen to me. I'm all he has."

"Shhh. It's all right." He finally released her locket to pull out his handkerchief. Gently, he dabbed at her face, the crisp linen soaking up the teardrops.

"You're the only one who knows. The only one who understands. Those men killed my brother. He was stolen from me forever by the Black Rose Society." She nearly spat the name. "He was going to buy a ship and name it after me, then sail the world and begin his own shipping company. He was a good man, a trustworthy brother. I loved him."

She choked on the last words, nearly undone, and her eyes filled again. Big fat droplets streamed down her cheeks, and she stared at him, so alone, so much in pain, grieving for the twin who had been ripped from her life.

In the face of such raw heartache, he could only do what any other man would do in his place. He gathered her into his arms and held her.

She sank into his embrace, her fingers curling into the lapels of his coat as huge sobs wracked her small frame. Murmuring soothing words, he urged her into one of the intimate grottoes so no one wandering down the path would see them. Then he held her, while she wept out her anguish into his shoulder.

He smoothed his hands over her back, crooning words of comfort in her ear. She seemed too petite to carry such a huge burden on her shoulders, but her spirit would not be conquered. She would do right by her brother or die trying. If she had been a man, he would have respected her tremendously.

But she wasn't a man. The sweet curves pressed against him reminded him firmly of that. And because she was a female, he held her in even higher esteem for her sense of honor and duty to her slain brother.

Beautiful, intelligent, loyal. Anna Rosewood was a hell of a woman.

Her sobs quieted, and she remained within his embrace, her breathing a series of long, deep shudders. He rested his cheek against her hair, closing his eyes and inhaling the sweet scent of roses that clung to her. He was content to hold her, the hush of the night surrounding them, the moon bathing them in cool, silvery light.

He could stay that way forever and die a happy man.

She lifted her head. Moisture clung to her lashes, and a hollow pain still lingered in her eyes. She sniffled. He raised a hand to her cheek and smoothed his fingers across the damp planes of her face, his tender smile reassuring.

She just looked at him, studied his face inch by inch with the fascination of someone examining the Elgin marbles. She paused at his mouth, eyes narrowing in feminine interest. His body tightened with a hot surge of need.

Then she pressed her lips to his, and he fell headfirst into the maelstrom.

He couldn't have her, but he couldn't resist her. He didn't want to want her, but he hungered for her with his very blood. Her willing kiss ensnared him, cast him into a whirlpool of desire that spun his thoughts and tangled his will in knots.

He fisted his hands behind her back even as he pulled her closer. She clung to him and tormented him with her lips and teeth and tongue, wearing down his willpower like rushing water over sand. He joined in the kiss, helpless to resist a moment longer. She gave a soft groan of triumph that shot straight to his loins and fed the fire.

He tugged her deeper into the shadows, and she clung to him like ivy to mortar, pliant in his hands.

Helpless against the need that worked its will on her, she yielded to his guiding hands and desperate caresses. Everything inside her glowed hot, and for the first time since last he held her, she burned with life.

Anthony was gone; but she was here, and she was on fire.

Rome's touch burned away the cold ache of grief and filled her with the delicious heat of desire. She wanted to bask in this wonderful feeling forever, to forget the darkness that had haunted her in the many months since her twin's death.

And the nightmares.

Rome gathered her to him as if insatiable for her, his hands greedy with need. She lost herself in his embrace, gloried in this dance of life as he swept his mouth down her neck. A sharp keening surprised her as it burst from her throat.

Had such joy ever existed before?

His hand cupped her breast, and her thoughts whirled away like autumn leaves. Pleasure spiked through her as he brushed a thumb over her nipple. Scandalous! Dear God, such sensations could not be borne . . .

"I need you." His rough mutter jolted through her like lightning. "God save me, but I need you, Anna."

"How do you do this to me?" She laid a hand along his cheek, drawing his gaze to hers. "How can you lay your hands on me and shatter every truth I thought I knew?"

"You do the same to me. You make me forget." He cupped her bottom and pulled her into the rigid length straining against his trousers. "I can think of nothing but having you."

"I need to forget." She kissed his lips, then held his face between her two palms. "Make me forget, Rome."

He gave a low growl that thrilled her, then tugged her over to the stone bench hidden from the path by hedges and flowering trees. She went willingly, desperate to push away the pain, starving to feel the pleasure once more. A tiny voice in the back of her mind begged her to beware the consequences, but she stilled it.

Fifteen months of mourning. The agony of it left her breathless and bruised inside. But Rome's touch washed away the pain, made her glory in her heart beating and her blood pumping. Before Rome, she had felt as dead and cold as the marble statues in the garden. But now—Dear Lord, *now* she lived.

She sat on the bench, and the cool stone momentarily jerked her from her passionate haze. The voice of caution whispered again, and she strained to hear it. Then Rome sat beside her and pulled her into his lap, and the glimmer of uncertainty winked out.

His hardness nestled against her bottom through thin layers of clothing, demonstrating his need for her. Right or wrong, she wanted this man with a hunger that shocked her.

He kissed her again as he slid his hand beneath her skirt. His fingers brushed her ankle, calf, knee. Her skin tingled in the wake of his caress, arousing her own demanding passion.

She wrapped her arms around his neck and kissed him back, lost in sensation, trembling with the force of her own ardor.

"I remember how you felt." He traced her ear with the tip of his tongue. "How you looked. How you sounded. I want that again."

Her heart skipped. "Oh, God."

"You're beautiful." He dipped his head and laved the curve of a breast plumped above the top of her bodice. "I want to touch all of you." His fingers edged along her thighs, light as fairy wings. "I want to watch you when the pleasure takes you."

His words wooed her with as much power as his caresses. Would he take her right here in the garden? Did he want her that much? Excitement rippled down her spine.

He nudged her thighs apart and slipped his hand between them as he nipped at her neck. He came to where the locket rested over her beating heart and flicked the ornament away, leaving it to dangle over her shoulder, as he dropped a string of sweet, succulent kisses down her breastbone, as his fingers reached the moist, hot folds between her legs.

Her head fell back as he touched her core, and the locket swung in time to his strokes, bumping her in gentle rhythm. It almost felt like someone was tapping her on the shoulder, trying to tell her something.

Then Rome slid a finger inside her, and her senses spun like a wild carousel.

"God, I want you," he rasped. "You're so wet and hot. I could slide right in, feel you squeeze me."

He curled his arm around her to fondle her breast, rubbing her nipple to an aching, rigid nub as his fingers glided over the slickness of her sensitive folds. She rocked in his arms, moving with an instinct that sang to her.

The locket kept tapping against her shoulder.

He leaned forward and rested his mouth over the turgid nipple, then breathed hot air through the silk of her dress. She arched her back as her senses jangled and her flesh throbbed.

"I want to see you." He tugged her bodice down, freeing her breasts, then stroking the bare, straining bud.

He cupped her plump flesh in his hand and took her aching nipple into his mouth.

A whimper burst through her lips as her head fell back, and she clung to him with fingers like claws. Tension built, piling up like logs in the river. If he kept touching her breast and stroking her down *there*, she knew she would shatter into a thousand pieces.

She squirmed against him, restless with the passion surging through her veins. She felt as if she had to do something. Get something. Take something. Her hand slid down his chest in a silky caress, hesitated at his waist. She didn't know what to do, how to get what she craved. Frustrated, she wiggled her bottom against his hardness.

He gave a wicked laugh. "I know what you want," he murmured in her ear.

"I just want you," she whispered back.

"And I want you so badly I ache from it." Holding her gaze with his, he shifted her to the bench, though her legs still draped across his thighs. Then he took her hand and pressed it to the stiff ridge she had felt beneath her. "Do you see what you do to me? How desperately I want to be inside you?"

"Heavens." Fascinated, she traced her fingers over the bulge in his trousers.

"Bloody hell." He trembled and squeezed his eyes shut, then grabbed her wrist to stop her caress.

"Did I do something wrong?"

"No. Too right." He opened his eyes, not even bothering to hide the hot desire that throbbed in him.

"Rome." She pulled her hand from his grasp and wrapped an arm around his neck. "Don't leave me aching like this," she whispered.

He made a choked sound of need. When she took his hand and pressed it to her bare breast, that sound became a growl. He crushed her to him, taking her mouth in a kiss that frightened and thrilled her with its savagery. He jerked at the fastenings of his trousers with one hand, and once he'd freed himself, he took her hand and pressed it to his hard, hot flesh.

She gave a gasp that was swallowed by his kiss. Following the guidance of his fingers, she stroked the velvety length of his naked flesh, taking perverse feminine pleasure from his groans of encouragement.

"I want to slide inside you," he whispered hoarsely between kisses. "I want to feel you around me, all that sweet wetness easing my way."

"Oh, my." She clung to him, utterly scandalized by his daring and yet thrilled by it, too. Had ever a man wanted her so much?

"Oh, my God!"

The strident female voice doused their ardor like a bucket of cold water. They looked up to see Lavinia standing at the entrance to their hideaway, her face stark white with shock.

Reality returned with a crash. Anna struggled out of Rome's lap, the seriousness of her situation hitting her like a tidal wave.

"Rome," Lavinia gasped, "what have you done?"

"Wait for me on the path, Vin." With a few swift motions, Rome refastened his clothing.

Lavinia's expression grew furious. "Wait for you on the path? Do you think me a child, Roman?"

"I only ask for a moment of privacy. For Anna."

She flicked a glance at Anna, then pressed her

lips together, clearly biting back blistering words. "Very well," she snapped. "I will wait *two minutes*, Roman!" Spinning on her heel, she stalked away.

Anna struggled to set her dress to rights, unable to meet Rome's gaze. Tears stung her eyes. What had she done?

"Allow me." Deftly, Rome straightened her clothing, while she sat helpless as a doll. "Anna? Are you all right?"

She raised her eyes to his. "We are ruined."

"No, we're not. It's Vin. I'll talk to her."

"She saw—" She choked to a stop.

"I know." He stroked her cheek. "I'll fix this. I promise." He leaned forward and scooped his forgotten handkerchief from the ground, then pressed it into her hand. "Dry your tears and compose yourself. I will speak with my sister."

Compose herself?

She stared in disbelief as he rose and walked away. As if it were simple to compose herself after they had both come so close to scandal!

With trembling hands, she straightened her bodice and turned the locket around. It had opened somehow. She stared down at Anthony's dear face and winced at the guilt that pinched her.

She had done it again, blithely fallen into Rome's arms and allowed him to take liberties. Begged him to, even. Her face burned as she remembered how she'd pleaded with him to make her forget.

And he had done so. Quite skillfully.

Forget the pain of her grief, yes. But how could she have forgotten Anthony and her objective to bring his murderers to justice? How could she have forgotten her duty to her parents, to Haverford?

She buried her face in the handkerchief. Wicked, wanton girl! Rome had become a bad habit, like blackberry trifle. And she craved him as much as she had ever craved her favorite dessert.

"Are you mad?" From the other side of the hedge, Lavinia's urgent whisper made Anna flinch. "How dare you seduce that innocent girl!"

"Calm down, Vin," Rome said.

"Calm down? You lied to me, Roman."

"I didn't. This was an accident."

"An accident is when you fall off a horse. Corrupting your cousin's fiancée in the garden is not an accident, it's just *wrong*. Have you not learned anything from Father's mistakes?"

"If you give me a moment to explain—"

"I don't need an explanation, Rome. I saw what I saw. Certainly more than any sister ever should! You're just lucky it was I who found you and not some gossip."

"You're overreacting."

"Hardly! Anna is missing, and so were you. Luckily, I am the only one who has put the two incidents together and came looking out here."

"Bloody hell."

"I should say," Lavinia shot back. "Now we

must return her to her mother, who is frantic by the way, with some plausible explanation."

"I will think of something."

"*You* cannot appear anywhere in the tale we are about to tell, Roman. There are those who would point to you and say the apple doesn't fall far from the tree."

Rome made a sound between a growl and a sigh of frustration.

"And I would be one of them," Lavinia added.

"What?" Rome thundered, clearly outraged.

"You just tried to seduce Haverford's intended," Lavinia shot back. "Did you think for a moment how the consequences of that would affect you? Me? Mother? Or were you thinking at all?"

"I never intended—"

"It was stupid," Lavinia interrupted, her tone sharp and merciless. "Anna would have been ruined, and everyone would have looked at you and seen our father's son. How could you, Rome? You've worked so hard to overcome this, and you're so close to obtaining that diplomatic position. Yet you'd throw it all away by seducing an innocent girl who is promised to another."

"Damn it, Vin." Rome's voice had dropped so low, Anna could barely hear it. "I never meant for this to happen."

"Your actions affect us all, Rome. Mother would never be able to show her face in society again if this got out. It would affect *you* and *me*, *my husband* and *his* career, not to mention my unborn child! And I will protect my family, even if it means I must protect them from you."

"I'm sorry, Vin."

"I'm not ready to forgive you, Rome. Now, I will take Anna back to the ballroom and avert the scandal. Lord knows I will think of something to say!"

The scrape of determined footsteps announced Lavinia's arrival moments before she appeared in the clearing. Anna sighed and stood. Her legs shook, and her knees appeared to be made of pudding, but she remained upright. To her surprise, Lavinia did not scold her at all. "Anna, thank goodness I found you. Your mother is overset."

"I'm sorry I worried her."

"Well, it's time to fix that." Lavinia swept her with a glance that missed nothing. "You look well enough, except for your eyes. Were you crying?"

Rome appeared behind his sister and drew Anna's gaze like a starving man to . . . blackberry trifle.

"She was crying," he confirmed. "I found her here weeping and lent her my handkerchief."

Lavinia sent her brother a look of disbelief, then snatched the handkerchief from Anna's hand and pressed it into her brother's. "Go away, Roman. You've done quite enough."

Rome's jaw clenched, but he said nothing.

Lavinia turned her attention back to Anna. "Why were you crying? Was it because of Roman's unconscionable behavior earlier this evening?"

"No." Anna touched her locket and drew strength. "I was thinking of Anthony."

Lavinia's brow smoothed. "Oh, Anna, you poor dear."

Anna nodded her thanks at the sympathy. "Your brother did lend me his handkerchief. He was trying to comfort me."

"I have no doubt of that." With a fierce glare at Rome, Lavinia linked her arm through Anna's. "Allow me to take you back to the ballroom. We will tell everyone that you were undone by memories of your brother and that I was with you while you sought privacy to regain your composure."

"Thank you," Anna whispered.

"And as for you, Roman . . ." Lavinia shot him another dark look. "I would advise you to remain here until any chance of speculation has passed."

His lips thinned in response to her scolding tone, but he gave a jerky nod and stood aside as the two ladies returned to the ballroom.

Once they had disappeared from sight, his fingers crushed the handkerchief still in his hand.

He felt like a schoolboy who had just received a whipping. Lavinia's words had striped him like a lash, drawing blood in her righteous anger.

And she had been right. Damn it, she had been completely correct in everything she said.

Had he lost his mind? What had just happened? Had he indeed attempted to make love to Anna Rosewood in the middle of a garden—again? He must be daft to take such a chance.

Or in love.

The idea halted his thoughts like a hand at his throat. Good Lord, could it be true?

He let out a harsh sigh and stared up at the sky as if he might find answers there. But the stars only glittered back in mocking omniscience. *Did* he love her? He admired her, certainly. Was attracted to her—too much so. Was she the sort of woman he could spend the rest of his life with?

Bloody hell, yes.

Damn the sentimental poets, but it had to be true. He was in love with Haverford's woman. What the hell was he supposed to do now?

He shoved the handkerchief in his pocket. There was nothing he could do. Anna was not free to return his affections—though from her response to his kisses, she certainly did. But where did that leave them? Clandestine meetings and longing looks across the ballroom? Anna deserved better.

Haverford deserved it, too.

He sat down on the bench where only minutes ago she had wrapped her arms around him and begged him to stop the ache. He swept a hand along the smooth, cool stone, remembering how sweetly she had given herself into his arms. She was so responsive, so open and giving, such a passionate woman.

They could never be alone together again.

It was the only solution. Anna wasn't meant for a life of scandal. She wasn't meant to live in the shadows, subject to the callous snickers of those who thought themselves better. She didn't deserve to walk through her days as an outcast, as his mother had. But that future was all he could give her.

And he had no desire to follow in the footsteps of his sire.

Yet he knew as certainly as he knew his name that if the opportunity presented itself to hold Anna in his arms again, he would not be able to resist it. And that way lay disaster for them both.

Anna deserved the life she would lead with Haverford. She would become his countess and bear his heirs and live in comfort and luxury until the end of her days. She would never want for anything—but Rome. Haverford was a much better catch than an ex-soldier with a modest income and dreams of travel and diplomacy.

Yet with Anna's stubborn determination to pursue the Black Rose Society surrounding them, the chances of ending up alone together increased. As long as Anna believed him the only one she could talk to about her brother and about the society, she would continue to seek private moments with him. That he could not allow.

The society had proven how dangerous they could be, and he could not tolerate Anna putting her life in danger again. As much as he longed to do so, he did not have the right to protect her, and any efforts in that direction would only incite the very scandal they wished to avoid.

There was only one way to avert complete ruin for both of them. Only one way to prove his love for her. He would bring this society to its knees.

And he would begin by speaking to Haverford.

Chapter 15

The day after the Severley ball saw Anna
burning with determination to continue the
investigation into her brother's death.

She had spent the morning at Bond Street, the
ever dour Bliss trailing behind her, going from
jeweler to jeweler with the note portraying the
symbol of the black rose tucked in her reticule.
None of the shopkeepers had ever seen the figure.
She would inquire at different shops tomorrow.

Since Rome had gone back on his word, she
had taken matters into her own hands, as she had
intended from the beginning.

She could not credit that she had believed him
when he claimed they could be partners. She
should have known better. Clearly, it was just a
ploy to get her to forget about the investigation.

Had his actions last night been more of the same?

Her face burned as she remembered that he had not been the one to make the first advance. She glanced over at Bliss, who sat across from her in the carriage, but the maid stared out the window with her usual expressionless mask in place. Anna looked the opposite way to hide her blushing cheeks.

Her distress over her brother's death could not explain why she had thrown herself at a man. Her behavior at the Severley ball shamed her. She had just wanted to forget the grief that haunted her daily, draw comfort from someone who knew the truth.

But her attraction to Rome had proven too strong, and she had willingly fallen into his arms.

Had she no care for herself? Her reputation? Not only had she betrayed her understanding with Lord Haverford, but she had engaged in wanton embraces with a man who intended to break his word to her. Attractive as he was, Rome Devereaux still acted less than a gentleman at every turn.

But given her response to him, could she actually call herself a lady?

She had come very close to disgracing herself completely. If Lavinia had not been coolheaded enough to concoct a story about Anna's becoming distraught with grief upon hearing acquaintances discussing her brother, Anna's mother might very well have learned the truth and been ruined and mortified along with her daughter. Instead, her mother had been quite sympathetic and called for their coach immediately.

But how many times would there be someone to rescue her from her own folly? Sooner or later, her luck would run out.

She had crossed many boundaries since she had started her quest, and it seemed the more times she wandered into the forbidden, the more blurred the strictures binding her became. She liked the freedom she had discovered, gloried in the brief glimpses of passion that Rome had shown her.

But once she brought the Black Rose Society to justice, once she married Haverford, she would settle back into the rigid mold of a well-bred lady. Oh, she would have a bit more freedom in society as a married woman, and a countess at that. But she couldn't help but wonder if Lord Haverford could show her the delights Rome had.

If any other man could.

Dear Lord. She had to stop thinking this way! It was bad enough she had fallen into his sensual trap, but now his sister had witnessed their reprehensible conduct. While Lavinia had successfully averted a scandal, Anna knew she must have questions.

Which was why she was on her way to the Emberly residence that afternoon with the hope of begging Lavinia's forgiveness.

She had been informed by her mother only

hours ago that they were to accompany Lord Haverford on a trip to Kent for a house party. They were to leave on the morrow.

Mama was in raptures, for she felt the earl might finally offer for Anna in the comfort and privacy of his country home. Anna, however, could not leave London without visiting Lavinia and determining whether or not they were still friends.

As the butler admitted her to the Emberly home, she prayed she could make everything right.

Rome presented himself in Haverford's study at the earliest hour still considered civilized. He had tossed and turned most of the night. Between his realization of his feelings for Anna and trying to get safe passage out of the country for Peter, his emotions had worn down to the raw edges of reason.

It would be a relief to turn the care of Anna over to Haverford. And it would be a torment.

When Rome entered his cousin's study, Haverford was seated at his desk, his head bent over a missive. He glanced up as Rome entered, then hastily refolded the letter and stuffed it back in the envelope. "Good morning, cousin. Please, sit down."

"Good morning." As he settled into one of the leather-bound chairs, Rome glanced at the envelope Haverford tossed aside and noted it was from the Fellhoppers. "I do hope Fellhopper hasn't run into more problems with his sheep."

Marc threw a startled glance at the letter. "Not at all. In fact, Miss Fellhopper has penned me a letter of thanks for assisting her brother with his difficulties." He yanked open the top drawer of his desk, tossed the letter inside, then closed the drawer firmly. "Now, what can I do for you?"

Rome took in the genuine interest on Marc's face and felt like the worst sort of bastard. This man had helped him past some of the more formidable obstacles society had to offer, and in the meantime, Rome had betrayed Marc by tasting the carnal delights of his cousin's intended.

It was good that he was here now. What he was going to do was the right thing, no matter how much it tore at his heart to watch Anna wed another man.

"I need to speak to you about a delicate matter," he began.

Marc sat back in his chair, concern etched on his face. "Are you in some sort of trouble, Rome?"

"No, not really." He selected and discarded words in his mind. "It concerns Miss Rosewood and an organization called the Black Rose Society."

"What is the Black Rose Society, and what does Anna have to do with it?"

And what do you have to do with Anna? Rome heard the words as if they had been spoken, though his cousin hadn't said any such thing.

Good old Marc. Always diplomatic, always fair. Hear the facts first before judging. But Rome caught the flicker of doubt that flashed through his cousin's eyes. The damage Rome's father had left behind haunted the family still, and Rome had no desire to add to it.

Somehow he must convey the urgency of the situation without hurting his cousin.

"Allow me to begin at the beginning. Do you remember Richard Brantley?"

"Yes, your friend who died on the battlefield."

"Correct. On his deathbed, he asked me to look after his younger brother, Peter." Marc gave a nod, and Rome continued, "Recently Peter became entangled with an organization called the Black Rose Society. They are a club of hotheaded young bloods who fight duels against each other in some sort of competition."

Marc shook his head, a glimmer of amusement curving his lips for an instant. "I remember such games. We played them at university."

"This has gone beyond games, cousin. They duel with swords. For money."

The lightheartedness vanished from Marc's expression. "Good God. All those recent deaths by sword. Are they related?"

"They are." Rome didn't bother to keep the disgust from his voice. "The bastards who run the organization make the members put up funds before they compete. Whoever wins the match takes half the purse, and the organization takes the other half. Worse yet, they are death matches fought at gunpoint."

"Dear God." Marc couldn't hide his shock. "And young Peter is involved?"

"He wants to leave the organization, but I fear for his life." Rome intentionally omitted mention of Peter's recent duel. "I am assisting him in leaving the country."

"Wise, I think," Haverford agreed. He tapped his fingers on the table. "Have you gone to the authorities with this information?"

"I will as soon as Peter is safe. I've arranged passage for him on a ship to America that leaves in two days' time."

"I see your point. Peter is just a boy. Better he is gone before this gets ugly."

"Exactly."

"If you need my assistance in this matter, do not hesitate," Marc said, his eyes going hard and flat. "Villains like this cannot go unpunished."

"I will bring them to justice," Rome swore.

Silence fell for a moment. Then Marc looked straight at Rome and asked, "What does Anna have to do with all this?"

Rome heard the question behind the words, saw the flash of apprehension behind Marc's usual calm, and was glad Lavinia had stopped him in time that night in Severley's garden. "She believes her brother was a member and subsequently killed in a duel."

"Really." Clearly surprised, Marc scratched his jaw. "Has she informed her parents?"

"I believe she has, but apparently they don't

share her opinion. So she has been investigating the matter on her own."

"What!" Marc sat straight up. "Is she mad?"

"My sentiments exactly. I have been following the trail of the Black Rose Society and on more than one occasion, I observed Miss Rosewood on a quest to learn the truth about her brother."

"I can't credit it." Haverford shook his head. "She seems such an obedient, well-behaved young lady."

"She was very close to her brother. Twins, I believe."

"Still, there are certain standards of behavior a lady must follow."

Rome bit back instinctive words of defense. Didn't Haverford realize how lucky he was? "Which is why I'm here. Miss Rosewood is very loyal to those she loves, but I believe that loyalty is putting her in danger."

"And so you come to me?"

"Yes. Am I correct in believing that you and Miss Rosewood have an understanding?" *Say no. Please say no.*

"We do have an understanding. I have every intention of asking her to be my wife."

Though he had expected the answer, Rome's heart plummeted. "I have done what I could to try and divert the lady from pursuing this matter. I've spoken to her and tried to convince her to leave such things to men, but her love for her brother keeps her focused on this path. I have come to the conclusion that only a husband, or an intended husband, can successfully protect her."

"You are right." Marc seemed to visibly relax. "It is my duty to see to her safety."

"She is a strong-minded woman," Rome warned. "If you outright forbid her to do something, there is no guarantee she will obey."

"It seems as if you have come to know her well."

There it was again, that question hiding behind the words. "I have been attempting to dissuade her from continuing her quest," Rome explained, uncomfortable beneath Marc's gimlet gaze. "For a short while she had me believing that she would cease her actions, but the recent death of Robert Chambers has fueled her energies all over again."

"I take it she knew him."

"They were childhood playmates." Marc contemplated the situation, and Rome added, "As I said, she is loyal."

"A good quality in a wife," Haverford remarked. "I take it you intend to bring this matter to a conclusion in short order?"

Rome nodded. "As soon as Peter is safely gone, I will see the Black Rose Society destroyed. This I promise you."

"As it happens, I have invited the Rosewoods out to my estate in Kent, so Anna will be away from London and safe under my protection."

"Excellent," Rome said. Inside, his heart clenched, but he had to accept that Anna belonged to Haverford. Unlike his father, he would do the honorable thing.

"I have also invited the Emberlys," the earl continued.

"Lavinia is thrilled, I'm sure. Will you invite the Fellhoppers as well?"

Marc cleared his throat. "Of course. I'm certain Anna will enjoy Miss Fellhopper's company." He stood. "Thank you, Rome, for bringing this to my attention."

Rome rose as well. "I just want to do what is right and keep Miss Rosewood safe."

"Coming to me was the right thing to do," Marc said, with a genuine smile. "If she's to be my wife, I had better start as I mean to go on. The lady sounds like she needs a firm hand to guide her, and I can give her that."

But can you give her love?

Rome pasted an answering smile on his face. "I'll not keep you longer, cousin. Good day to you."

"Remember," Marc said, as Rome headed for the door. "If you need help, don't hesitate to contact me."

"I will." But as he left the room, his smile faded.

I had everything I needed in this world, and I just gave it away.

"You can't see him anymore."

Anna blinked in confusion. A moment ago, she and Lavinia had been discussing the latest fashions pictured in the ladies' magazine open between their two chairs. "I'm sorry, what did you say?"

Lavinia sighed. "I apologize for blurting that out, but we must talk, Anna. About the Severley ball."

"Oh." Cheeks burning, Anna glanced away. "I know what you must think of me—"

"Oh, no!" Lavinia leaned closer, unmindful of the magazine that slid to the floor. "I do not blame you, Anna. Really, I don't. My brother can be quite charming, this I know."

"I do not deserve your kindness." Anna sucked in a breath. "I knew what I was doing. I am as guilty as he."

"I do not think so. Rome is quite a bit older than either of us and is worldly. He could have ruined both of you in the garden that night. I'm just glad I found you in time."

"I am expected to marry Lord Haverford. How can you not hate me?"

"I do not hate you, but I *will* caution you." Lavinia pinned Anna with a sober gaze. "Our father ran away with the old earl's betrothed, and we all suffered greatly as a result of the scandal. If it happened again, I don't know if the family would ever recover."

"I do not intend to run away with your brother," Anna assured her. "I would never do such a thing."

"Then what *are* you doing?"

Lavinia's quiet question shook her. What *did*

she hope to accomplish with such fast behavior? "I don't know," she finally admitted, searching her friend's face for an answer. "These encounters just seem to happen."

"They must stop immediately. Hear me in this, Anna. Roman finally has a chance at the future he has always dreamed about, but it can only happen if he remains free of scandal. These interludes . . . sooner or later you will be discovered. And when that happens, your reputation will be soiled beyond redemption, and Rome will never have the successful career he deserves." She sat back in her chair. "Neither of you deserves that. You must stop seeing my brother, Anna. It is the only way to avoid disaster."

"I know." Her heart screamed in protest, but she believed in her soul that Lavinia was right.

"You must be the one to do it, Anna. Refuse to see him. Give him only the barest of civilities when you encounter him socially. Do not go off alone with him under any circumstances."

"All right," she whispered.

"Be strong, Anna." She sighed. "I have come to know you a bit, and I think that you must care for my brother to take such risks. If you do, you must do what's best for him. He can have no future with you when you are promised to Haverford."

"I never meant for any of this to happen."

"But it has happened, and you are the only one who can ensure that it will not happen again."

"You're right." Anna lifted her chin with determination. "I cannot let this continue."

"If you love him, free him."

Love him?

Did she love this man who struggled so hard to live an honorable life? This man who fought to make his dreams come true, who was so protective of his family? This passionate man who constantly put himself between others and harm?

"I do love him." Even as the words slipped from her lips, she knew it was the truth. Shocked, she could only gape at Lavinia, who looked back with a mixture of sympathy and concern. "Dear heavens, I hadn't even realized it myself."

"Love has a way of tangling everything. If I didn't think you loved him, I would cut you from my social circle without hesitation. But because I can see it whenever you look at him, I find I am not so mean-hearted." She squeezed Anna's hand between both of her own. "And if I see it, then others might, too. Woman to woman, Anna, I beg you to do the right thing."

Her heart grieved even as her mind accepted the truth. "I will."

"That is all I can ask." With effort, Lavinia rose from her chair. "I fear I must curtail our visit today, Anna. I do not feel quite the thing all of a sudden."

"What's the matter?" Anna rose, too, alarmed by Lavinia's pallor.

"Probably just the babe." Lavinia bent down to

pick up the magazine off the floor, then tilted precariously as she stood back up. Anna's firm grip on her arm prevented her from falling. "Good heavens! Thank you, Anna."

"You had best lie down," Anna said. "And do not fear for your brother any longer. You have opened my eyes."

"I'm glad." Slowly, Lavinia walked Anna to the doorway of the parlor. "I feel so much better after our conversation."

"I was worried I had lost your friendship," Anna said, "and that I could not bear."

"It might have come to that," Lavinia admitted, "had you been resistant to the plan. But you love him."

"I love him." Tears stung her eyes, and she bit her lower lip to stop its quivering. "But I love him enough to save him. Thank you for showing me the truth, Lavinia. And I do hope you feel better."

Lavinia gave a wan smile. "I have more bad days than good lately. However, I am told it will pass. I expect to see you at Haverford's house party."

"I look forward to it," Anna said. "Perhaps with so much distance between your brother and me, what I have to do will become easier." Squeezing her friend's hand in farewell, she moved into the hallway.

As Anna waited to be shown out, Lavinia made her way slowly up the staircase. Dour Bliss appeared in the company of the butler, and Anna waved her on ahead. The woman marched outside to the carriage as if keeping time with a military troop. Anna took up her reticule and followed.

When she stepped outside, she saw her carriage waiting. Bliss was already climbing inside. And Rome Devereaux was making his way up the steps toward her.

She froze where she was, conscious of the servants all around, of the people walking down the street, of the interested stares of the occupants of passing coaches.

She had promised Lavinia—and herself—that she would have nothing more to do with Rome. Cold civility, that was the thing. But when he looked at her with that familiar green gaze, her insides softened, and her heart yearned.

With effort, she kept her expression politely distant. "Good afternoon, Mr. Devereaux."

"Miss Rosewood." He stopped a couple stairs down from her, putting them almost at eye level. "How are you today?"

"I am well."

"I'm glad."

Silence. Aching, dreadful silence where they watched each other with wary, hungry, hopeful eyes. Memories of his kiss haunted her, like an exquisite dream that had slipped through her fingers upon waking.

"Your sister is not feeling well," she said finally. His brow furrowed with concern as he glanced at the house. "Oh. I had hoped to speak to her today."

"Another time perhaps."

"Another time," he echoed, his voice heavy with wishes unspoken. He brought his gaze back to hers. Waiting.

He still wanted her. It was there in every inch of his body, in the way he leaned slightly toward her, as if unable to stay away. She wanted to step into his arms and lose herself in his embrace, but they stood in front of all of London, like players on a stage. No matter how they longed for each other, this was not meant to be.

Her eyes stung with sudden moisture, and she dug blindly in her reticule.

"Anna . . ." His hoarse whisper nearly broke her will.

"I've something in my eye," she said, and yanked a handkerchief from her bag. Something white fluttered to the pavement as she raised the delicate lace to dab at the welling tears.

Rome bent and picked up the much-folded paper.

"Give that back." Anna snatched it from him and, in her haste, dropped it again.

They both bent to retrieve it and found their faces an inch away from each other.

Anna straightened with a rush, and Rome followed suit more slowly, bearing the worn letter in one hand. The note had fallen open, and he stared at the familiar symbol.

"Good God, Anna, what are you doing with this?"

"It was Anthony's." She nipped it from his fingers and crammed it back into her reticule.

"Anna, wait!"

"Good-bye, Mr. Devereaux." She paused to take one last look at his beloved face, then hurried to her waiting carriage, before he saw how much leaving him tore her heart to pieces.

Hidden from view, he watched the carriage pull away with a frown. So, that was where the missing letter had gone. No doubt Anthony Rosewood had passed it on to his sister in hopes of betraying the secret of the society.

Well, he'd learned his lesson, hadn't he?

From his hiding place across the street, he watched Rome Devereaux turn around and descend the steps without ever knocking on the door, then head off down the street. He waited until Rome had disappeared from view, then cautiously stepped from the shadows.

He had finally discovered what had become of the lost missive. The mystery had taunted him for over a year, the only loose thread in an otherwise perfectly woven plan. But now he knew where to find it.

And he planned to get it back.

Chapter 16

⁓OↃↃ⌒

"This is your chance, Anna," Henrietta whispered.

Anna closed her eyes tightly for an instant, focusing on Charlotte Fellhopper's lovely soprano. They had just finished their first dinner at Haverford Park, and the earl had coaxed Charlotte into an impromptu performance. Of course, that was not enough to stop Mama when she had something on her mind.

"Use this opportunity to encourage the earl," Henrietta continued in a low tone. "The Season is almost gone, and you must secure an offer from him."

"Mama, not now." Anna kept her attention on Charlotte, not wanting to appear rude to those around her.

"You should be sitting beside him," Henrietta whispered.

Anna glanced at the earl, who sat in the chair nearest the pianoforte with Charlotte's brother beside him. Haverford appeared mesmerized by the performance.

"I refuse to disrupt the musicale," Anna breathed. "Now, please, Mama!"

Charlotte finished her song, and Anna joined in the riotous applause.

"Do play another," Haverford said, as Charlotte made to rise from the bench.

"I'm certain there are others who wish to play." Cheeks pink, she hesitated in leaving the bench and glanced around the room. "Mrs. Emberly? Anna?"

"I fear I cannot sing a note," Lavinia replied cheerfully.

"That's not quite true," said Henry, who had arrived just after dinner. "I believe you can sing *one* note."

This brought laughter from the entire group.

"And I do not sing or play at all," Anna said. "My talent lies with watercolors, I fear."

"Definitely don't want the gel to sing," Admiral Rosewood added, with a deep chuckle.

"Quentin!" Henrietta sent her husband a warning look, then turned a sweet smile on those assembled. "My Anna is quite talented."

"I'm certain she is," Haverford agreed gallantly.

"Would you like to play?" Charlotte asked again.

Anna shook her head. "I cannot compare to you. Please, do continue."

"I would love to hear you sing again," Haverford said eagerly.

Charlotte dropped her eyes, her pink cheeks darkening even more. "Very well, my lord." She sat down at the keyboard and began another tune.

Henrietta sat back in her chair with a scowl. "I do not like the way he looks at her," she murmured so only Anna could hear.

Anna rolled her eyes and sat back to enjoy the performance.

"I can't thank you enough," Peter said, tossing back an ale. "You've saved my life, Roman."

Rome leaned forward across the gouged wooden table. "Have a care with your words," he warned, grinning for the sake of those watching. "You never know who's listening."

"I thought we'd lost any followers." Suddenly wary, Peter glanced around the rowdy dockside tavern. No one paid him any mind as the other patrons drank and sang and fondled the barmaids.

Rome shook his head and took a swallow, then plunked down the tankard. "Stop acting like a virgin at Almack's, Peter. This crowd can smell uncertainty like a pack of wolves smell blood."

Peter stiffened. "If you seek to comfort me, you're not."

"Just remain calm. Captain Morrow has assured me of your passage, and the ship leaves at dawn. All is well."

Peter wrapped both hands around his tankard and stared down into the foamy depths. "It will be so odd not to live in England anymore."

"You'll be alive," Rome murmured. "That's enough."

"True." Peter raised his tankard. "To you, Roman. For saving my life."

Rome clanked his tankard against Peter's and drank. Then he plunked the empty vessel on the table. "Let's go."

"Where?"

"To your room." Rome stood and weaved his way across the room to the staircase, hoping to make anyone watching believe him foxed. "We'll stay together tonight, then I will see you off in the morning."

"No, we won't. I'm not a child." Peter stomped up the stairs behind him and followed Rome down the hall. "You have your own room right across from mine, Roman. I'll be safe enough with you right there. You needn't hold my hand all night."

"Peter—"

"Roman, please. I'm a grown man." They stopped outside Peter's room.

Seeing the determination in the younger man's eyes, Rome sighed. "Promise you won't leave the room without me."

"I won't. Thank you, Roman," he said, his hand on the door latch. "I would not be alive if not for you."

"It is both my duty and my pleasure to be of assistance."

"Good night, Roman."

"Good night, Peter."

Rome waited as the boy stepped into his room and locked the door behind him. "Are you watching, Richard?" he murmured. "I've kept my promise."

Anna came down to breakfast the next morning to find the Fellhoppers there before her.

"Good morning, Charlotte. Mr. Fellhopper."

"Good morning, Anna." Charlotte smiled as she sipped her hot chocolate. Dennis peeked out from behind the morning paper to briefly acknowledge Anna's greeting and grab his coffee cup.

"You're both up early this morning," Anna said as she selected her breakfast from the sideboard, then moved to the table.

"In Leicestershire, we rise very early," Charlotte said. "We just can't seem to sleep much past sunrise!"

"Sheep rise early, too," Dennis said, from behind the *Times*.

Charlotte giggled, then abruptly quieted as Haverford strolled into the room.

"Good morning, all," he said briskly, then began loading a plate from the sideboard.

"Morning, Haverford," Dennis said. "Price of wool looks very promising this morning."

"Excellent!" Haverford sat down next to Anna. "You ladies both look delightful for such an early hour."

"We rise early at home in Leicestershire," Charlotte offered.

At the earl's inquiring look, Anna shrugged. "I simply could not sleep."

Haverford frowned. "I do hope the bed was comfortable. You must tell me at once if we should change your room."

"No, my lord, the bed was quite comfortable. My own thoughts kept me awake."

"Hate it when that happens," Dennis muttered, from behind the paper.

Charlotte leaned forward. "I find that a cup of tea before bedtime sends me right to sleep, Anna. Perhaps you might try that."

"I might," Anna replied, then set about slicing her ham.

"I find that tea keeps me awake," Haverford commented, salting his food.

"My special tea would lull you to sleep," Charlotte said, then blushed red. "Forgive me, my lord, for being so familiar."

"Nonsense," the earl said, with a shrug of his shoulders. "There are times when I could use such a remedy."

"When we all could use such a remedy," Dennis commented.

"Would you like to accompany me on a ride, Anna?" Haverford asked. "I have a mare that is spirited, but well suited for a lady."

Anna couldn't stop the grin that spread across her face. "I would quite enjoy that, my lord. Thank you for the invitation."

"My pleasure." The earl turned his attention to the Fellhoppers. "You are both invited as well."

"Excellent," Dennis remarked, folding his paper. "I could use a good morning gallop."

"Thank you for the invitation, my lord," Charlotte said quietly. "I would quite enjoy that."

Haverford stood. "Then let us all plan on meeting in the foyer in an hour. Is that enough time for you ladies to ready yourselves?"

Charlotte nodded.

"Of course, my lord," Anna replied.

"Excellent! Until then." The earl strode out of the dining room.

Charlotte rose from the table almost immediately. "I must go change into something more appropriate for riding. Are you coming, Anna?"

Anna indicated her half-full cup of chocolate. "Do go without me, Charlotte. I shall meet you in the foyer."

Charlotte gave a quick nod and hurried from the room.

"My goodness, Mr. Fellhopper, but your sister is quite eager to be out of doors!"

He never took his eyes from the front page of the paper. "She loves to ride."

* * *

Finally alone in his rooms, he took a bracing breath and pulled the black velvet pouch from its hiding place.

Did he dare do it now? She was going riding. The timing would be perfect.

But there would be other people around. He certainly didn't want any witnesses to this particular act!

Haverford met his own eyes in his looking glass. Anyone who looked hard enough might see the conflict he fought with his conscience. He hadn't realized the truth about Anna until recently, hadn't put together all the pieces of this intricate puzzle.

But this new information changed nothing. He would do what must be done.

He opened the bag and shook the ring out into his palm. The gemstone glittered in the morning sunlight, and he closed his hand around the cursed bauble. The responsibility and loyalty tied to it chafed like a noose around his neck. How could he have known it would come to this?

He shoved the ring back in the bag, then tucked it away into its hiding place. Not yet. Later, he would summon the courage to take care of the matter.

It would be quick and quiet. Then the matter of Anna Rosewood would be put to rest.

Finally.

He left the room, slamming the door so hard that it rattled the swords mounted on the wall.

* * *

The docks were bustling in the morning. Food vendors called out to passersby, hawking their tasty wares. The aroma of fresh food mixed with the scent of aged wood and brine in the air. Beneath it all lurked the dank odor of things left too long near the sea.

Rome stood with the sun shining its warmth down on him, taking some of the morning chill from the air. Shading his eyes, he looked at the place where Captain Morrow's ship, the *Mary Louise*, had sat at anchor. All that remained was sea and sky.

He'd awakened early and gone to Peter's room to fetch him. There had been no answer to his knock. Finally, the innkeeper had unlocked the room, and Rome had discovered an empty bed. Curse his hide, but the proud young man had left without him.

He'd hurried to the docks in hopes of saying good-bye, but the *Mary Louise* had already set sail.

He hoped the stubborn lad found happiness and peace in America.

He turned back toward his horse. With Peter safe, he could concentrate on bringing to justice the brigands who called themselves the Black Rose Society. He had an appointment tomorrow with Edgar Vaughn to talk about the diplomatic position, and while he was there, he intended to ask a few subtle questions of his own and determine if the man was indeed as guilty as he appeared.

He mounted his horse and set about navigating the pedestrian-clogged streets.

The traffic was worse than usual. He followed along behind a hired hack, using it to cleave a path through the throng that he and Sisyphus could easily traverse. But when the hack stopped abruptly, his gelding almost crashed into it.

"Easy, fellow." Patting the horse's neck, Rome craned his neck to see what was going on. He noticed a crowd gathered outside the tavern where he and Peter had shared their last ale together, but the people pushed and shoved so close to each other that he could see nothing else.

"What the devil is going on there?" he murmured, frowning. He didn't like coincidences, and the fact that all the interest was focused on the tavern where he had last seen Peter sent his instincts tumbling over one another like hissing snakes.

He tried to maneuver to a closer position through the mass of spectators, but the mob only pushed him aside. The jangle of alarm that pricked the flesh at the back of his neck would not go away.

Frustrated, he dismounted and eased his way through the crowd, leading Sisyphus behind him. The closer he got to the tavern, the more tightly the masses pulled together, forcing him to push his way through with more roughness than he had originally intended.

"Watch it there!"

"Easy, guv!"

A cold glare hushed up the complainers, and he continued to move forward.

"—found him this morning, just like that."

"—lying in the alley like a sot—"

"—killed by that gang of cutthroats what use swords—"

Swords.

Ice shot through his veins and froze his heart in his chest. Uncaring of the protests, he thrust forward through the onlookers. As he reached the front, he saw the man lying facedown in the alley.

Familiar blue coat.

Dark hair.

Outstretched hand with the family ring of the Brantleys on one pale, still finger.

"Peter!" He charged forward. The extended arm of a watchman halted him abruptly.

"Keep back if you please," the burly fellow said.

"Damn you, let me through! *Peter!*"

The watchman looked at him with interest. "You know the bloke?"

"Yes, I know him!" Rome snarled. "Now let me through!"

The watchman narrowed his eyes as if considering planting him a facer, then called over his shoulder, "Anson! This fellow says he knows the poor sod."

A tall, thin watchman pulled away from the group gathered around the body. "Is that right?"

"Yes, that's right," Rome said. "If I could but see his face . . ."

Anson gave a short nod. "Let him pass, Higsby. But leave the horse behind."

Rome handed the reins to a startled Higsby, then ducked under the man's arm and hurried to the body. As he got there, one of the watchmen rolled the victim onto his back.

Dark eyes stared up at him, wide and empty, and a blossom of blood seeped through the fine blue material of what had once been an elegant coat.

"Dear God." The strength poured out of his body, and he sank to his knees beside the cold corpse of the boy he was supposed to have protected. "Peter, my God."

"Do you know the deceased, sir?" Anson asked, his face softening with compassion.

"Peter." Rome could barely say the word beyond the grief that choked him. "Peter Brantley."

Idling the day away on horseback was not conducive to her investigation, Anna thought. She hated being trapped in the countryside when she could be in London, searching for clues. But her mother had taken control of matters, and all she could do was go along.

"You must attract his lordship's interest and hold it long enough for him to offer," Henrietta whispered as she walked beside Anna to the foyer.

"Yes, Mama." Dressed in her favorite dark green riding habit, Anna gripped her riding gloves tightly in her hand. She hated playing the marriage game. It struck her as a huge waste of her time when she had a killer to locate.

"You must converse with him. Amuse him. Time is running out, Anna."

"I understand." And she did. Her mother wanted her to flirt with Haverford, to seduce him into the web of matrimony with womanly guile.

Her heart wasn't in it, but she would do her duty.

"There he is. My, how dashing he looks."

Not as dashing as his cousin. "Don't fret, Mama. I know what to do."

"Keep him away from Miss Fellhopper," Henrietta hissed, before putting on her social smile. "Good afternoon, everyone! I hear you're going riding."

"We are," Dennis said. "How are you this morning, Mrs. Rosewood?"

"Not as excited as my Anna. I don't ride well, though my daughter has an excellent seat."

"It should be great fun," Charlotte chimed in.

"A good gallop always clears my head," Haverford said, smiling at Charlotte.

Henrietta nudged Anna. Rolling her eyes, Anna swept up to the earl and laid a hand on his arm. "I do apologize for holding up the party," she murmured.

"Nonsense." Haverford patted her hand. "We are all here now."

"I trust you will pick out a suitable mount for me, my lord."

Haverford smiled. "I already have the perfect mare in mind for you."

"I'm sure she will suit quite well." Anna kept the smile on her face, though she detested playing the vapid society miss. Out of the corner of her eye, she saw her mother give a slight nod, a pleased smile curving her lips.

"Your comfort is my priority," Haverford assured her, then sent a warm look to Charlotte. "As is yours, Miss Fellhopper. I take care of my guests."

Charlotte giggled. With effort, Anna kept her mouth fixed in a smile. "I am eager to see your estate, Lord Haverford. Especially the sheep."

The earl beamed. "It will be my pleasure to show them to you." Keeping Anna's hand on his arm, he led the group toward the front door.

"Have you had any trouble with the spring lambs, my lord?" Charlotte asked.

"Not at all," the earl replied, then launched into a detailed discussion of the trials of lambing.

Casting a glance back at her beaming mother, Anna made a mental note to learn more about sheep in the coming months. Apparently, she would need it if she were ever to have a conversation with her future husband.

Rome stepped into the darkness of his rooms. He'd drawn the drapes that morning, and the place looked like a tomb. Numb, he went to the window and pulled aside one of the curtains.

The descending sun hung over London, lighting the sky in shades of orange and yellow and bright, bloody crimson.

Peter was dead.

He squeezed his eyes shut against the tears that wanted to come. His jaw trembled with the effort, but finally he won the battle and pushed the emotion back into a small, safe place in his mind.

There would be time for that later.

For the moment, he still had his duty. He had failed in his promise to Richard, had failed to keep Peter alive. But how? He'd been so careful, had planned every step meticulously. And still the society had found Peter—had found him and murdered him.

He'd failed Peter. But he would *not* fail in bringing Peter's murderers to justice.

He clenched his fingers into the material of the curtain as the grief struggled to rise up again. Had he the luxury, he would indulge in the cleansing emotional breakdown over a bottle of strong whiskey. But if he were to punish the Black Rose Society for their crimes, he needed to be clearheaded and focused.

He had allowed himself one drink to control his emotions after the discovery of Peter's body. Now he needed to think like the soldier he was and track down the murderous dogs who had so callously slain a barely grown youth.

He changed his clothes, requiring something

more casual than a morning coat for ease of movement. He settled on his favorite riding coat, then went to his trunk and took out his pistol, his derringer, and a wickedly sharp knife. These he concealed on his person.

A familiar, cold detachment settled over him as he armed himself. He'd watched comrades fall in battle, and he'd grieved even as he'd continued to fight. But this was different.

The Black Rose Society took advantage of youth, exploited it, then cut it down without a hint of remorse. They were a different sort of enemy from the foreign armies he'd fought in the past. They were vermin, a disease that had spread for far too long. They had no honor, no principles.

Therefore, neither would he.

He slipped a pouch with all his available funds into his pocket. Before the night was through, he might indeed have to flee the country. The authorities took a dim view of killing, even if done for the right reasons.

Once he was ready, he stood for a moment, taking in the modest comfort of his home and making sure he hadn't forgotten anything.

Then he turned and left his rooms, shutting the door behind him without looking back.

It was time to find Edgar Vaughn.

Chapter 17

Her mother would have considered the riding outing a disaster.

Anna sat before her dressing mirror as Lizzie arranged her hair. She had tried her best to attract the earl, but their conversations had stumbled along awkwardly. Lord Haverford was a serious man, not one skilled in the art of flirtation.

Not like Rome.

Her heart clenched at just the thought of him. She closed her eyes for an instant, searching for strength, then opened them again and met her own gaze in the mirror.

She had shadows beneath her eyes. The dark smudges gave testament to restless nights, the dreams that had plagued her when she had managed to find a rare few moments of slumber. Most nights, she lay awake for hours, thoughts spinning through her mind like autumn leaves in the wind.

She missed Rome.

It was wrong. She was promised to another man and had no right to such traitorous longings. But her heart would not listen; it yearned for the man who could make her blood sing with a touch.

She had tried to flirt with Lord Haverford today, but a simple pleasure that came so easily with Rome had proven a chore with the earl. Her gaiety had been forced, and she hated loitering in the country while her mission stagnated back in Town.

Rome had once called her clever.

Lord Haverford had seemed much more interested in the Fellhoppers and their talk of sheep than her attempts to amuse him. How was a woman to enchant a man whose only interest was the wool market? He had not been rude about it; in fact, he had tried to include her in the conversation. But she was an admiral's daughter, not a farmer's. His entire discussion on shearing had lost her almost from the beginning.

Was this her future then? To listen to dissertations on sheep farming for the rest of her days? Would he talk of the dratted beasts even in their marriage bed?

Every moment with Rome had left her feeling vibrant and alive, sizzling with passionate emotions and new ideas. With Haverford, her brain had gone numb with talk of sheep and farming. His gentlemanly touches—helping her to mount and dismount, touching the hand she rested on his arm—left her unmoved.

Her future loomed before her, predictable and safe. The earl's money and title would grant her a life of comfort in exchange for the heirs she would bear, but would she suffocate wrapped in such luxury?

She loved Rome. Passionately. Unreasonably. His very presence made her skin tingle and the blood rush through her veins in merry ecstasy.

But Haverford was her future. A good man. A wealthy man. They would probably rub along tolerably well for the most part, but would that lead to love?

Or would she go to her grave with only the distant memory of real love to comfort her?

She was doing the right thing. But even as she tried to convince herself, her eyes welled with tears. Her looking glass reflected every emotion as her face crumpled, and the illusion of strength dissolved. She caught a brief glimpse of Lizzie's expression of alarm, then rested her head on her folded arms and cried out the sorrow she had carried with her since the day she had bid her love farewell on the steps of Lavinia's home.

Lizzie patted her shoulder, making soothing noises, as Anna wept, the loss of her romantic dreams more than she could bear.

Rome arrived at the building that housed diplomatic affairs just after five o'clock. Most of the offices were closed up and dark, but light shone from Vaughn's office, and the door stood open. The stalwart Pennyworthy was nowhere to be seen.

Vaughn himself sat bent over his desk, carefully scrutinizing a stack of papers in front of him. Rome slipped into the room, then closed the door behind him with a soft click.

Vaughn's head came up in alarm. "Devereaux! What the devil are you doing here at this hour?"

"I couldn't wait until Wednesday for our appointment." Rome took a chair across from the desk. "Let's talk now instead."

Vaughn's eyes narrowed. "What are you about, Devereaux? Are you foxed?"

Rome gave a short bark of laughter. "Hardly, though the notion holds a certain appeal, I must admit."

"I don't have time for cryptic discussions, my boy. I have quite a bit of work to do. You can see yourself out."

"I think you can make time for this conversation, Vaughn. Let's talk about the Black Rose Society."

"Ah." Abandoning his papers, Vaughn sat back in his chair, a cool smile curving his lips. "I wondered if you had recognized the ring that day."

"Oh, I recognized it." Rome stretched his legs out before him in a casual pose, knowing he could leap to his feet at a second's notice.

"You know what it is, what it means."

"I do. I just want to hear it from your lips."

Vaughn cocked his head to the side. "Just what is this about, Devereaux? Why do you come to me now when you saw the ring days ago?"

"I have my reasons."

Vaughn sighed and rose from his chair. Rome tensed, but the man only prowled from behind his desk, rubbing the back of his neck with one hand. "Lad, we're not going to get anywhere with these mysterious answers of yours."

"I came here to question you, Vaughn, not the other way around."

"We'll see about that." He'd always known Vaughn looked older than his years, and the diplomat proved it by yanking a sword from the wall and falling into a fighting stance in the blink of an eye.

Expecting such a movement, Rome drew his pistol at the same time.

Vaughn glanced down at the pistol pointed at him. "Not very sporting of you, Devereaux."

"This isn't about sport." Rome rose, keeping the weapon trained on the other man. "This is about death. And you will answer my questions."

"I see all that I heard about you is true," Vaughn said, with a bark of laughter.

"The Black Rose Society," Rome began. "What—"

Vaughn's leg came up. Numbing pain shot up Rome's arm as the kick connected with his wrist. The pistol flew out of his hand and hit the floor, skidding across the room.

"Yes, let's do talk about the Black Rose Society." Vaughn pointed the sword at Rome's throat. "I've been watching you, Devereaux. Waiting for this moment."

"And here it is. You must be pleased."

Vaughn's eyes narrowed. " 'Tis I who will ask the questions, my boy, and you will answer them."

"As you wish." Quick as a blink, Rome swept a heavy book from the desk. The resounding thud broke Vaughn's concentration for only a moment, but it was all Rome needed. He darted away from the sword and grabbed its mate from the wall.

Vaughn's expression of shock melted into one of pleased challenge. He saluted Rome with his blade. Rome did the same, and both men eased gracefully into fighting stance.

The battle began with the first tentative scraping of metal on metal, each of them exploring the other's skill. Swish, scrape. Swish, scrape.

Vaughn thrust unexpectedly. Rome parried. They stood frozen there for a moment, eyes locked as fiercely as their weapons. Then Vaughn slowly smiled. Rome gave a nod, and the duel exploded.

Vaughn attacked. Rome countered a wicked slash, and the vibration of sword meeting sword traveled up his arm. He tightened his grip and came back at his opponent, forcing the older man backwards with a thrust.

Vaughn dodged the blade, then came back with rapid swordplay that demanded all of Rome's concentration. They moved around the room in the intricate dance of combat, nearly equal in their skill, fiercely matched, blades glittering in the candlelight.

"They taught you well," Vaughn admitted, sweat beading his brow.

"The battlefield taught me." Rome drove Vaughn back a step.

"I can claim the same." Vaughn pressed onward again with a surge of strength.

Rome parried the attack. "Death is more than you deserve."

"I welcome death, if it means I take you with me." Vaughn pushed forward, his blade lightning fast.

"Haven't you sent enough men to meet their maker?" Rome panted.

"More than you, I'd imagine." Red-faced with exertion, the older man still fought with surprising vigor.

"Bastard." Grim-faced, Rome stepped up his pace.

"I cede that title to you." Vaughn twisted in an unexpected maneuver that wedged them together, face-to-face, blades locked at the hilt. "Only the most vile of villains could murder a boy like Peter Brantley."

"I agree." Rome shoved against Vaughn, but the other man spun and locked their weapons together again. Rome leaned in, putting pressure on the other man's grip. "And I will avenge his death with your own, old man."

Vaughn blinked. "What the devil are you talking about?"

"Peter Brantley. You murdered him."

"I didn't." Puzzlement etched his face. "You did."

"What game is this?" Furious, Rome shoved the other man away.

"No game." Vaughn held up his hand when Rome would have charged forward. "Hold a moment. I thought you killed Brantley."

"No, you did. Or someone else in your Black Rose Society." Rome leaned into fighting stance again. "Now let's finish this."

"My society? Hardly." Vaughn lowered his sword. "I am not a member."

"You have the ring."

"I do. I removed it from a member of the society that we captured some time ago."

"Lies. Raise your sword, coward."

"I'll forgive you that because I believe you to be grieving. Devereaux, I was under the impression that *you* were a member of the society."

"Me?" Completely startled, Rome carefully rose from his stance. "You're the villain here."

"No, I'm investigating the villains."

"So am I."

The two men faced each other across the oriental carpet, wary.

"Does this mean," Vaughn finally asked, "that we are fighting on the same side?"

"Unless you're lying."

Vaughn shook his head and threw down his sword. "There is my weapon. I can show you the notes I have kept of my investigation to prove the truth to you."

"I might be lying, in which case you're foolish for discarding your weapon."

Vaughn simply pinned him with a look. "Are you lying?"

"No."

"Then we will simply have to trust each other."

"That could prove hazardous."

"My instincts tell me you are on the side of right, Devereaux." Vaughn stepped backwards toward his desk, keeping his eyes on Rome. "I just can't fathom how you became involved. Was it Brantley?"

Rome nodded, grief and confusion clogging his throat. "Keep your hands where I can see them."

"I will." Vaughn moved behind his desk and removed a thick set of papers from a drawer. "I have friends in the Home Department, and one of them asked for my assistance in this matter due to my years of experience and fascination with swords." His expression grew stony. "I have seen too much of death to allow these miscreants to murder our bright youth."

Rome said nothing, merely stepped forward

and glanced at the papers. Names, dates. Going back over a year.

Rome remained silent, the memory of Peter's lifeless eyes still too fresh. He raised his gaze to Vaughn's. "Tell me about the ring."

"We had an informant for a brief time, a boy who wanted to leave the society. One night he got word to us that a duel was about to occur, and I took a team of men to stop it. Everyone got away but one man."

"Whom you interrogated, I assume."

Vaughn nodded, then sighed. "He refused to talk. He wore that ring, so we believe he was a high-ranking member of the society."

"The Triad."

Vaughn raised his brows. "Yes."

Rome turned away, sword at his side now. "What happened to him?"

"He managed to hang himself, the cur. Gone without ever telling us a word." Vaughn shuffled the papers. "I suppose Brantley involved you."

Rome gave a stiff nod. "I made a deathbed promise to his brother on the battlefield."

"We thought you were a member. You attended a dinner party at Vauxhall Gardens not long ago."

Again Rome nodded. "You had men there?"

"One. They discovered him quickly." His mouth thinned. "And murdered him."

"I'm sorry."

Vaughn accepted the sympathy with a bob of

his head. "You walked out of that party with no mask, so we were able to identify you."

"And thought I was one of them. I would have done the same." Rome leaned the sword against the desk.

"Your name and the rumor of the lost note were the only trail we had to follow."

"Lost note?"

"It was the talk of the party. I'm surprised you didn't hear of it. It went missing about a year ago." Vaughn gave a hard little laugh. "The precious Triad was mad to find it. It was a trail, you see. Evidence that they existed. They would kill to get it back."

Even the breath in his lungs stilled. "Does it contain the symbol of the society?"

"Yes, it matches the rings the members wear. Apparently, when someone received the symbol in the post, he was supposed to report to a pre-destined meeting place to be taken to the duel."

Anna.

That day on Lavinia's steps replayed in his mind like some horrible nightmare. Anna possessed the missing note, a scrap of paper the society would kill to recover. Her life was in danger, and she had no idea.

Vaughn peered at him, brows beetled in concern. "Devereaux? Are you all right?"

"Fine." He studied Vaughn's face, torn. He'd admired Edgar Vaughn all his adult life—until he'd suspected him of belonging to the Black

Rose Society. Even with all of Vaughn's research laid out before him, he remained unsure of the diplomat's allegiance. Was he indeed an ally? Or was he a clever foe trying to mislead Rome with cunning words and believable details?

Did he dare confide in Vaughn? Or would he be knotting the noose around Anna's neck by doing so?

Her life was too precious to be wagered on a guess.

"What is it?" Vaughn asked, studying Rome's face with narrowed eyes. "Come, Devereaux, we must work together if we are to put an end to the society."

Time was running out. "I know who has the note"

Vaughn's face lit with interest. "Tell me."

"I believe it's at Haverford Park." Rome crossed the room and picked up his fallen pistol, then tucked it safely away.

"Wait! Where are you going? You can't just walk off like this!" Vaughn came out from behind the desk. "Damn it, Devereaux, we're not finished here!"

"I am." He headed for the door. "I will contact you if I need assistance, Vaughn."

"Blast it, Devereaux, come back here! I can help you!"

But Rome kept going, closing the office door behind him.

* * *

"I wish Mama had agreed to come," Lavinia said, as she sat with her husband, Anna, and Henrietta in Haverford's drawing room.

Emberly patted his wife's hand, the small diamond in his pinky ring glittering in the soft light. "Now, my sweet. You know your mother dislikes socializing."

"She doesn't dislike it," Lavinia protested. "She's simply too humiliated to be seen anywhere but *en famille*. The instant she discovered the Fellhoppers were going to be here, she changed her mind about attending."

All of them glanced at the Fellhoppers, who sat with the admiral and Haverford at the card table, playing a spirited game of whist.

"It could have been quite the intimate coze," Mrs. Rosewood remarked, sipping a glass of sherry, "had it been kept to just family."

"Then you and I would not be here, Mama," Anna reminded her.

Henrietta gave her a patronizing smile. "Nonsense, daughter. You know it is just a matter of time before we are family in truth."

Anna rolled her eyes and glanced apologetically at the Emberlys. "I do not seek to presume, Mama."

A squeal of feminine laughter came from the card table. Henrietta sent a disdainful look at the players. "Some people do, apparently."

Anna was saved from covering her mother's rudeness by the entrance of the butler, Leighton.

"Mr. Roman Devereaux," the butler announced. Moments later Rome appeared in the door, windblown and exhausted, and Anna's heart skipped.

"Rome!" Haverford called out. "What ever are you doing here?"

Rome nodded acknowledgment to the other people at the table as he came to stand by the earl. "It is urgent I speak with you, cousin," he murmured.

"I see." Haverford rose. "If you will all excuse me . . ." The two men left the room, and Anna's chest grew tight. Breathing became a chore as she watched the door swing closed behind that tall, familiar form.

"Don't be too obvious," her mother murmured. "We mustn't let his lordship think you fast."

Anna just closed her eyes and focused on calming her quivering nerves, leaving her mother to her incorrect assumption.

"I wonder what brings your brother here?" Emberly mused. "He looked as if he's ridden his horse into a lather."

"I don't know." Lavinia frowned after the two men. "I do remember he had said he intended to stay in London." She cast a puzzled glance at Anna.

Anna shook her head ever so slightly. She had no idea why Rome was at Haverford Park, but the urgency and unexpectedness of his arrival certainly left her at sixes and sevens.

Lavinia pursed her lips as she considered the

matter, then gasped. "Oh! I do hope nothing has happened to Mama!"

Emberly squeezed her hand. "If that were the case, he would have come to fetch you. No doubt 'tis some sort of man's business. Do not worry."

"I agree with your husband," Henrietta said. "Mr. Devereaux would surely tell you immediately if your mama needed you at her side."

Lavinia took a deep breath. "Very well. I will simply wait until he has finished speaking to Marc before I quiz him."

"Sound thinking." Emberly agreed.

But she glanced at Anna again, and the worry in her eyes sparked Anna's own. What *was* Rome doing here? And worse yet, how in the world could she keep her distance from him when every beat of her heart demanded otherwise?

Lavinia twisted her fingers together, and Emberly rested his hand over hers. "My dear, do not overset yourself. If you like, I will go and tell your brother to come speak to you the instant he has finished conferring with Haverford."

"Oh, would you, Henry? That would make me feel so much better."

"Of course, my dear." Henry rose and smiled down at her. "I shall be back momentarily."

As Emberly left them, Anna's mother said, "You are fortunate in your husband, Mrs. Emberly. He clearly cares for you a great deal."

"Thank you, Mrs. Rosewood. I am indeed blessed, though Henry is gone quite a bit to his political meetings. I do wish he could spend more time at home."

"There are other wives who see their husbands but once a year," Henrietta continued. "A woman must appreciate the moments her busy husband can spend with her. Isn't that right, daughter?"

Hearing the lesson behind the words, Anna answered by rote. "Yes, Mama." Surreptitiously, she glanced toward the door. Lavinia coughed loudly, and Anna jerked her attention back to her companions to meet Lavinia's warning gaze. At the silent reminder, Anna's wild speculation about Rome lurched to a halt. She struggled to pick up the conversation. "I shall certainly remember that when I am wed."

"If more daughters listened to their elders, there would be more content wives," Henrietta declared.

"A woman should always be content and grateful for what she has," Lavinia said. "Everyone is happier for it."

"Indeed, Mrs. Emberly, I believe you have hit upon the root of the problem." Henrietta nodded and sipped her sherry. "If more of our young ladies learned to appreciate their lot in life and let go of foolish, romantic notions, we would all be the better for it."

"I agree," Lavinia said, looking straight at Anna. "The heart leads without reason, and those who follow it often find themselves the victims of disaster."

Before Anna could formulate a reply, Emberly rejoined them.

"I'm sorry, Lavinia," he said, taking his seat beside her. "They have closeted themselves in the study. I expect we will have to wait until they return before you can speak to your brother."

"Thank you for trying, Henry."

Emberly smiled, and his affection for his wife shone in his normally sober dark eyes. "Anything to make you happy, my sweet."

Chapter 18

Haverford closed the door to the study and locked it, then walked toward his cousin. "Rome, what are you doing here? Has something happened?"

Rome paced the floor of the study, too restless to sit. "Peter is dead."

"What? Good God!" Haverford grabbed the back of a chair, his eyes wide with shock. "When? How?"

"Early this morning. And by the sword, of course." Rome gave a harsh laugh. "The bloody Black Rose Society."

"I'm so sorry."

"I was supposed to protect him." The slash of guilt still ripped at his insides. "I thought I had a good plan. No one should have been able to find him."

"They must have been following him."

"That's my guess." Grief tried to drown him, but he fought back the wave with effort. There would be time to mourn later, when his duty was done.

"I take it there is some danger that brings you here."

Marc's smooth, practical tone helped Rome to regain control of his roiling emotions. "Yes. Anna . . . Miss Rosewood is in danger."

Marc sat down. "Tell me."

"She has something they want, something that belonged to her brother. They would kill to get it."

"Really. Do they know she has it?"

"I don't know." Plagued by agitation, Rome picked up Haverford's letter opener off the desk. The elegant silver instrument resembled a miniature sword, hilt and all. He turned the piece over in his hand, watching the light play on the blade.

"What is this mysterious something?" Marc asked, raising his brows as he plucked the letter opener from Rome's fingers.

"Oh, sorry. It's a note to her brother from the society. Apparently, they are mad to get it back lest it lead the authorities to them."

Marc frowned. "I see."

"I just learned of this and came straightaway to warn her."

"Don't you mean to warn *me*? After all, I am responsible for Miss Rosewood's safety."

"To warn *all* of you." His fear for Anna would betray his true feelings if he did not choose his words carefully. Frustrated, he took the letter opener from Marc and tossed it on the desk. "Cousin, I have ridden a long way to bring you this news. I only just found out myself. Let's formulate a plan."

Marc drummed his fingers on the arm of the chair. "How did you discover this complication?"

"Vaughn."

"Edgar Vaughn? What does he have to do with this?"

"He's investigating the society."

"Really!" Marc adjusted his spectacles. "And he told you this?"

"Yes. I will tell you the whole of it later, but for now, let's just focus on the fact that the society wants that note back, and Anna has it."

"And we can't confirm if they know she has it," Marc mused.

"The best course of action would be to get it from her," Rome said, sitting on the edge of the desk. "I don't think they would be keen to kill her unless she gets in their way."

"Why do you say that? Aren't these men murderers?"

"Yes, but the death of a young woman under mysterious circumstances would generate more attention than they would like."

"Whereas young men being slain by the sword could just be attributed to impetuous youth and a boy getting into deep territory with unsavory elements."

Peter's lifeless face flashed through Rome's mind, and he clenched his jaw. "Yes. Even if they used a method other than the blade, the death of an otherwise healthy young lady, especially one of Miss Rosewood's social standing, would cause a considerable uproar."

"So you believe they may simply try to steal back the note?"

"Yes."

"What if they don't find it?"

Coldness settled over Rome, freezing his expression in a hard mask. "Then they might risk harming her. At that point, they would fear for their very existence."

"So it is up to us to protect her. Unless Mr. Vaughn is going to assist?"

"I didn't tell him everything. I'm trying to keep Anna out of it." Rome got to his feet and prowled the room.

Marc rose as well. "So only you and I stand between Anna and these blackguards? You're playing a deep game with our lives, Rome."

Rome stopped dead and glared. "Would you rather I betray her to the society? What if they don't know she has the note? By calling in the authorities and surrounding your house with armed guards, we would tell the society where to find their missing communication, as surely as if we had taken out an advertisement in the *Times*."

"You're exaggerating."

"Am I?" Rome strode across the room to loom over Marc in subtle intimidation. "Peter is dead, and I was careful with him. If they are watching Peter, then they may be watching me."

Marc simply looked at him with those calm gray eyes, unthreatened by Rome's greater height. "In which case, you may have led them to our doorstep."

"Damn it!" Rome turned away, irritated by his own shortsightedness. "You're right."

"But then again," Marc mused, ever unflappable, "if you had not come, we would not know of this danger. At least now we can prepare."

"I suppose you're right." Rome settled back on the edge of the desk again, determined to keep his emotions in check and think like a soldier. "So let's make a plan. Will you ask Miss Rosewood for the note, or shall I?"

Marc hesitated before answering, his expression pensive. "You have said that Anna is obsessed with learning more about her brother's death. If that's true, do you suppose she will just hand the note over to us?"

Rome gave a bark of laughter. "Hardly. Anna Rosewood is a stubborn woman."

"So you've said." Marc raised his hand and tapped his chin with one finger. "I suppose we will have to steal it."

"Agreed. And I should probably be the one to do it."

Marc raised his brows. "Why you? This is my house."

"I picked up quite a few talents in the military." Rome grinned. "Don't look so shocked, cousin. It was all for the good of England, you know."

"Indeed." Marc shook his head. "Very well, tell me your plan."

"You will distract Miss Rosewood and the rest of the guests with an outing of some sort. I will cry off—exhaustion after my bruising ride. While you are gone, I will go into Miss Rosewood's room and search for the note."

"That should work. I shall give the servants the afternoon off so you are not disturbed."

"Excellent."

"And once you've found the note, you can give it to me, and I will put in my safe."

Rome thought it over, then nodded. "A good plan. Even if the society believes she may have the note, once they search her room and don't find it, they may well believe the rumor was a mistake."

"And with it snug in the safe, we can hold it to turn over to the authorities."

Rome got to his feet. "Shall we try this tomorrow afternoon?"

"I've already offered to take my guests on a picnic tomorrow, so that will work out splendidly."

"Good. Together we will make certain Miss Rosewood stays safe."

"I had best return to my guests," Marc said. "And you should change your clothing and join us. I'm certain you must have alarmed Lavinia with your rather abrupt arrival."

"No doubt you're right." Rome blew out a hard breath. "I will reassure her, Marc, but then I will retire to my room. I'm not good company tonight."

"Of course." Sober-faced, Marc nodded. "I'm sorry about Peter, Rome. He was a good lad."

"He was." Rome walked with Marc and waiting while the earl unlocked the door. "And I will find who did this to him, no matter how long it takes."

"Rome!" Lavinia cried. She jumped to her feet as her brother entered the drawing room and would have run to him except for her husband's restraining hand on her arm.

"Propriety," he murmured. "And have a care for your state."

"Very well." She shook off Emberly's grip and hurried at a quick walk to meet her brother.

Henrietta leaned close to Anna's ear. "I'm glad Mr. Devereaux has arrived," she whispered. "Perhaps he will distract Miss Fellhopper."

Anna struggled against her own distraction. Freshly shaven and in clean clothes, Rome drew her gaze despite her best intentions. He lingered on the other side of the room, listening to his sister with one ear while greeting the players at the card table.

Then he turned his attention toward her.

Their eyes met for one sizzling second. Her breath caught, and her heart skipped, and her flesh warmed. She nearly stood up, except her mother leaned in again.

"See how she can't take her eyes from him? Perhaps his handsome face will distract her from the earl."

She sat back in her chair with a soft thud, appalled at how she had nearly betrayed herself.

Rome approached with Lavinia by his side. "Good evening, Mrs. Rosewood, Miss Rosewood." His gaze lit on Anna for an instant, then moved on. "Emberly, good to see you. When did you arrive?"

"Just last night. I had expected to be delayed, but my schedule cleared unexpectedly."

"Mine as well."

"You were right, Henry," Lavinia chimed in as she took her seat again. "It was just a business matter."

"She had feared some fatal accident had befallen your mother," Emberly told Rome.

"I'm sorry I worried you," Rome said with a smile at Lavinia. "I was coming out here anyway, and a business acquaintance asked that I pass an important message to Marc."

"I thought house parties bored you," Lavinia teased.

Rome cast a smile at the group, lingering for half a second longer on Anna. "This one promises to be quite stimulating."

Conscious of Lavinia's watchful gaze, Anna kept her own expression polite. "Lord Haverford has suggested a picnic tomorrow, Mr. Devereaux.

Are you certain you will find so mundane a pastime entertaining?"

"Of course he will!" Henrietta exclaimed, with a chiding look at her daughter.

"On the contrary, I find I am quite fatigued from my journey this evening."

"How disappointing." Mrs. Rosewood gave a charming smile. "But you will join us for dinner, I hope? Miss Fellhopper has promised us a concert afterward. She has a lovely singing voice."

He glanced over at Charlotte. "I look forward to hearing her."

Anna followed his gaze, where pretty Charlotte laughed and teased her brother over a hand of cards. Her heart twisted with pathetic jealousy, and she had to turn away. She must control her emotions. Rome was an eligible gentleman, and Charlotte was an unmarried lady. He had every right to admire her, to even pursue her if he chose.

Just because Anna had been foolish enough to lose her heart to a man she could not have did not mean Rome should not find happiness elsewhere.

She withdrew into herself as the conversation continued around her. Curse the man! He wasn't supposed to be here, confusing her with all these forbidden emotions. He was supposed to be safely in London while she did her best to lure Haverford into a marriage proposal here in the country. His very presence tempted her to forget about honor and follow her heart.

But this she could not do. Her family depended on her to make the excellent match they had arranged for her, and she had no wish to create such a scandal that it would ruin Rome's chances at a future.

And he knew that, drat him. He knew their association was wrong, and yet here he was, standing before her. She knew that nothing so inconsequential as a house party would have drawn him away from London and the investigation of the Black Rose Society. That meant that something had happened to bring him here—something to do with the society.

She needed to talk to him alone and find out what he was doing here, then she would do everything in her power to make certain he left again with all possible haste.

Because as long as Rome Devereaux was close enough to see, hear, and touch, there was no way on this earth she could ever muster the strength to agree to marry another man.

At long last, the house fell silent.

Rome had expected to slip into a deep slumber upon returning to his room, given the exhausting events of the past couple of days. But his mind would not rest, and so he had lain in bed, tossing and turning amongst the tangled sheets, images of Peter's lifeless body haunting him.

Finally, he had given up on sleep and turned to whiskey for comfort.

He stood before the window, moonlight bathing his nude body beneath the open dressing gown, his third glass of whiskey in his hand. Outside, the manicured lawns of Haverford Park glimmered in the soft, silver light of the moon, as if painted by the faerie folk.

If a man believed in that sort of thing.

He tossed back a swallow of whiskey. A man like him only believed in the pistol in his hand and the woman at his side. What he could see, taste, and touch. Feelings were foreign to him, uncomfortable. He had gotten into the habit of suppressing his emotions if they interfered with his work.

Love refused to be suppressed.

His throat clogged, and he sucked in a deep breath to keep the unmanly tears at bay. Another swallow of whiskey helped. Damn it, he would not bawl like a babe over what he'd lost.

Anna. Peter.

Peter was dead. Gone. Never to return. The immediate danger around the note had seen to it that Rome could not even attend the funeral. No, he must stand by and watch over the woman he loved.

Watch her with another man.

He choked back the last of the whiskey, then grabbed the bottle off the night table. All his life, he had tried to act with honor. Was this his reward? To lose the boy he was supposed to protect? To fail his fallen friend? To stand by, helpless, as the woman he loved wed another man?

.

When would it be his turn to step out of the shadows and live in the sunshine?

A sound outside his door made him tense. Quietly, he set down the bottle and glass, then tied the sash of his robe with two efficient tugs. The scrape of the latch sent him to his night table, where his pistol rested in the drawer. As the door slowly creaked open, he ducked to one side of the window and blended into the shadows.

A figure in white slipped into his room, closed the door silently, then began to creep toward the bed. Rome stepped out of hiding, pistol extended. "That's far enough."

The figure stopped. "Rome?"

Anna.

"What the devil are you doing here?" He lowered the pistol, then went to the night table and shoved it back into the drawer. "Get out."

"I need to speak to you." She came forward into the rectangle of moonlight reflected through the window. Though she looked the part of an innocent lady in her modest white nightdress and wrapper and her hair streaming down her back in luxuriant waves, he knew what passion lurked inside her.

Wanted it.

"It's important. You know I would not take such a risk otherwise."

"I'm warning you to leave." He grabbed his whiskey bottle and poured a generous glass.

"What's happened?" She moved toward him, her face soft with concern.

"What are you talking about?" He turned his back on her, didn't dare look at her. He held up the bottle. "I'm having a drink is all."

"I know something has happened, Rome. Nothing less than utter disaster could have pulled you from London at this time."

He curled his hand around his whiskey glass and bent his head. "Peter Brantley is dead."

"Oh, no," she gasped. "Was he the one . . . was he the friend you had in the society?"

"He was." He turned to face her, gripping his glass tightly to keep from reaching for her. "The society killed him. He's dead because he tried to leave the country."

She tilted her head, her luxuriant hair spilling over her shoulder. "Did you come here to tell me about it?"

He gave a harsh laugh. "Hardly. Don't you remember? I told you I cannot be your partner."

Confusion flickered across her face. "Then why are you here and not at Peter's funeral?"

Unable to stop himself, he touched her cheek. "Because of you."

She sucked in a breath and took a step back. His hand fell to his side. "But you just said . . ."

"You're in danger, pet. That note of your brother's? Apparently the society would kill to get it back." His lips twisted. "I'm here to make sure you stay alive."

"Oh." She glanced down at her hands, tangling her fingers together.

"Did you think I was here for some other reason? Undying love?" He chuckled, the sound bleak even to his own ears. "Duty brings me here, Anna."

"I see." When she raised her head, unshed tears glimmered in her eyes. "That is all to the good, I suppose. When do you plan on leaving?"

The question sliced his heart. "Eager to be rid of me?"

"You're a complication, Rome. It's just a matter of time before his lordship makes an offer for me, and I don't want any hint of our past to ruin that."

"Do you think I would tell him? Good God, Anna, I owe that man everything I have!"

"I know. I'm sorry." She took a shuddering breath, and he couldn't help but notice how her breasts shifted beneath the thin lawn of her nightclothes. "But when you are here . . . Dear Lord, Rome, but I can't think. I can't see anyone but you."

"That's not the way to make me leave here." He threw back his head and inhaled deeply, struggling for control. "I just lost Peter. I was supposed to protect him. I can't lose you, too."

She gave him a sad smile. "I was never really yours, Rome."

"The hell you weren't." She flinched at his profanity, and he gave her a wicked smirk, whiskey fueling the frustrated anger racing through his veins. "You come apart in my arms, Anna. I may not have the right to claim you, but you can't say that you were never really mine."

"We both know the right thing to do here."

"Stay apart? Is that it?" He set down the whiskey. "Is that what you want?"

She closed her eyes, pressing her lips together as a tear slithered down her cheek. "It's what we have to do," she whispered.

"Is it so wrong to love you?"

Her eyes sprang open, her lips parting in shock.

He gave a grating laugh. "Yes, I love you. I didn't want to, but I didn't have a choice." He stepped closer, the scent of her luring him over the boundary of propriety. "I just lost a good friend to the sword of the enemy, and the woman I love is promised to marry another man. It seems to me I don't have much more to lose." He laid his palm alongside her cheek.

The tenderness of his caress belied the cut of his words. She nuzzled her face against his hand for just a moment, his merest touch sending her heart beating in a quick, steady rhythm. "I didn't come here for this," she murmured.

"Why did you come here, Anna?" He speared his fingers into her hair, his gaze intense. "Into my room, so late at night?"

"To find out why you're here. When you're leaving." His scent teased her, and she had to bite the inside of her cheek to keep from kissing the wrist only inches from her mouth.

"I'm here for you. And I'm not leaving until I know you're safe." He slid his hand to the back of her neck and pulled her forward until their foreheads rested against each other. "I will always be there for you, Anna. Watching you. Protecting you. Loving you."

Her throat tightened. "Don't make this any harder."

"I'm not asking for anything."

She lowered her gaze to his throat, lest he see the desperate hunger in her eyes. "What will you do when the danger is past?"

"Leave here. Leave England, maybe." He let out a long, whiskey-scented sigh. "I can't be around you without wanting you, and I won't dishonor you or Haverford that way."

She swallowed hard, the lump in her throat the size of a plum. "Thank you."

He shuddered, then pushed her away. "Go back to your bed, Anna. Having you here, in my room, is more than I can resist. Especially now."

Bereft without his touch, she stood numbly and watched him reach for his whiskey glass again. His hand trembled as he lifted it to his lips. "You cared for Peter very much."

He swallowed, then nodded, setting down the glass. "I promised my friend on his deathbed that I would watch over his brother. Peter was like my own sibling." His voice roughened on the last word, and he turned away, leaning forward to rest both hands on the night table. "Go back to bed, Anna."

He was mourning. It was there in the taut

planes of his face, the stiffness of his posture. The half-empty whiskey bottle told the tale, as did the barely eaten tray of food on the bureau.

He was hurting, he was grieving, and he was alone.

And she couldn't walk away.

She came to him, sliding a comforting hand down his back. "Tell me about him."

"I can't think when you touch me." He shrugged her away, then walked to the window. "He was a good lad. A bit hotheaded, always thinking he was more adult than he was. He was due to come into his inheritance when he turned twenty-five, and it frustrated him that he had to wait." His mouth curved. "He would have done well for himself."

"I'm so sorry, Rome."

"I've lost men before, but never someone so close to me." He glanced at her, his face stark with emotion. "If anything happened to you, Anna, it would destroy me."

"Oh, God." Had anyone ever loved her that much? The tears won the battle, overflowing in streams down her face. How could she give him up? How could she possibly walk away from him to marry another man?

"Anna, what is it?" His eyes narrowed in alarm, he came to her, grasping her arms to peer into her face. "What's the matter, my darling girl?"

The genuine concern in his voice, in his eyes,

smashed through the walls of her defenses. Her barriers came tumbling down, demolished by the gentle power of love. She looked up into his beloved face, hiding nothing any longer.

"I love you, Rome. And I don't know how I will live without you."

Chapter 19

Her quiet whisper ripped through him like a pistol ball. "What did you say?"

"I love you. I've tried not to, but it doesn't work." She threw herself into his arms, pressing her sweet body against his. "Oh, Rome, what are we going to do?"

He shuddered and held her, his senses drowning in the soft, sweet-scented female that filled his arms. "Anna." He closed his eyes, rubbed his cheek against her fragrant hair.

"How can love be wrong?" she murmured into his shoulder. "It feels right. Like destiny."

He struggled to regain control, but the whiskey and his raw emotions burned through his weakening attempts at discipline. "You know how things are." He smoothed his hands over her back, greedily filling his palms with her silky tresses, stealing a moment before he had to walk away. "We can't be together."

"Because of a promise made between fathers." She pulled back enough to look up into his face. "It's not fair."

"I know." He should push her away, make her go back to her room.

But his hands would not obey his commands.

Her dark eyes looked fathomless in the moonlight. "I can see no man but you," she whispered.

"Sweet Jesus, Anna," he breathed, squeezing his eyes closed. "I haven't the will to resist. You must help me."

"I don't want you to resist." She slid her arms around his neck. "I want you to touch me. And kiss me. And make me feel all those wonderful feelings again."

His breathing stopped, and maybe his heart, too. "Anna . . ."

"I want to make you as wild as you make me. I want to make love with you, Roman."

"Dear God." His self-control trembled like a new foal, shaky and unsure.

"Tomorrow will come soon enough," she murmured, brushing her lips along his jaw. "But tonight is ours."

He fisted his hands in her wrapper. "I want you more than I want to breathe," he rasped, sweeping his hungry gaze over her face. "And I haven't the strength to walk away."

"Then don't." She pressed her mouth to his.

Any lingering resolve crumpled like paper in a roaring fire. She was everything he'd ever wanted and couldn't have. She was beauty and intelligence, courage and passion. And she wanted him.

For this one night, she would be his.

He lost himself in the comfort of her arms. Her kisses soothed the pain that tore at his heart, and her small hands swept away guilt and loss and longing.

Somehow he peeled away her wrapper, leaving her clad in her plain white nightdress. The moonlight touched on the fine lawn, and through the thin, pale cloth, he could see the shadows of her nipples and the feminine mound at the juncture of her thighs.

The sight excited him more than total nudity would have.

Her small hands settled at his waist and tugged at the knot of his sash. As the fabric parted, his erection rose proudly into view. She made a small sound of pleasure and closed her fingers around him. He groaned.

"I've wanted to see this again," she said, caressing him. "I want to see all of you."

He gave a rough laugh and stilled her curious fingers. "Easy, my love."

She bit her lower lip, her eyes widening with dismay. "Did I do something wrong?"

His heart clenched with love for her. "No. But there's no rush, and I want to play, too." He lowered his mouth to her throat, nipping the tender flesh there as he tugged her closer with his hands on her bottom. His erection nestled between her thighs, pressing against her hot mound. He rubbed himself against her in a slow, sensuous rhythm.

"Oh!" Her fingers dug into his shoulders.

"That's it, my love." He swept his open mouth along her throat. "Let yourself go."

She closed her eyes as sensations washed over her. His hands . . . his mouth . . . his hardness rubbing her *there* . . . She gave herself up to his greater experience and let him lead the way.

He took her mouth, his kisses slow and intoxicating and tasting of whiskey. He cupped her breast, and her mind spun as if she'd had too much sherry. He seemed to know every sensitive spot on her body, bringing each to life with a taste or touch.

When he took her nipple in his mouth right through her nightdress, coherent thought ceased all together.

She shoved his robe off his shoulders, and it dangled from his arms, moonlight gilding his muscular body. He let go of her for a moment to shake free of the garment, and even that brief instant was too long a time without his touch.

Then he came back to her, his naked body a work of art to her inexperienced eyes. He pulled her close, one arm firmly around her waist, the other hand cupping the back of her head. He took her mouth in a deep, carnal kiss that demanded everything she had to give.

She gave it, willingly—anything he asked, everything she was.

Her breasts ached, and the place between her legs felt hot and swollen. He held her to him as if he couldn't get close enough, his kisses slow, demanding, and insatiable.

His flesh warmed hers even through the thin lawn of her nightdress. At first she was grateful for the garment, but soon it became less like protection and more like a barrier. When he grabbed a handful of the gown and dragged it over her head, she helped him discard it.

As the nightdress hit the floor in a crumpled heap, he stopped and just studied her from head to toe. His intent regard should have embarrassed her, but instead she found herself easing her shoulders back to present her breasts more fully. He reached out to smooth a hand along her bare hip, and her nipples tightened in reaction.

"You were made for moonlight," he said, then pulled her back into his arms for another heated kiss. Flesh to flesh they stood, bathed in eerie silver light, greedy hands clinging to smooth skin, pulses galloping in equal frenzy.

Glorious. His hand on her bare bottom sent a thrill zinging straight to her loins, and his hardness nudged her thighs apart, sliding between them to rest snugly against her aching flesh.

"Come to bed," he murmured, nipping at her lower lip.

She nodded, unable to speak. He took her hand and led her to his bed, then with a simple gesture urged her to lie down. As she clambered onto the bed, he caressed her bottom again, and she hurriedly flipped onto her back, cheeks burning that he had been looking so closely at that part of her body.

She had settled into the middle of the mattress. He chuckled, then hooked an arm around her waist, urged her closer to the edge, and turned her so her legs hung off the bed.

"That's nice." He flashed a smile and nudged her knees apart so he could step between her legs.

Her heart skipped madly at their position. He looked down at her, and she realized he could see every inch of her most private places. She flexed her fingers against the coverlet, somehow knowing that if she tried to cover herself, he wouldn't allow it.

"Don't worry, my sweet." He stroked his fingers along her throat and down her body, between her breasts, over her belly to rest on the damp, curling hair between her thighs. "I just want to admire you. You're so beautiful."

His eyes glowed with sincerity, and her tense muscles slowly relaxed.

"That's it." He tangled his fingers in her private curls, stroking her as sweetly as if she were a kitten. "Let me make you feel good." His other hand glided along her thigh, testing the firm flesh with gentle squeezes.

A soft gasp escaped her lips as his thumb glided over her pleasure button.

"Yes, that's right, my sweet." The hand on her thigh smoothed its way up her torso to her breast and plumped the sensitive flesh. "Just lie back and let me love you."

Their encounters in the garden paled beneath this tender onslaught. He touched her everywhere, kissed her in places she had never thought to be kissed. He murmured words of praise about her beauty and her passion. Each caress spiked her breathing and tripped her heart. Her body became his plaything, his hands those of a master who knew exactly where to touch, when to tease.

Every inch of her flesh ached for him. Her nipples strained for his mouth; her skin grew damp with perspiration. By the time he finally leaned over her, his erection poised at the entrance to her body, she thought she would go mad with wanting him.

"You are everything a man could want," he murmured, looking deep into her eyes. "I love you now, and I will love you for the rest of my life."

"Rome." She raised a trembling hand to his face. "I want no man but you."

He nuzzled her hand, his eyes closing for a brief instant as he savored the contact. Then he took her hand and linked it with his, smiling down at her with a tenderness that made her heart roll over in her chest. "Hold on to me, my love. The first time is usually difficult for a woman."

Their fingers still entwined, he kissed her as he guided himself carefully into her virgin passage.

It stung. Her whimper got lost in their kiss, and she clenched her fingers around his, her other hand gripping his shoulder. Steadily, he pressed on until the full length of him filled her completely.

He stilled then, lying on top of her with their bodies joined, kissing her and caressing her until the discomfort finally eased.

When he began to move, she tensed, but the pain had passed. Gradually she relaxed, lost in the fascinating sensation of his body joining with hers. He lengthened his strokes, hooking an arm beneath her knee to tug her leg over his hip. The position seated him even more deeply within her, bringing a startled gasp to her lips.

He halted. "Am I hurting you?"

"No." She arched her hips, desperate for more of him. "Please don't stop."

"My love." He pressed a kiss to her lips. "This is only the beginning."

She curled her other leg around him, locking her feet together behind his back as he picked up the rhythm again. She linked her arms around his neck, buried her face in his shoulder, and held him close, as if she could absorb all of him into her.

When he groaned and shuddered with his pleasure, she tightened her arms and legs around him as tears trickled down her cheeks.

Her passion had saved him.

Rome lay crosswise on the bed with Anna in his arms, more content than he had any right to be. The biting grief of Peter's death had dulled to a deep sorrow, and he knew with certainty that he would be able to get through another day.

But he didn't look forward to sunrise. With the light of the new day, Anna would leave him.

She shifted in his arms. "Are you awake?"

"Yes." He kissed the top of her head. "How are you?"

"Fine." She turned her face into his chest. "A bit sore, I suppose."

"I'm sorry about that. I tried to be careful."

"I know." She untangled herself and rolled to her other side, facing away from him. "I'm glad you were the one," she said softly.

He rolled toward her, fitting his body spoonlike to hers with an arm around her waist. "I also know," he murmured close to her ear, "that you didn't finish." His hand drifted downward.

"More?" she gasped as he slid his fingers between her legs.

"Not more. Still." He knew what she liked now and used that knowledge to arouse her. "You didn't finish. But you will."

"Rome!" She arched into his hand as the familiar excitement trickled into her veins. "Oh, my goodness."

"I know what you like." He nuzzled her neck, his fingers gliding over her damp flesh. "Sometimes a woman needs more."

"Oh, my. *Oh, my!*"

He rolled her onto her back, still caressing her, and took one nipple into his mouth. She stretched out, hands above her head, and gave him full access to her body. As her blood began to burn, she closed her eyes and surrendered to the building desire.

"Making love is about two people," he murmured against her skin. "And now it's your turn."

When she cried out her pleasure a short time later, it was his name she called.

The first glow of dawn lit the room when next Anna opened her eyes.

She lay wrapped in Rome's arms, the bed-clothes tangled around them. She stretched a little, and her body protested with unfamiliar aches in strange places. Rome murmured in his sleep and pulled her closer.

She looked up into his face, committing every detail to memory. The way his eyelashes looked against his skin, the way his beard darkened his jaw in the morning.

The way he held her like he would never let her go.

But it was morning, and the real world awaited

them. Their magical night had ended, and Anna knew she would take every minute of it to her grave. Gingerly, she slid out from beneath Rome's arm and slipped from the bed.

It felt strange to walk around naked in daylight. She padded to the middle of the room and picked up her nightdress from the floor, then slipped it over her head. Moderately covered, she next sought out her wrapper.

Once clothed, she went to the edge of the bed and looked at Rome. She didn't want to leave him; she wanted to crawl right back in bed with him and relive the night all over again. But the sun was rising, and people would be searching for her.

She and Rome would return to their normal lives and pretend nothing had happened.

He muttered in his sleep, then turned over, presenting her with his back. Just the sight of that long, lean expanse of flesh started the fires burning all over again.

She made herself turn away. She and Rome did not have a future together, and that was that. They would have to continue with their normal lives, and when they came in contact with each other—as they would, given that Marc was Rome's cousin—they would just have to try to avoid each other.

Her lover murmured in his sleep and turned flat on his back, his dark hair falling over his brow in boyish disarray.

Her heart fluttered like a bird's wings in her

breast, and she struggled to take a deep enough breath. Who was she trying to fool? Did she really think she could avoid him? Or pretend nothing had happened between them?

She had to. Somehow she had to learn to handle his presence, to control the wicked desire that tried to work its will on her every time she set eyes on him.

She had changed since she had first begun her quest. No more was she sweet Anna Rosewood, who always did what her parents bid her without the slightest complaint. She had tasted the heat of passion in the arms of a forbidden lover and had lied continuously to her parents about her where-abouts for the past year.

She had become someone she didn't know.

Was it dishonorable to give herself to the man she loved, especially since she was about to marry someone else? And what about Rome? What would happen to him if the secret got out? The scandal would destroy him.

She couldn't let Rome lose all chance of a future because of her.

Somehow she would convince him to leave Haverford Park. What had he said—that An-thony's note would draw the society to her?

Well, then, she would just give Rome the note. Perhaps if he thought the danger was past, he would go back to London and end this torment for both of them.

At one time, she would have protected that last link with her brother like a mother tiger with her cubs, but now she realized that Rome would do that for her. She could trust him to uncover the truth about Anthony's death and bring the Black Rose Society to justice.

She took one last look at him, then turned away from the bed. She'd best get back to her own room before someone discovered her missing.

She made it all the way back to her room unseen and had just laid her hand on the door latch when Lavinia came out of nowhere.

"What are you doing?" she hissed. Clad in her nightdress and wrapper with her hair a tangled mass of curls down her back, her face was pale and etched with fatigue. "Are you mad? Are you trying to *ruin* my brother?"

"Hush, before someone hears you." Anna glanced up and down the hall. No one was there. She opened the door and grabbed Lavinia by the arm, pulling her into the room. The instant the door clicked closed, Lavinia folded her arms and glared.

"Well? Would you like to tell me why I just saw you coming out of my brother's room at this hour of the morning?"

"I will tell you all, but if you don't keep your voice down, you will cause the very scandal you so wish to avoid."

"Fine." Lavinia lowered her tone to a whisper.

"Now explain what I just saw, if you please."

Anna's face heated. "I'm sure you can fathom the details for yourself."

"You spent the night with my brother? Here, beneath Haverford's roof?"

Anna folded her arms around her middle. "We love each other, Lavinia."

"This cannot happen again." Lavinia swept a hand over her mouth. "History cannot repeat itself."

"We have no intention of its happening again."

Lavinia pushed a hank of hair out of her face. "A Devereaux cannot steal the bride of the earl a second time. It would absolutely destroy this family."

"He has no intention of stealing me." Anna sat down on the edge of the bed and gestured for Lavinia to take the chair in front of her vanity table. "We love each other, Lavinia, but we understand the situation. Neither one of us intends to cause any sort of scandal."

"How long has this been going on?" Vin asked quietly.

"Just last night." Anna sighed, accepting Lavinia's disappointment. After all, Rome's sister wasn't making false accusations, and her concern came from love for her brother. "He received news that Peter Brantley died, and he was grieving. The rest . . ." She shrugged. "The rest just happened."

"Sweet heavens." If possible, Lavinia paled even more. "This is a very volatile situation,

Anna. If it had been anyone but me in the hallway just now, you and Rome would have both been ruined."

"I know." Anna dropped her eyes, twisting her fingers. "It was not something we planned. I tried to do what you said, to stay away from him. I couldn't know that he would follow us out here."

"I will speak to him today and ask him to go back to London. If he doesn't, Anna—" Lavinia waited until Anna met her gaze. "You will have to make certain you are chaperoned at all times. Next time it might be someone else who sees you in the hallway. Like Haverford. Or your parents."

"I will."

Lavinia stood, her expression troubled. "I am appalled at your conduct. I know you love my brother, but you are promised to my cousin. Only my love for Roman is preventing me from taking this tale to Haverford."

Shame flooded her. "I know. If it helps at all, I've rather shocked myself."

"No, it doesn't. See that you stay away from my brother, Anna. This is your only warning."

Lavinia swept out of the room, leaving Anna stunned and shaking behind her.

Chapter 20

Rome slept late into the day. When he finally rose, he discovered the rest of the household had already left for the picnic.

Just as well, he thought as he made his way to the breakfast room. He could go into Anna's room, find the note, and leave Haverford Park without even seeing her. Callous it might seem after the night they'd spent together, but he didn't trust himself around her. There was no way he'd be able to hide his feelings in front of the others, not after he'd made love to her.

He came into the breakfast room, hoping to find some remnant of food left over, and stopped dead in the doorway. Lavinia sat at the table, a cup of tea in front of her.

"Good morning, Rome," she said, unsmiling. "I've been waiting for you."

"Vin, what are you doing here?" Fruit and cheese had been left on the sideboard. Rome grabbed a plate and began piling it with food. "I thought you were supposed to go on a picnic today."

"I was. I told Henry I didn't feel well."

"Again?" Plate in one hand and coffee in the other, Rome sat down across from his sister. "Perhaps the house party is too much for you, Vin. Maybe you'd best go home and rest for a few days."

"I'm going nowhere, Roman Oliver Devereaux. I am staying right here, no matter how sick this babe makes me, to keep an eye on you and Miss Rosewood."

Rome choked on the coffee he had just sipped. Wiping his mouth with his napkin, he glanced around, noting there were no servants to be seen. Haverford had given them all the day off, he remembered.

Which meant that Vin didn't have to mince words.

"I met dear Anna in the hallway this morning," she continued, idly stirring her tea. "She had just left *your* room and gone back to her own."

"I'm sure she was just lost."

Vin dropped the spoon on her saucer with a loud clank. "Don't even try and lie to me, Roman.

I know what happened. Just be glad it was I who saw her and not Haverford."

"She was gone when I awoke." He reached out and touched his sister's hand. "It was a mistake, Vin. One we have no intention of making again."

"It is not just a mistake," she whispered, pulling her hand from beneath his. "It is a potential disaster. Roman, after the way we grew up, I would expect you to have more control."

"Don't you think I know that?" He fisted his hand where it rested on the table. "Damn it, Vin, I love her."

His raw words echoed in the silence.

"I suspected as much," she finally said, her tone sad. She reached for him now and placed her hand over his clenched one. "Rome, you are so close to achieving your dream. I just don't want something like this to destroy you."

"I'm not our father, Vin." He turned his hand so their fingers entwined. "I have no intention of making the same mistakes he did."

"I'm glad of that."

"But I must admit, feeling the way I do about Anna, I begin to wonder if I haven't judged him too harshly all these years."

She snatched her hand back. "I can't agree."

"I accept that." He curled both palms around his coffee cup. "I've never felt this way about anyone before, Vin. I've tried to do the honorable thing, but my heart keeps leading me back to her."

Her face softened. "You love her that much?

Enough to risk hurting your family and ruining your future?"

"I do." He let out a long sigh. "If things were different, I could have courted her openly. Why did she have to be Haverford's intended?"

"They're not engaged yet," Vin pointed out. "They just have an understanding."

"And as to that—why is he hesitating? Why doesn't he just offer for her and do away with all of this uncertainty?"

"I don't know." Vin sipped her tea. "Perhaps he had the ring reset and is waiting for the jeweler. Or perhaps there is something in the marriage settlement that needs to be addressed."

"Or maybe he has no intention of asking her."

Vin put down her teacup with a sharp click. "I know that look, Roman. What are you thinking?"

"I'm thinking that Marc has not asked Anna to marry him. Maybe he never will."

"Roman . . ."

"Should I stand by as my love grows cold while Marc dithers? Or should I act now, while Anna is still unattached, and offer for her myself?"

"You promised you would not follow in our father's footsteps!"

"I'm not. Father ran off with the old earl's affianced bride. That was the scandal; they were already betrothed, and of course, Father was already married. What if I declare myself to Marc? Tell him how I feel about Anna? Perhaps we can yet be together."

"Dear Lord." Lavinia buried her face in her hand. "You will ruin us all, brother."

"I won't. I promise you, Vin, I won't. But I have to follow my heart."

"I know you do." She lowered her hand and met his gaze head on. "I was going to ask you to go back to London, to forget this thing with Anna. But I can see now that you will never do that."

"I can't. Not if there's a chance we can be together."

"Then I ask this one thing of you: please do this with honor. Don't tear apart our family again."

"I promise." He grinned, eager as a lad on holiday. "I will talk to Marc before I do anything. Perhaps I am right, and he has no intention of offering for Anna."

"I have been waiting for the right moment," Lord Haverford said as he walked with Anna along the path through the woods. On the other side of the trees, they could hear the rest of their picnic party screeching with laughter as they competed to see who could skip a stone the farthest. "It never seemed to come, so I will have to make my own."

"The moment for what, my lord?"

Haverford stopped right in the middle of the path and took her hand. "I have spoken to your father, Anna, and he has given me his consent to ask you to be my wife."

Though she'd expected it, hearing the words still stunned her.

Haverford reached into his pocket and withdrew a small velvet pouch. He tugged it open and poured the contents into his hand. The Haverford family engagement ring sat nestled in his palm, the deep blue sapphire surrounded with diamonds glittering in the sun.

"I've been carrying this with me for several days," he said, as she stared mutely at the ring. "It belonged to my mother and my grandmother before her."

"It's beautiful," she managed.

"You haven't yet given me your answer, Anna. Will you marry me and be my countess?"

She raised her gaze to his, words jamming in her throat. Finally, she squeezed out a reply. "I would be honored, my lord."

He grinned. "Thank goodness. For a moment, I thought you were going to refuse me." He slipped the empty pouch into his pocket, then took her hand and slid the heavy sapphire onto her finger. "It fits well. I'm glad. Shall we tell the others?"

She nodded, still unable to speak. Her conflicting emotions had tangled up her insides and stolen her voice. As he led her back to the rest of the party, she glanced down at the glittering heirloom ring adorning her finger.

Never had she seen so beautiful a key to a prison.

* * *

She had accepted Haverford's suit.

Dressed for dinner, Rome slowly made his way down the hall. His plans to search Anna's room spiked by Lavinia's presence, he had instead spent the afternoon preparing to approach Anna about their future. He'd even girded himself to speak to Marc, hoping he could find the words to explain the situation without reopening the wounds left by his father's ill-conceived actions.

But it was too late. She was betrothed, and nothing would stay Haverford from his course.

"Rome." Anna stepped out from behind a statue of Zeus throwing a thunderbolt.

"Anna, what are you doing here?" He took in her pure white dress and the flowers in her hair. "You look beautiful." His gaze dropped to the Devereaux sapphire adorning her hand.

"I don't know if you've heard, but I have accepted an offer from Lord Haverford." She traced the ring of diamonds around the sapphire. "I wanted to tell you myself."

"I had heard. Congratulations." He forced a smile.

"You don't have to pretend." Her dark eyes searched his face. "I know you're not happy about this."

"What I feel doesn't matter here." Somehow he managed to keep the words from choking him. "We knew it was going to happen."

"Yes." She bit her lower lip, then dug into her

reticule. "Here. I believe this is what you need." She pulled out a much-folded piece of paper and handed it to him.

He took it, barely believing that she had so readily handed it over. He unfolded it and found himself looking at the symbol of the Black Rose Society. "I thought you would have wanted to keep this. In memory of your brother."

"I did want to keep it, but I also know that as long as I am in danger, you are bound here by your stubborn pride." She sniffed, her eyes misting. "Take it and go back to London, Rome. Bring the Black Rose Society to its knees so I know my brother's murderers have been brought to justice."

"Anna." He reached for her, but she flinched away.

"Just leave here so that I don't die a little bit every time I look into your eyes," she whispered, then turned away with a sob and hurried down the hall, late for her betrothal celebration.

Somehow she made it through dinner, though every time she glanced down the table and saw Rome, a shard of pain pierced her heart. When the ladies finally retired to the drawing room, she got a brief respite.

"Congratulations on your betrothal, Anna," Charlotte said. She glanced down at the engagement ring, and some fierce emotion flashed across her face too quickly for Anna to identify it.

"Thank you, Charlotte."

"Yes, congratulations," Lavinia said. She looked weary, and leaned back in her comfortable chair as if she would fall asleep right there.

"Are you feeling ill again?" Anna asked, genuinely concerned.

"I've been ill rather constantly for the past few weeks," Lavinia said. "It keeps me awake, so I haven't been able to sleep very well."

"You poor dear," Henrietta said. "I remember those days. Have you tried weak tea and toast?"

"It is practically all I can eat these days."

Before she could say anything more, the door opened to admit the men. Anna noticed Charlotte sending one more quick glance at the Devereaux sapphire before the blond woman turned to greet the men with her usual social smile.

Henry Emberly came over to his pale, fading wife. "Lavinia, dear, are you still unwell?"

"If I could only sleep one night through, I'm certain I would feel so much better."

"My poor dear."

Rome walked in behind the other men, and Anna found her gaze drawn to him. He glanced at her, a visual caress that made her tingle to her toes. Then he noticed Lavinia and frowned. "You really do not look well at all, Vin. You should probably retire early tonight."

"For what purpose? All I do is toss and turn."

Haverford came up to Anna and laid a hand on

her shoulder. She jumped. "What's happening?" the earl whispered.

"Lavinia is ill," Anna replied softly. "I believe it is affecting her ability to sleep."

"Poor thing." He stepped away, and suddenly she could breathe again. "Lavinia, I have a recipe for a toddy my grandmother swore by. Would you like me to have Cook brew some for you tonight? It's supposed to put you right to sleep."

Lavinia looked up at him with tears in her eyes. "I will try anything at this point, Marc."

"Very well, then. I will see to it."

Rome rested his hand on Lavinia's shoulder, then glanced over at Anna. His green-eyed gaze spoke of love and secrets and whispers in the night.

Her heart bumped in her chest, like hatboxes in the boot of the carriage. Her mind touched on images from last night—the memory of his hands and his lips and the wicked surprises he had revealed to her. They had spent the whole night making love, then sleeping, then waking to enjoy each other again.

How in heaven would she be able to sleep in her cold, lonely bed tonight with the memories of last night haunting her?

Marc walked past her to summon a servant, and she touched his sleeve. He stopped. "Yes, my dear?"

"Would you ask the cook to send me one of

those toddies, too?" she asked. "I'm certain I shall not sleep a wink with the excitement today."

Haverford smiled. "Of course." He touched her hand, then went to summon the servant.

Anna turned back to the rest of the party, studiously avoiding a pair of knowing green eyes.

Before Haverford even reached the door, Leighton entered the room. "Mr. Edgar Vaughn," he announced.

Edgar Vaughn entered the room. "Good evening, Lord Haverford."

"Vaughn." Clearly puzzled, but ever the charming host, the earl welcomed his unexpected guest. "May I offer you a drink?"

"That would be splendid. It was a long ride from London."

Haverford glanced at his cousin. "Rome, would you please get Mr. Vaughn a drink while I have a word with Cook?"

"Certainly." Rome sent an enigmatic glance at Vaughn, then went to the sideboard. "What's your pleasure, Vaughn?"

"Brandy."

Rome poured a glass and brought it to the older man. "What are you doing here?" he murmured.

"I followed you." Vaughn gave him a mocking salute, then sipped from the glass. "Go along with what I say, and by the by, it's all true."

The earl came back. "Mr. Vaughn, I must admit surprise. What are you doing here?"

"Business with your cousin, actually." Vaughn

turned to Rome. "We must discuss that problem with the Russian ambassador, Devereaux. It's rather urgent."

Lavinia sat straight up in her chair. "Roman, did you accept the diplomatic position?"

Rome sent a baffled look at Vaughn, who clapped him on the shoulder as if they were close friends. "Of course he did. Didn't you tell your family, Devereaux?"

"Uh . . . no."

"How could you not share such news?" Emberly came over and shook his hand. "Congratulations, Roman."

"Yes, congratulations!" Haverford clapped him on the back.

Lavinia launched herself out of her chair and into her brother's arms. "I'm so proud of you!"

Next came the Fellhoppers, then the Rosewoods with congratulations. Last came Anna, her face luminous with pride, her eyes dark with longing. "Congratulations, Mr. Devereaux. You deserve such a distinguished position."

"Thank you, Miss Rosewood." Rome turned to Vaughn. "You must wish Lord Haverford happy," Rome said. "He and Miss Rosewood have just become betrothed."

"Well, then, this is a night of celebration, isn't it?" Vaughn said with a chuckle.

Rome watched Anna as she went back to Haverford's side, silently mourning for what he could never have. "Quite."

Chapter 21

There was no reason for him to stay.

Rome carefully folded the note and tucked it into a hidden pocket of his satchel. Anna was safely engaged to Haverford and he could return to London and finish his mission to bring the Black Rose Society to justice.

He tucked his satchel in a corner. He would leave first thing in the morning with Edgar Vaughn, since Haverford had offered the man a room for the night.

Vaughn's unexpected appearance had thrown him, but a short, private conversation with the man had proven enlightening.

While Vaughn had indeed followed him with the intent of working together to end the reign of the Black Rose Society, apparently the diplomat had also decided to give him the position after all. They would work together on this mission, then Rome's diplomatic career would begin. After working so long and hard toward his dream, he could hardly credit that he had at last achieved it.

His glance fell on the bed. Most of his dream, that is.

The huge bed mocked him with its emptiness. Anna belonged to another man now, and there was no way they could ever be together. He walked over and smoothed a hand along the mattress. How was he supposed to sleep here, knowing she was so close and yet forever forbidden to his arms?

He clenched his hand in the coverlet, his heart aching with loss. First Peter, then Anna. Was there any use in loving when the heart could be so easily rent by it? He pictured a night of tossing and turning while his demons laughed at him in his mind. Blast it all, he should have asked for one of Haverford's hot toddies.

He jerked away from the bed. Grandmother's toddy wouldn't have been enough anyway. He needed whiskey.

He stalked out of the room, his destination Haverford's liquor cabinet in the first floor study. If he couldn't have peace, he would take oblivion.

But somehow, he found himself in the hallway near Anna's room.

Fool. That way lay nothing but more heartache.

Still he lingered there, watching her door, thinking about her dressed in her nightclothes and wrapped in the covers.

Thinking about undressing her and unwrapping her.

Idiocy. Everything had fallen into place as expected, and he could ruin all if he tarried. She belonged to Haverford. She wore his ring.

And he was not his father.

The scrape of a footstep made him tense. Lavinia? No, she was safe in slumber, thanks to Grandmother's toddy. Anna? His heart skipped a beat, excitement flooding his veins. Wait, no, it couldn't be Anna. She had taken Grandmother's toddy, too.

So who else would be sneaking around the house so late at night?

He slipped into a shadowed niche and waited.

Someone walked softly down the hall, no candle lit, as if they knew the way. Rome hadn't brought a candle either, but he had good vision at night and knew the house intimately from childhood. Anyone else should have needed light to navigate the labyrinth of hallways.

The whole situation took on a sinister cast. He tensed, ready to act on a moment's notice.

"Devereaux?" came a whisper. "Blast it, where did you go?"

Rome frowned and stepped out of the niche. "Vaughn?"

The other man startled. "Damn it, man, you move like the wind."

"What are you doing skulking around the hallways?" Rome asked.

"Looking for you. I saw you leave your room and thought you were doing a bit of reconnaissance. Good idea with all the danger afoot."

Rome seized on the excuse. "Exactly."

"If you're taking this wing of the house, I'll patrol the other," Vaughn whispered.

"Excellent notion." At least the activity would get him away from Anna's door.

"I've brought my pistol," Vaughn whispered. "I'll fire it off in case of emergency."

"Very good."

"We'll share our findings in the morning, unless something happens before then. Be careful, Devereaux."

"You, too, Vaughn."

Vaughn gave a single, quick nod and went back the way he came, headed for the other wing of the house.

Rome started in the other direction. He probably should have told Vaughn that he had the note in his possession. There would be time enough for that in the morning, he supposed.

Whiskey abandoned for the moment, he set about patrolling the wing he'd been assigned.

She should have taken that toddy.

Anna flipped over, tugging the coverlet up

around her shoulders. She had come within a breath of drinking down the honey-flavored beverage, but reconsidered.

Did she really want to forget last night's events?

Earlier, she had thought she might enjoy lying in her bed, reliving her one and only night with the man she loved and had offered the toddy to her mother, whose excitement about the wedding had left her jittery and overstimulated. Now she wished she had taken the dratted thing.

Well, at least one of them would sleep tonight. Anna's fond memories had quickly turned to teasing bits of torment as the hours passed, and slumber eluded her. Had she really thought she would enjoy reliving that night, when there was no way she would ever again sleep in Rome's arms?

Foolish girl. She was engaged to be married to a kind man who would provide for her always. She should accept her lot and be grateful. Instead, she longed for a man she could not have.

She heard a sound in the hallway, and her heart leaped. Rome? Had he come to her?

She nearly sat up in the bed, but her engagement ring caught on the bedsheets, reminding her of how matters stood. She couldn't welcome him, no matter how much her heart sang at the thought. She had pledged herself to Haverford of her own free will, and she must honor that pledge, no matter how much she longed to be with Rome. Sucking in a shuddering breath, she forced herself to remain still, as if lost in slumber.

Hopefully he would leave when he saw she was sleeping, because if he woke her with a kiss, she knew she wouldn't have the strength to send him away.

The door creaked open. Her pulse sped up, and her hands trembled with the effort it took to remain still. Someone crept into the room, footsteps a soft scuffle in the silence of the night.

The temptation to throw back the covers and invite him to join her was unbearable.

She expected him to come to her bedside, to whisper her name. But instead he went to her vanity table and quietly began looking through her things. What in the world . . . ?

She shifted just a bit so she could see him. The lean shadow of a man froze at her movement, but when she remained still, he continued his search. He finished at the vanity and went toward the wardrobe, passing the window as he did so.

Moonlight gleamed off the hilt of the sword buckled at his waist.

Anna gasped as fear shot through her. The tiny sound betrayed her, and the intruder turned in her direction. Abandoning her pretense, Anna threw back the covers to slide from the bed. He leaped on her, his heavy body flattening her back against the mattress. Gripping her hair painfully near the scalp, he jerked her face close to his.

In the soft light of the moon, she saw he wore a mask.

"Where is it?" he demanded, in a guttural whisper.

"What?"

He jerked her head back. A whimper escaped her lips. "The note. Tell me, or I'll snap your neck."

"I don't have it."

"Liar." He jerked her head again. "Tell me."

"I don't!"

"Then you're of no use to me." He released her with a jerk, grabbed a pillow, and pressed it down over her face. "Poor dear, you were supposed to be asleep," he hissed. "Why didn't you drink your toddy? Is this the behavior of an obedient wife?"

That voice . . . it sounded familiar. Her mind struggled for the association even as she gasped for breath. But her lungs drew no air. He was smothering her!

Suddenly he lurched away. There was a smash of breaking glass. She threw the pillow from her face and sat up, sucking in sweet, fresh air.

"Bastard." Rome loomed over her fallen assailant, a broken lantern in his hand. "Looking for something?"

The masked man leaped to his feet and charged at Rome. The two men crashed to the floor, rolled. Rome's broken lantern skidded away. They punched. Kicked. The masked man jumped on top of Rome and closed his hands around Rome's throat.

Anna jumped from the bed and grabbed the pitcher from the bureau, then swung it at the intruder's head. He raised an arm at the last instant and knocked the pitcher from her grasp. It flew across the room and shattered.

Rome shoved the man away and scrambled to his feet. The masked man leaped up and escaped through the French doors leading out to the terrace that ran the length of the house.

Rome grabbed Anna by the shoulders. "Are you all right?"

She nodded, still stunned by the attack.

"Good." He pressed a hard kiss to her lips, then shoved her toward the bedroom door. "Go for help." Then he plunged through the French doors in pursuit of the villain.

The terrace led out to a sweeping dining area off the ballroom. Thanks to a night with a nearly full moon, Rome was able to keep his prey in sight. The man would either have to descend the stairs into the garden or escape through the house.

He raced past Haverford's room and saw the gleam of crossed swords on the wall. He stopped. Better to face this enemy armed and with help from his trusted friend, Vaughn. Going back to his cousin's bedroom, he jerked at the handles to the French doors, but they were locked. He pounded on the glass. No answer. He peered into the room and made out the dim shadow of Haverford's bed. Empty.

"Bollocks!" With a silent apology to his cousin, he braced himself and then rammed his elbow through the glass by the handles. Careful of the razor-sharp shards, he reached inside and unlatched the door. It swung open.

He charged into Haverford's room and took in the multiple sets of swords mounted on the wall. Ah, that one. He grabbed an elegant rapier. This had always been his favorite when fencing with Marc.

Armed, he raced back out to the terrace, hoping the intruder had not evaded him.

His intimate knowledge of the house aided him as he sped along the terrace, dodging objects. He poured on the speed, and as he came upon the open patio, he saw his assailant racing for the stairs that led to the garden. With a roar, he leaped, tackling the intruder.

They crashed to the hard stone of the patio, and his sword skittered away. He rolled off the intruder and scrambled over to retrieve his fallen weapon. When he turned around, the other man had just gotten to his feet.

Upon seeing the sword, the masked man laughed. "You think to challenge me to a duel? Have you any idea how many men I've killed?"

Rome took his stance, blade at the ready. "I know how many boys you've killed."

His opponent growled with displeasure and whipped out his sword. "I will be happy to add one more kill to my list."

He leaped forward, taking the offense in a move that surprised Rome.

Swords clashed as they exploded into battle. The masked man was good—better than good. He was clearly a master. But Rome had rage and grief on his side. This blackguard had tried to kill Anna and had probably lent a hand in Peter's death as well. There was no way on this earth he would escape this time.

He was fast. Rome parried a quick volley of blows, barely able to keep time with the swordsman. Their blades locked, and he gave a shove, sending the other man stumbling back.

Rome had greater height and weight on his side, but the other man's slender build gave him an edge when it came to agility. The masked man darted here and there, his blade slashing wickedly. The Society ring on his right hand gleamed in the moonlight, the bloodred ruby a sign of the Triad.

This was no ordinary member. He was one of the leaders.

A lucky swipe drew blood from Rome's cheek.

"So sorry," the other man sneered, then laughed in glee, his blade flashing again.

Rome parried, then pressed in with his own attack. He may not have fought many duels, but he had the experience of the battlefield to guide him. He feinted and drew blood with a quick slice to the rib cage. His opponent danced away, but not in time to avoid the blow completely.

"You think to best me?" Voice harsh with rage, the masked man stepped up the pace.

Rome kept up, but barely. Already he gasped for breath, his heavier build starting to work against him. Blood dripped from his cheek and trailed down his collar. Sweat trickled down his temple. Their sword hilts locked again, and Rome shoved the other man, unlocking their weapons and sending him staggering backwards. Pressing the advantage, Rome charged forward with a cry, determined to cut down this murderer once and for all.

At the last second, the masked man moved his sword out of the way and brought up his other hand. Rome saw the knife an instant too late. He dodged and took the brunt of the blow just beneath his collarbone.

Pain seared through his flesh. He sucked in a breath, struggling for coherence, determined not to lose this battle.

Someone shouted, and a shot rang out. The masked man shoved Rome away and escaped down the stairs. Rome pressed a hand to his wound, blood flooding through his fingers as he staggered and fell. He lay there, gasping, fighting against the blackness that edged his vision.

Running footsteps. The hysterical babble of voices. Again, the harsh crack of a pistol.

"Got the bastard!" Vaughn's triumphant cry.

Someone knelt beside him and gently urged him onto his back. Marc. Still clad in his dressing gown, the earl examined his wound, his mouth grim. "It's bad," he said.

The admiral appeared behind Haverford, offering a handkerchief. "Use this until we can get him inside."

Marc took the snowy linen and pressed it to the puncture. Rome's breath hissed out from between his teeth as the pain tried to take him again. "Bloody hell!"

"Easy, Rome. It's over." Marc laid a comforting hand on the uninjured shoulder. "Vaughn shot the blighter."

Vaughn appeared and knelt on his other side. "Young Fellhopper's watching over the body. What's happening here?"

"Knife just under the collarbone. Way too much blood. May have nicked an artery." Marc glanced at Anna's father. "Admiral, please have someone summon the surgeon at once."

"I will." The admiral hurried away.

Marc looked at Vaughn. "The two of us might be able to carry him, or I can call for a litter."

"Carry him."

"Very well." Marc and Vaughn positioned themselves to lift Rome's weakening body.

"Wait." Barely able to keep his wits about him, Rome grabbed Vaughn's sleeve. "The Black Rose. Who?"

"Emberly." Vaughn shook his head, clearly surprised. "It was Emberly."

"Oh, God." He turned pleading eyes to Marc. "Look after Vin . . ."

"I will. Now stop talking and save your strength for healing."

"This is going to hurt," Vaughn warned, and when they lifted him, his head spun with searing pain, and his stomach churned, and the rest of the world faded blissfully away . . .

Chapter 22

⌒◯◯⌒

The news left everyone reeling in shock.

Upon waking to discover that her husband was not only dead but had tried to kill her brother, Lavinia fell into numb despondency. The added news that Rome hung on to life by a thread sent her completely into hysterics. The surgeon prescribed laudanum.

Anna lingered around the house like a ghost, waiting for news of Rome. She sat in the parlor, her embroidery hoop dangling from her unmoving hands as she stared out the window at the bright, spring day.

The doctor had deemed his condition extremely serious. The good news was that the blade had missed his heart. The bad news was he still might die from the excessive blood loss.

No one would tell her more than that, and she wanted to scream at the frustration of it. To the casual observer, she was nothing more than a future relative. How could anyone know that if Rome's heart stopped beating, so would hers?

Henrietta bustled into the room. "Lavinia's mother has arrived, thank goodness. That poor girl will need her family about her at this difficult time."

"I feel for Mrs. Devereaux," Anna said quietly. "Her son is at death's door."

"Yes, we mustn't forget about dear Mr. Devereaux." Henrietta sat down on the sofa next to her daughter. "He uncovered the plot, after all. Imagine, that killer dined with us and played cards with us, and all the while he was a member of that terrible Black Rose Society."

"We were all fooled," Anna agreed. She poked her needle through the cloth.

"And did you hear what Mr. Vaughn said about Anthony? That he was helping bring the society to justice? Oh, my poor son." She sniffled. "You were right, Anna. His death was the result of foul play. I only wish we'd listened to you."

"He was doing what he thought was right, and it was smart of him to go to Mr. Vaughn with his findings. He is a hero." Anna touched her locket for a moment, content that the truth about her brother's death had finally been brought to light.

Henrietta pulled a lacy handkerchief out of her

pocket and dabbed at her eyes. "The surgeon came by this morning."

Anna dropped her embroidery. Taking a calming breath, she leaned down and scooped it off the floor. "What did he say? I hope Mr. Devereaux is recovering."

"He is still not doing as well as we'd hoped, though both the physician and Lord Haverford are quite close-mouthed." Henrietta eyed her daughter. "You appear to care very much for Mr. Devereaux."

"He will soon be family, won't he?" Her heart pounded, and her fingers shook as she tried to maintain her composure. "And he was helping Mr. Vaughn learn the truth about Anthony."

"Yes, I like him quite a bit. He's a brave man, and an honorable one."

Anna set aside her embroidery, unable to sit still for another moment. "I believe I will seek out his lordship and see if he is willing to take me into his confidence."

"Excellent idea, daughter. Begin as you mean to go on."

Anna found his lordship in the garden. She paused on the path, the leaves of a hedge hiding her from sight. He was not alone.

"I cannot fathom the events of last night," Charlotte said. She sat on a stone bench with a handkerchief crumpled in her two hands. "Dennis insists we leave today."

Haverford sat next to her, leaning forward, their shoulders barely touching. His clasped hands dangled loosely between his knees. "I'm sure your brother just wants you to be safe." His gaze swept Charlotte's face in a moment of unveiled affection.

"But the danger is past. I do not understand his haste to be away from here."

"Would you like me to talk to him?"

"Oh, would you?" She turned to face him, her lovely face filled with hope.

He nodded, clearing his throat. "Of course."

Silence fell between them, and such an intimate silence that Anna wondered why she had not seen it before.

"Thank you, my lord," Charlotte finally whispered.

Haverford just nodded again.

Anna came forward, deliberately scuffing her shoes against the stone pathway. The two jolted, and Haverford sprang to his feet, guilt flickering across his face as if he'd been caught with his hand in her reticule.

"My lord, there you are. I've been looking for you." Anna smiled at the other woman. "Good afternoon, Charlotte."

"How are you, Anna? I trust you have recovered from your terrible ordeal last night."

"I am well, thank you." Anna looked at Haverford. "May I speak to you a moment, my lord?"

"Of course."

Charlotte got to her feet. "I'd best go find my

brother." She glanced one last time at Haverford. Anna only caught a moment of it as the woman turned toward her, but the longing and misery in Charlotte's eyes matched what she saw in her own gaze in the mirror.

How could she have been so blind?

Haverford watched Charlotte walk away, then gave Anna a benign smile. "How can I help you, my dear?"

"I'd like to know how Rome is doing."

Haverford's expression grew serious, and real worry deepened his voice. "Not well. He's been running a fever since last night. We must hope for the best."

"Will he die?"

"I won't lie to you. It's a possibility."

"Dear Lord." She turned away from him, taking a moment to tame her unstable emotions before she betrayed herself.

"I didn't realize you cared so much for my cousin, Anna. It pleases me that my family is so dear to you even after so short a time."

She squeezed her eyes shut. How could she bear it? The man she loved lay on the brink of death, and she could not even comfort him. How would she go on without him?

"Anna? Are you all right?"

She opened her eyes, and through her blurry tears, saw the sapphire-and-diamond engagement ring on her finger. How could she go forward with her life, living a lie?

She turned to Haverford, searching his face for some grain of truth. "Why did you ask me to marry you?"

His unguarded look revealed a moment of surprise before the polite mask fell back into place. "Because I admire you, of course."

"I don't think that's the only reason."

He frowned. "Anna, what are you about? These questions are most unseemly."

"Not as unseemly as marrying for the wrong reasons." She took a deep breath and plunged forward. "I don't love you, Marc."

His expression cleared. "Is that all? Love will come, Anna. I believe mutual respect and friendship make for a harmonious union."

"And I believe the truth makes for a harmonious union. So please trust me enough to tell me. Did you offer for me because you want me to be your wife, or because you were honoring a promise made by your father?"

"Well, of course, honor comes into it," he blustered. "I've always known I would ask you to marry me when the time came."

"And I've always known I would accept." She looked down at her ring, then slid it off her finger and handed it to him. "But I realize now I made a mistake. I would make you a terrible wife, Marc."

Shock wiped the courteous façade from his face. "But you have accepted my offer! Are you jilting me?"

"I am." She folded her hands over his, closing

his fingers over the precious heirloom. "I love your cousin, Marc. I am hoping you will not be angry about that. We met and developed feelings for each other before you ever proposed marriage to me, and I was wrong to accept you when I knew my heart lay elsewhere."

"You're in love with *Rome*?" He nearly shouted the words. He raked his hand through his hair in a frustrated gesture she had never seen him use.

"Yes." She stared imploringly at him. "Neither one of us chose this, and neither of us wants to hurt you. Rome may die—" The words nearly choked her. "He may die, and I would rather live the rest of my life alone with the memory of our love than wed for the wrong reasons."

"I don't know what to say. I cannot fathom it. Twice this has happened to my family. *Twice!*"

"It's not the same. Look past your wounded pride." She pried open his fingers so the sapphire glittered in the sunlight. "Isn't there someone else you would rather give this to? Someone your heart longs for?"

"I . . . it doesn't seem right."

"Nothing could be more right."

"You love him that much?" Marc asked. "Enough to withstand the gossip that may surely come of this?"

"If tongues wag, I shall not care. But I don't think there will be any gossip. The only people who know you and I were engaged is the intimate circle of friends and family here with us. A notice was never sent to the newspapers."

"No, I had planned on doing that once we returned to London." A hint of hope lit his features as he stared down at the ring.

"Even if it meant I would be branded a jilt for the rest of my life, I wouldn't change my mind." Anna touched his hand, then waited as he raised his gaze to hers. Joy glowed in his eyes as he began to accept the possibilities, and she smiled, glad that someone might find happiness in this complicated tangle. "Go and find her, Marc. Ask her to be your bride. Follow your heart."

Still he hesitated, searching her eyes. "Are you certain, Anna?"

She laughed. "How typical of you, Marc, to still question the rightness of this. I am more certain than anything in my life." Her eyes misted. "There will be no scandal. Go and ask Charlotte to marry you. And whatever happens, be happy."

He closed his hand around the ring. "If you're sure this is what you want." He started to walk away, then stopped and turned back to face her. "About you and Rome . . . I understand. And if it all works out, you have my blessing."

"Thank you."

He hurried off, his pace as animated as a schoolboy's.

And Anna let the tears finally fall.

* * *

"You did *what*?" Henrietta shrieked.

Anna didn't even flinch at her mother's shrill tone, having known when she returned to the parlor that the news would not be taken well. "I have given Lord Haverford back his ring. We are no longer engaged."

"I cannot fathom it. This is a nightmare. That my daughter could be so foolish as to *jilt* an *earl*!"

"I didn't love him."

"Love! Dear God, I have birthed a romantic!" Henrietta laid a hand over her eyes and slumped on the sofa, moaning softly.

Anna sighed, well acquainted with her mother's histrionics. She went to the door and caught the attention of the butler. "Leighton, please have Bliss fetch my mother's hartshorn. Oh, and if you know where my father is, would you send him here?"

"Right away, miss."

She turned back to her mother, who lay barely moving on the sofa. "I have sent for Bliss, Mother."

"You have killed me," Henrietta moaned.

Anna shook her head and moved to the window to look out on the sunny gardens. She caught a glimpse of Marc walking with Charlotte, both of them chattering and laughing. The sapphire ring glittered on Charlotte's left hand.

A small smile touched her lips. Whatever happened, she had done the right thing.

The admiral rushed into the room, Mr. Vaughn on his heels. "Henrietta? What's happened?"

"I'm afraid I gave Mama some bad news," Anna said, turning away from the window.

The admiral sat on the sofa beside his wife and patted her hand. "Henrietta? Henrietta, it's Quentin."

"I've broken off my engagement to Lord Haverford," Anna said.

"What? Well, no wonder she swooned." Her father patted Henrietta's cheek. "Come now, my dear. It isn't as bad as all that."

Bliss entered the room, as implacable as ever. "Here is the hartshorn." The admiral took it from her and waved it under her mother's nose.

Henrietta sat up, coughing, waving away the pungent agent with one hand. "Enough, enough!"

"There you are." Quentin handed the smelling salts back to Bliss, who sat down on the other side of her mother and began comforting her.

"My word," Vaughn said with a shake of his head. "And I thought all the excitement had already happened this morning!"

Anna's puzzlement must have shown on her face.

"We searched Emberly's things," her father said, "and we found a membership list for that dratted society. Emberly was the leader."

"I have the list in a safe place." Vaughn grinned, a glint of danger in his eyes. "We will disband the villains soon enough, and the other two leaders will be arrested as soon as I get back to London."

"My heavens," Anna whispered, raising trembling fingers to her locket. It had been so long since she had first started her quest, that it was hard to believe it had come to an end.

"Have you all lost your senses?" Henrietta rasped, still catching her breath. "Does no one else understand that my daughter has thrown away her future?"

"Now, Mama."

"A countess!" Henrietta exclaimed, spreading her hands. "You would have been Lady Haverford! Love comes, Anna. You don't always have it at the beginning, but over time—"

"I'm in love with someone else."

Silence greeted her words, then Henrietta exploded to her feet. "Someone else! Who?"

Anna swallowed hard as all eyes focused on her. "Roman Devereaux."

"Mr. Devereaux? You had an earl for your fiancé, and you jilted him for a *mister*?" Henrietta's eyes rolled back in her head, and she swayed again. The admiral and Bliss caught her beneath the arms and helped her sit down on the sofa.

Vaughn stepped forward as everyone else fussed over her swooning mother. "Devereaux is a good man," he said quietly. "He will make a good diplomat. I wish you all the best."

"Thank you, Mr. Vaughn."

"A mister!" Henrietta cried again.

Vaughn turned his attention on her mother. "Yes, a mister. Mrs. Rosewood, that mere 'mister' saved your daughter's life and brought a dangerous criminal element to justice. You should be grateful your daughter has such good taste."

"But the earl—" Henrietta began.

"The earl is engaged to Miss Fellhopper," Anna said.

"Miss Fellhopper?" Her mother's eyes bulged. "I told you she was dangerous," she muttered.

"I'm sorry, Mama. I know you wanted me to be a countess, but my heart did not agree." Anna folded her hands in front of her and held her mother's gaze. "I'm in love with Rome, and if he asks me to marry him, I will accept."

"You will not! I—"

"Henrietta," the admiral said quietly, stopping her midbreath. "Leave Anna alone."

"But . . ."

"She was right about Anthony, and we didn't listen." He took his wife's hand and squeezed it. "Any fool could see she was miserable with Haverford. Roman Devereaux is clearly a good soldier and fully capable of taking care of our daughter."

"But I wanted so much for her." Her mother's voice broke, and she looked at Anna. "Do you really love him?"

"I do," Anna said, lifting her chin with pride.

Henrietta sniffled. Well," she acquiesced after a moment, "at least he is related to an earl."

* * *

Sunlight beamed in through the window, blinding him as he opened his eyes. With a groan, Rome tried to turn over, but a stabbing pain in his shoulder stopped him cold.

It all came back to him. The Black Rose Society. The swordfight. Marc. Emberly.

"You're awake." A soft, feminine hand brushed the hair from his forehead. "The surgeon said you were out of danger, but I didn't dare believe him while you slept so deeply."

He blinked, certain he was dreaming as the face of his beloved slowly came into focus. "Anna? What are you doing here?"

"Waiting for you to wake." She bent and kissed his forehead. "You scared me," she whispered.

"How did you get in here? Does Marc know?"

"He's the one who told me to stay by your side."

"I don't understand."

"I'm no longer engaged to him."

"But . . ." He glanced at her bare finger. "Your ring?"

"I gave it back to him. He's proposed to Charlotte."

"Charlotte!" His mind stumbled, and his heart seized with hope. Did that mean . . . ? Impossible! "Marc would never go back on a promise."

"I'm afraid I'm the one who broke the promise. I told him I was in love with another man." She leaned close and nuzzled her cheek near his. "So, my love, it seems I am a jilt. What do you think about that?"

Her playful whisper unleashed the joy he could no longer contain. He curled his good arm around her, holding her close, amazed at the change of circumstance. "I think you should marry me straightaway to avoid the scandal."

She laughed. "I'm glad you offered, since I told my parents I intended to accept if you proposed."

The bedroom door clicked open, and someone cleared a throat loudly. Anna straightened, and Rome's arm slid back onto the bed. "Yes, Bliss?"

Without a word, the maid entered the room and made herself comfortable on a chair. Her unflinching dark gaze never left the two of them.

Anna sighed. "I believe my mother has sent Bliss to chaperone us."

"A good idea. I wouldn't want any rumors of a hasty wedding to plague our future." He smiled at her, but his eyelids were already growing heavy. "How is Vin?" he managed to ask.

Anna sighed. "Not too well. She is devastated, of course. Your mother is with her."

He nodded, then reached for her hand, playing with her fingers. "And Marc? He really understands?"

"Yes. He's very happy with Charlotte. They talk about sheep all day long."

He gave a sleepy chuckle. "I thought it was he for a moment, you know."

"What?"

"I thought Marc might be the leader." He yawned, then tilted his head to better see her. He could barely keep his eyes open. "I broke into his room for a sword, and he wasn't in bed."

"He was with my parents and me, checking on everyone else."

"Huh. Typical." He closed his eyes just for a moment.

"Rome?"

"Hmmm?"

"Are you going back to sleep?"

"Mmm-hmm." He felt her fingers slipping away from his and tightened his grip. "No. Stay."

"You want me to stay with you?"

"Mm-hmm. Forever."

"All right, my love." She stroked her fingers through his hair again, her other hand curled softly in his. "I'll stay forever."

He closed his eyes in utter contentment.

All his dreams had finally come true.

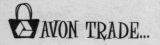

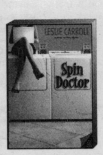